REVENGE AT BURIAL ROCK

BLOODY JOE MANNION BOOK TWO

PETER BRANDVOLD

WOLFPACK
PUBLISHING
— EST 2013 —

Revenge at Burial Rock
Paperback Edition
Copyright © 2022 Peter Brandvold

Wolfpack Publishing
5130 S. Fort Apache Rd. 215-380
Las Vegas, NV 89148

wolfpackpublishing.com

Paperback ISBN 978-1-63977-249-0
Large Print Hardcover ISBN 978-1-63977-503-3
eBook ISBN 978-1-63977-251-3

REVENGE AT BURIAL ROCK

and, keeping his voice down,
gest--"

as the front door opened. He
black-clad stranger step through
e and holding his hat. When he
rned to the room, took a few
carefully on his head, took a few
aise and then disregard the four
sitting at the table before him,
plankboard bar beyond them. Ma
d the bar—a stout, brown-haired
y face, mean eyes, and wearing an
siderable waist.

two other customers—two Mexican
a table against the far wall, drinking
cribbage. There'd been three but the
his six bits to Ma Howard and gone
is ashes hauled by one of Ma's fat

d the tall stranger with his gaze. As
es on him, the man stopped suddenly,
k over his shoulder. Again, the man
e with that uncomfortably probing one
n, he quirked that knowing smile then,
d and Lucky, pinched his hat brim and
e bar.
is hat, set it on the bar, and ran a hand
is long, thick, black hair.
r poison, mister," Ma Howard said in her
t-toned voice.
he said and slapped his hand down on

sharp *crack!* made the three drovers jump in

CHAPTER 1

"WHAT FER CRYIN' IN THE QUEEN'S ALE DO WE HAVE
here?" asked Lucius "Lucky" Brocius as he stared out a
dirty front window of the Beartooth Inn along the Rio
Grande River in southwestern Colorado Territory, south
of Del Norte.

Lucky had made the inquiry with no little awe in his
tone.

Sitting to his left and nursing his own bottle of beer
and a whiskey shot, Cable Coffee thumbed his ratty hat
up off his forehead and followed his fellow cow puncher's
gaze out the window. A man on a tall, handsome cream
horse was just then pulling up to one of the two
hitchracks fronting the road ranch.

The man was strikingly put together. He was very tall,
and he wore a long, black leather duster over a black,
three-piece suit with a black foulard tie and a red and
gold vest over a white shirt. A bright, gold-washed chain
hung down from the vest's left watch pocket. He wore a
black leather patch over his left eye.

Long, coal-black hair hung straight down from the
black, bullet-crowned, broad-brimmed hat he wore.

There wasn't a stitch of gray in that hair, but the man had to be in his fifties at least. Maybe his sixties. His broad, severely chiseled face was as craggy as the siding on a long-abandoned barn. Finely and deeply lined, the skin was drawn taut across the flat planes of his cheekbones.

As Cable watched the man swing lithely down from the fine cream then walk up and loop the reins over the hitchrack, the man looked up suddenly, the broad, black hat brim coming up to reveal the man's eye. Cable's shoulders tightened when he saw that eye. It was the jade of a mountain meadow in late spring, and it seemed to look right through Cable even through the building's dirty front window.

The corners of the man's broad mouth quirked under his thick, black mustache, as though something about the subject of his inspection amused him.

Cable felt the heat rise in his cheeks. He lowered his gaze to his shot glass, which he suddenly saw he was squeezing so hard between his thumb and index finger that both appendages had turned bone white.

"Strange lookin' fella," Cable rasped out.

"You know who that is?" Lucky asked in a hushed tone, watching the tall, black-clad man loosen the cream's saddle cinch, stretching his lips back from his teeth with the effort.

"Who?" asked Toad Barker, sitting across from Lucky and to Cable's right. He was tall and thin and sun-wizened though only twenty-six years old, and his own battered, cream Stetson was shoved up off his forehead, a wing of sandy blond hair hanging down over his right eye. He held a loosely rolled quirley to his lips and was thoughtfully puffing it as he stared at the stranger through the window.

Lucky leaned forward over the table, his features set

Cable looked at Luck
said, "So, what are you su
He stopped abruptly
turned to see the tall,
the door, ducking a littl
closed the door, he t
seconds to set his hat
more seconds to appr
obvious cowpunchers
then headed for the
Howard stood behin
woman with a dough
apron around her co
There were only
punchers sitting at
tequila and playing
third one had paid
upstairs to have
whores.
Cable followe
though feeling ey
and glanced bac
caught Cable's e
of his own. Aga
glancing at Toa
continued to th
He doffed
back through h
"Name you
pinched up, fl
"Whiskey
the bar.
The loud

I
lo

wan

S
beer 1
the na
killed t
in land
seven me
yards out
Longshot.
reward on h

Lucky
sentence.

Toad stuck
puffed, and sai

"Wanna kee
abuse and eatin
enticingly. "Or yo
down to Mexico?"

CHAPTER 1

"WHAT FER CRYIN' IN THE QUEEN'S ALE DO WE HAVE here?" asked Lucius "Lucky" Brocius as he stared out a dirty front window of the Beartooth Inn along the Rio Grande River in southwestern Colorado Territory, south of Del Norte.

Lucky had made the inquiry with no little awe in his tone.

Sitting to his left and nursing his own bottle of beer and a whiskey shot, Cable Coffee thumbed his ratty hat up off his forehead and followed his fellow cow puncher's gaze out the window. A man on a tall, handsome cream horse was just then pulling up to one of the two hitchracks fronting the road ranch.

The man was strikingly put together. He was very tall, and he wore a long, black leather duster over a black, three-piece suit with a black foulard tie and a red and gold vest over a white shirt. A bright, gold-washed chain hung down from the vest's left watch pocket. He wore a black leather patch over his left eye.

Long, coal-black hair hung straight down from the black, bullet-crowned, broad-brimmed hat he wore.

There wasn't a stitch of gray in that hair, but the man had to be in his fifties at least. Maybe his sixties. His broad, severely chiseled face was as craggy as the siding on a long-abandoned barn. Finely and deeply lined, the skin was drawn taut across the flat planes of his cheekbones.

As Cable watched the man swing lithely down from the fine cream then walk up and loop the reins over the hitchrack, the man looked up suddenly, the broad, black hat brim coming up to reveal the man's eye. Cable's shoulders tightened when he saw that eye. It was the jade of a mountain meadow in late spring, and it seemed to look right through Cable even through the building's dirty front window.

The corners of the man's broad mouth quirked under his thick, black mustache, as though something about the subject of his inspection amused him.

Cable felt the heat rise in his cheeks. He lowered his gaze to his shot glass, which he suddenly saw he was squeezing so hard between his thumb and index finger that both appendages had turned bone white.

"Strange lookin' fella," Cable rasped out.

"You know who that is?" Lucky asked in a hushed tone, watching the tall, black-clad man loosen the cream's saddle cinch, stretching his lips back from his teeth with the effort.

"Who?" asked Toad Barker, sitting across from Lucky and to Cable's right. He was tall and thin and sun-wizened though only twenty-six years old, and his own battered, cream Stetson was shoved up off his forehead, a wing of sandy blond hair hanging down over his right eye. He held a loosely rolled quirley to his lips and was thoughtfully puffing it as he stared at the stranger through the window.

Lucky leaned forward over the table, his features set

with a conspiratorial air. "That, gentleman, is none other than the cold-blooded regulator 'Longshot' Hunter Drago!"

"Never heard o' the man," Cable said, staring out the long, narrow window right of the door.

The tall stranger had moved up onto the stoop and, having removed his hat, was washing his face at the washstand, soaping then splashing the water in his face and shaking his head, making his long, black hair fly. He lifted his head to wash his neck then lowered it to wash the back of it, gritting his teeth.

"Never met him, neither," Cable continued. "If I had, I'd remember. I'd remember meetin' some hombre who looks like he does, sure enough."

"Who the hell is Longshot Hunter Drago?" Toad wanted to know, blowing smoke out his nostrils.

Still leaning forward over the table, Lucky sleeved beer foam from his mouth, and said, "Regulator. One o' the nastiest cold-blooded killers in the west. They say he killed twenty-seven men. Mostly workin' for big ranchers in land wars against nesters or rival ranchers. Twenty-seven men! Shot some of 'em from three, four-hundred yards out with a Sharps rifle. That's why they call him Longshot. Last I seen, there was a two-thousand-dollar reward on his head—*dead or alive!*"

Lucky nodded meaningfully to punctuate the sentence.

Toad stuck the quirley in his thin-lipped mouth again, puffed, and said, "So, what are you suggestin'?"

"Wanna keep workin' for Old Man Walsh, takin' his abuse and eatin' the slop he calls grub?" Lucky smiled enticingly. "Or you wanna pad out your pockets an' head down to Mexico?"

Cable looked at Lucky and, keeping his voice down, said, "So, what are you suggest--"

He stopped abruptly as the front door opened. He turned to see the tall, black-clad stranger step through the door, ducking a little and holding his hat. When he closed the door, he turned to the room, took a few seconds to set his hat carefully on his head, took a few more seconds to appraise and then disregard the four obvious cowpunchers sitting at the table before him, then headed for the plankboard bar beyond them. Ma Howard stood behind the bar—a stout, brown-haired woman with a doughy face, mean eyes, and wearing an apron around her considerable waist.

There were only two other customers—two Mexican punchers sitting at a table against the far wall, drinking tequila and playing cribbage. There'd been three but the third one had paid his six bits to Ma Howard and gone upstairs to have his ashes hauled by one of Ma's fat whores.

Cable followed the tall stranger with his gaze. As though feeling eyes on him, the man stopped suddenly, and glanced back over his shoulder. Again, the man caught Cable's eye with that uncomfortably probing one of his own. Again, he quirked that knowing smile then, glancing at Toad and Lucky, pinched his hat brim and continued to the bar.

He doffed his hat, set it on the bar, and ran a hand back through his long, thick, black hair.

"Name your poison, mister," Ma Howard said in her pinched up, flat-toned voice.

"Whiskey," he said and slapped his hand down on the bar.

The loud, sharp *crack!* made the three drovers jump in

their chairs then look toward the bar. They exchanged sheepish looks and grinned with embarrassment.

"What do you have to eat?" Drago asked the woman as she set a shot glass on the bar and pried the cork from an unlabeled bottle.

"Chili an' bread," the woman said, splashing liquor into the shot glass. "That's all I ever have. Chili an' bread."

"It's good, too!" Lucky Brocius offered over his left shoulder.

Drago turned his jade eye on him. "Is that a fact?"

"It is a fact. Ma's bread's good, too."

"Are you vouching for it?" Drago asked Lucky with an odd sort of vaguely menacing smile.

Lucky hesitated, colored a little. "Sure, sure," he said, suddenly not certain anymore.

"All right, then," Drago said, slapping his hand down on the bar again, making the three drovers jump again though not as violently as before. "Set me up a bowl of chili, then—would you, Ma? Do you mind if I call you, Ma?"

"Mister," Ma said, "as long as your money's good, you can call me any damn thing you want!"

With that, she gave him a slow blink then pushed through a swing door behind the bar and was gone. Drago turned sideways to the bar and said, "Obliged for the recommendation."

Lucky glanced over his shoulder at the man again and smiled. "No problem."

Drago picked up his glass and his hat and moseyed over to a table on the other side of the room from the three drovers. He casually slid a chair out with his boot, dropped his hat on the table, set his whiskey down, then slacked his long frame down into the chair with a heavy sigh.

Ma Howard came out a minute later with a wooden bowl of steaming chili and a small plate with two slices of crusty, brown bread. She set the chili and the bread on the table.

Drago looked over at the drover's table. "How's the ale here, gentlemen?"

Again, Lucky braved an answer. He lifted his own brown bottle with the cap hanging down by the wire. "Dang good. Ma brews it herself—don't ya, Ma?"

Ma only grunted.

"I'll have one of those to go with the chili, then, kind lady," Drago said with a wink at the woman.

Ma wasn't having any of it. She gave another slow blink, pulling down her mouth corners, then turned and slouched back around behind the bar and opened the beer bottle as she slouched back out and set the beer on Drago's table.

"Thank you, kind lady." Drago smiled at her again, winningly.

At least, he probably thought it was winning, Cable thought. It might have been winning had his eye not been such a piercing, off-putting green. He smiled the way a lizard would smile if a lizard smiled.

Cable didn't think they did. This fella shouldn't, either.

Cable, Lucky, and Toad sat in edgy silence. Each was keeping his own council about the reward on the killer's head. Two thousand dollars split three ways came to a little over six-hundred-and-fifty dollars. None of the three cow punchers had ever had that much money at any given time. Hell, Old Man Walsh paid them twenty dollars a month and found, and they could

go through almost that much in a single weekend in Del Norte.

Six-hundred-and-fifty dollars meant they could take a year off and stomp with their tails up in Old Mexico, serenading the senoritas. Not just serenading them, either.

Cable felt a smile tug at his lips. Lucky gave him a devilish, mind-reading smile and kicked him under the table. Toad heard the kick and Cable's grunt and barked out a clipped laugh before covering it with an even louder throat clearing. That made both Cabe and Lucky snicker. The snickers built until soon all three were snorting into their hands or arms, trying like the devil to stop laughing though, as was often the case, the harder you try the harder you laugh.

Like boys in church.

Finally, their muffled laughter dwindled and they turned their red-mottled faces toward Drago's table only to find that he was no longer there. Ma was giving the three drovers the wooly eyeball as she picked up the empty chili bowl and the shot glass from the killer's table.

The three drovers frowned at each other curiously then shuttled their gazes to the front window. The cream was still tied at the hitchrack.

"Privy," Toad said under his breath.

Lucky glanced at Toad and Cable in turn. "We gonna go after that two-thousand dollars? If so, now's the time."

Cable arched a skeptical brow at him. "While he's in the privy?"

"Shhhh!" Lucky said, scowling.

"Ma's in the back," Cable said. "And the Mescins don't understand English."

Toad looked directly across the table at Lucky. "Let's

go get that two-thousand dollars. Once we have it, we'll tell old Walsh what he can do with his job and his ranch and his nasty old wife and that mean dog of his—my ass still hurts where he tore a chunk out!--and let's high-tail it to *Mejico* before the snow flies!"

Lucky looked at Cable. "You in?"

Cable glanced at Toad. "If he's in, I'm in."

Lucky placed his hands resolutely onto the table and pushed himself to his feet.

Cable and Toad rose from the table, tugged their hat brims low, hitched up their pants and gun belts, and followed Toad across the room to the back. There was a short, dark hall and a door just ahead, buttery sunlight showing through the cracks between the door's vertical pine boards. Lucky stopped, glanced meaningfully at the other two coming up behind him, and then very quietly tripped the latch.

He winced as the hinges groaned as he opened the door.

"Slow, slow!" Cable whispered in his ear.

Lucky gave him an angry scowl then pushed the door farther open and stepped through it. Cable and Toad followed him into the backyard.

The single-hole privy, gray, splintered and listing precariously to one side, missing several shakes from its peaked roof, sat just ahead at the end of a well-worn path. The gray door was closed. The traditional half-moon was cut into the top.

The three cow punchers looked at each other nervously and walked very slowly and quietly toward the privy. Fifteen feet away from it, they stopped and slowly, quietly shucked their six-guns from their holsters. They spread out about eight feet apart, covering the front and one side of the privy

Stretching his lips back from his teeth, Lucky cocked his old Schofield, raised it, and extended it straight out from his right shoulder. Cable and Toad followed suit, aiming down the barrels of their own extended guns.

Lucky looked at them, grinned, and said, "*Now!*"

The old Schofield leaped and flashed.

Cable's own Scofield barked a second later.

Then Toad's Remington, which he'd won off a hand from the Tin Cup Ranch at an all-night poker game last summer in Buena Vista, belched smoke and flames.

The three guns kicked up a cacophony as the three punchers-turned-bounty hunters continued shooting, the bullets plunking through the privy's rotten boards until the poor, old sagging house was damn near honeycombed with them. Lucky had fired most of his through the door. Cable, most of his through the front left of the door. Toad had fired his into the side.

The house groaned and sagged.

No one inside the privy could have survived all those .44 slugs.

Lucky whooped and yelled, "Why, the old killer Drago's gonna rattle when he walks!" He lowered his smoking pistol.

"He ain't gonna do much walkin', I don't think," Cable said, sheathing his own weapon with satisfaction then walking up to the door, his spurs chinging.

He grinned victoriously over his shoulder at his pards.

Still grinning, he pulled the door open--and leaped a foot in the air, yelling.

He turned in horror to the other two cow punchers, stepping to one side so the others could see around him.

The privy was empty.

A man cleared his throat behind them.

Cable swung around with yet another horrified yell.

Drago stood off the saloon's right rear corner, the tails of his long, black leather duster jostling in the breeze.

He had his head canted skeptically to one side, smiling, deep lines stretching out from the corner of his lone eye. He had his fists on his hips and was holding the flaps of the duster back behind the big, pearl-handled Colt holstered for the cross-draw on his left hip.

"Smelly, nasty things--privies," he said. "Never use 'em myself. Prefer to do my business in the brush."

He glanced toward a stand of lilacs by the windmill to his left.

Cable's heart thudded.

His lower jaw hung to his chest.

The hand squeezing the Schofield in his right hand was slick with cold sweat.

He heard a trickling sound and looked over at Lucky to see water running down from inside the drover's pants leg and puddling on his boot.

The last human voice Cable heard was Toad's, who said, "I knew this was a bad idea," just before old Longshot Hunter Drago's face lost its smile. The legendary regulator drew that big, pearl-gripped Peacemaker so fast that Cable couldn't follow it with his eyes.

There was an ear-numbing cacophony of loud barks just before the world went dark.

All three would-be bounty hunters were dead before they hit the ground.

CHAPTER 2

THE BIG BLUE ROAN WAS THE FINEST STALLION "Bloody" Joe Mannion had ever seen.

He watched it now as it reared high in the round breaking corral that he and his junior deputy, Henry "Stringbean" McCallister, had built for it. The roan clawed at the sky with its front hooves and loosed a shrill whinny that rattled Mannion's eardrums.

The horse dropped back down with a heavy thud and took off running circles around the corral, shaking his head angrily and buck-kicking, sometimes slamming those savage rear hooves against the corral's stout, unpeeled pine poles—stout because Mannion had known what he and the corral would be in for when he'd ridden out and roped the wild stallion and brought it home to his seventeen-year-old daughter, "Vangie", short for Evangeline.

She stood looking through the corral with her father, hands entwined on a rail, smiling with her appreciation of the wonderful horse. Her brown hair was pulled back in a mare's tail that hung long down her back. She wore her customary attire--blue jeans and a red and white checked

work shirt, wide brown belt, and pointed-toed stock-
man's boots. Her pretty, blue-eyed, heart-shaped face was
olive from the sun.

Evangeline Mannion was not an indoor girl. She
preferred to be out in the fresh air and sunshine, either
working in the yard of the house she shared with her
father at the edge of Del Norte in the southern Colorado
Territory or working with her horses. She had two. This
would be her third.

At least she *had* enjoyed working in their yard. That
was before Whip Helton and four other hardcases had
burned the Mannion house to the ground and had
kidnapped and raped Vangie. Now, in the wake of that
tragedy, she was on the mend, but Mannion had not
started to rebuild their house just yet. Only the stables
and a square corral behind the charred ruins remained of
the original structure. He and Vangie were living in the
San Juan Hotel & Saloon owned by Mannion's lady
friend, Jane Ford.

Joe had wanted to gift Vangie the roan to get her out
of the hotel and back out in the fresh air and sunshine to
help her heal after her excruciating ordeal not to mention
the long mountain winter. At seventeen, she'd graduated
early from school, so without a house and a yard to care
for anymore, she'd needed something to get her up in the
morning, to bring the spark of life back to her eyes that
had been so flat and sad in the weeks following her
ordeal.

"Seems a shame to domesticate such a wonderful,
wild beast as the roan, Pa," she said now, her voice a little
forlorn though her eyes glowed brightly with appreciation of the fine horse just then dashing past her, whickering defiantly, black tail arched, black mane buffeting in
the breeze and glinting blue in the high-altitude

sunshine. The roan pranced high, eyes fierce, occasionally stopping to crow hop or to spin in a quick circle, dust lifting around him, then continue his defiant circular run around the corral.

"It is at that, darlin'," Mannion said. "But the ranchers he was getting crossways with by luring off their mares were getting ready to--"

Vangie reached over to press two fingers to her father's mustached mouth. "Don't even say it, Pa! I can't imagine anyone wanting to shoot such a fine beast as the roan! How *could* they?"

"Oh, they could, all right. Make 'em angry enough, and that stallion running off their blooded mares was doing just that. They didn't want to. They appreciate fine horse flesh as much as we do, but when it comes to money..."

"Yeah, I know—money," Vangie said, wrinkling her nose distastefully as she continued watching in wide-eyed fascination the bucking, lunging, snorting bronc.

Mannion smiled at his daughter. He was glad to have her back almost the way she was before Helton and his toughnut friends had treated her so badly. Mannion had run them down, killing four but only wounding Whip. Vangie had been the one to punch her chief molester's ticket after she'd pulled a gun off the body of the Spur Ranch's dead foreman, Quint Wayne. That had been when Helton's father, Garth Helton, had come to town with all his gun-hung waddies to demand Mannion release his son from jail.

All hell had broken loose that day. Fortunately, several of Del Norte's good citizens, including Jane Ford herself, had backed Mannion and his two deputies, Rio Waite and Stringbean McCallister, and, after the gun smoke had cleared, the entire Spur payroll had lain dead on Main

Street. Garth Helton alone had survived with only a shoulder wound. He'd returned to his ranch where he was stewing to this day, eight months later.

Mannion had let the old man live because he had a daughter who'd reminded Joe of his own sweet and eccentric Evageline.

"Think you can break this tough guy, Vange?" Mannion asked her.

"Oh, there's no breaking a horse like this one, Pa," she said, rubbing her forehead against Mannion's shoulder. "There's no breaking the spirit of a horse like this. I mean, *I* wouldn't, anyway. I *couldn't*. Maybe I can gentle him, though. In time."

"In time," Mannion said. "Gonna be a slow process."

"I'll enjoy every minute of it, Pa." Vangie smiled up at her father. "I'll rope him later, try to get to know him. Him, me." Her smile brightened. "Thank you for him. I'm sorry he's not free anymore, but I hope he can at least be my friend."

Mannion planted a kiss on his daughter's cheek.

Hearing the thuds of hooves and the clatter of wheels behind him, Joe turned to see his lady friend, Jane Ford, driving her leather-seated, red-wheeled chaise around the mounded ruins of his and Vangie's house, heading toward the breaking corral. He smiled, admiring the beauty before him.

Even pushing forty, Jane Ford was easy on the eyes. Thick tresses of curly, copper-red hair hung down past her shoulders. Her oval, freckled face with dark brown eyes and fine, aristocratic nose was so head-turning that her establishment, the San Juan Hotel & Saloon, was packed to the rafters every night and sometimes even for noon lunch. Her hour-glass figure, always clad in the finest gowns and jewels, was the same way—always turning heads until Mannion had to admit to pangs of jealousy. Jane's liquor, food, gambling layout, and the percentage girls she housed on the second and third floors of her fine establishment, were the best in Del Norte, maybe even in Colorado Territory south of Leadville.

Mannion had no idea how he'd landed a fish like Jane. They were from two far different worlds—she from a moneyed family in the St. Louis, educated in the finest finishing schools money could buy. An adventurous gal, she'd ventured out West to start a new life for herself on her own, and she was now a formidable business lady, indeed, respected across the territory. Mannion had been raised here in the territory when it had been even wilder and woolier than it was now. His father, Zebediah Mannion, had been a mountain man, his mother a quarter-blood Navajo raised on one of the first ranches in the Sawatch Range, near the Arkansas River.

Both were long dead now. Mannion himself was pushing fifty and feeling every hard year of it, from his early days fighting the Utes to taming towns on the wild frontiers of Kansas and Oklahoma during the days of the great Texas cattle herds and the violence that accompanied them up from Texas and lured it from all points of the compass in the forms of gunfighters, card sharps, snake oil salesman, and prostitutes.

"There's my ride," Mannion said as Jane drew back on the reins of the fine, high-stepping black in the traces.

Her brown eyes beneath the feathered, orange felt hat she wore to match her gown and velvet waistcoat were on the stallion still running and buck-kicking around the corral, snorting his defiance at being hemmed in, no longer free to run wild with his harem and his colts and to fight other stallions interloping on his territory. His shredded right ear was testament to his violent past.

"That's some horse," Jane said.

"That's some horse for some girl," Mannion said, kissing Vangie's cheek.

"Good morning, Joe. Good morning, Miss Evenge-line." Jane smiled her winning, toothy smile framed by broad, red lips and glanced toward a lilac hedge in full bloom nearby. "A fine spring Colorado mountain morning, is it not?"

"It sure is, Miss Jane," Vangie said. "Are you here to take my pa away from me today?" She smiled.

"'Fraid so, kid." Mannion gave his daughter's shoulders an affectionate squeeze. "Jane's takin' me to breakfast. You're on your own."

He looked down at Vangie with the old concern. For months, he hadn't wanted to let her out of his sight, feeling the fatherly urge to be near her and to protect her always. Finally, when she'd seemed well on the road to a full recovery, he'd had to let her go. The world was the world, and there was no saving anyone from it—not even his daughter. He hadn't been able to save his wife, dear Sarah, and he couldn't, in the end, save Vangie from it, either.

"Are you going to be all right?" he asked her.

Vangie smiled up at him, reached up to flick the broad brim of his high-crowned, black Stetson with her index finger. "I'm just fine with it, Bloody Joe. I have the roan to keep me company."

Mannion inwardly winced. He didn't like when Vangie called him by the old monicker. He preferred to see her far removed from that violent side of his life. She wasn't, however. The night Whip Helton had come to call had taught Mannion the folly of the notion. He was and forever would be "Bloody" Joe Mannion, uncompromising lawman often at war with his own worst nature. There was no separating that life from his daughter's.

Oh, he could maybe fool himself into believing that he could at times. But always, deep down, he knew he could not.

He could only try to be the best father Joe Mannion could be.

Aside from the night Helton had come to call and had burned his house and taken his daughter—Mannion had been drunk, having a dark night of the soul after killing an outlaw woman who'd tricked him into killing her—he wasn't doing half-bad. Of course, that night would always prey on his conscience. The night he hadn't been able to protect Vangie was a cross he'd have to bear for the rest of his life.

The wild stallion was his own feeble way of trying to make up for it.

"Be careful with the bronc," Mannion urged Vangie now. "He's as rank as they come. Maybe best wait till tomorrow to rope him. He's still got a lot of green to run off. Whatever you do, don't try to get on him for a good, long time."

"Don't worry, Pa," Vangie said with an indulgent smile then returning her attention to the roan. "This isn't my first rodeo. But I think he's already getting to know me. He keeps looking at me as though he's seen me somewhere before and is trying to remember where."

Mannion chuckled as he lifted his hat and ran his big, sun-seasoned hand through his long, silver-brown hair as he walked to the chaise. "Goodbye, darlin'. See you back at Jane's place tonight for supper."

"Goodbye, Pa. Goodbye, Miss Jane."

"Goodbye, Vang—" Jane stopped when galloping hooves rose behind her.

She and Mannion, who'd just climbed up into the carriage beside Jane, turned to see a rider coming toward them. It was the tall, lanky, long-faced Stringbean McCallister on his coyote dun. The twenty-three-year-old had a look of concern in his light tan eyes beneath the brim of his battered, cream Stetson. He wore his sandy hair long to partly cover the jug ears he was self-conscious about.

Stringbean reined up beside the carriage, thumbed his hat up onto his forehead, and leaned forward against his saddle horn. "Mornin' Marshal. Mornin', Miss Jane." He smiled as he turned to Vangie. "Mornin', Miss Vangie. Sure is a nice-looking hoss you have there. Gonna be able to get all that wildfire out of him?"

"I wouldn't want to get all the wildfire out of him, Stringbean," Vangie said, and smiled. "What's a horse without some fire in him?"

Stringbean chuckled.

"Thanks for helping Pa bring him in," Vangie added.

Stringbean, who once gentled horses himself before he got bucked off one too many times and wound up with a game hip and had applied to Mannion for the deputy town marshal's job, shook his head. "Boy, that was a job of work. Sorta like lassoing a hurricane—wasn't it, Marshal?"

"Sure was," Mannion said.

Stringbean smiled. "But we had a good time doin' it—didn't we...though the bronc sure didn't?"

"We sure did." Mannion glanced at the roan who was making moves as though fighting a fellow stallion, likely a bronc competing for the roan's harem or territory. "He did not. That's a lot of horse." He turned back to his deputy. "What brings you out this way? Any trouble in town?"

"Not sure," Stringbean said, running a gloved thumb along his clean-shaven jaw. "You always say you wanna know about any suspicious strangers in town, so I thought I'd let you know about three who just showed up this morning. Three big fellas. Look to have come a long way as their horses were all dusty and blown."

"Armed?" Mannion asked.

"For bear," Stringbean said.

CHAPTER 3

"Describe these three fellas, Deputy," Mannion said.

"Big, tall men—as big an' tall as you, Marshal." Mannion stood six-feet-four. "I'd say they're somewhere in their thirties. Two are bearded, one has a big handlebar mustache with waxed ends. I know cow punchers, and they're not cow punchers. All three got real serious, hard eyes and, like I said, they're well-armed. One has a Big Fifty rifle in his saddle boot."

"Might be market hunters," Mannion mused aloud.

"Might be," Stringbean allowed. "I just thought I'd mention 'em on account of how they gave me a suspicious feelin' and you're always sayin' you wanna know about suspicious-lookin' newcomers."

"Always good to go with your gut, and I trust yours, Stringbean," Mannion said.

That made the deputy's cheeks color a little. He sat up a little straighter in his saddle.

"Where are they?" Mannion asked him.

"They were havin' drinks in the Wooden Nickel but I heard one grumbling about heading out for breakfast."

"All right—I'll check 'em out. Thanks, Deputy. Good work." Mannion nodded and pinched his hat brim to the lad.

That made the young man sit up even straighter in his saddle and flush a deeper shade of red. "You got it, Marshal," he said with pride. "He drew his hat brim down and pinched it to the ladies. "Good-bye, Miss Vangie. Good luck with the bronc. See ya around, Miss Jane."

With that, he reined the dun around and booted it back in the direction of town.

Holding the black's reins loosely in her gloved hands, Jane turned to Mannion. "Want me to take you to the Wooden Nickel, Joe?"

"Nah," Mannion said. "I'll check 'em out after breakfast." He rubbed his stomach. "I'm so hungry my belly thinks my throat's been cut."

Jane and Vangie chuckled at the old joke. Mannion and Jane said goodbye to Vangie and Jane clucked the black into motion, turning the horse to head back in the direction from which she'd come and where Stringbean's dust was still sifting. Mannion grimaced at the remains of his and Vangie's house as Jane pulled the carriage around it, heading for the two-track trail that would take them the quarter mile to Del Norte.

Mannion had built the house out here in the trees for privacy for both himself and his daughter—a private, shy girl—when they'd first moved here five years ago from Kansas. Mannion had needed a change of scenery. Kansas had been where his dear wife Sarah had hanged herself when Vangie had still been a baby, and Joe hadn't realized until nearly twelve years later that he'd associated the town he and Vangie had lived in with that horrific suicide —Sarah leaping out of the fork in the big cottonwood in their yard with a rope around her neck.

She'd been suffering mentally for weeks. The doctor had told Mannion that young mothers sometimes fell into a mental abyss in the months after they gave birth, and that Sarah had needed his support. Mannion had been taming another in a long string of towns and hadn't given his poor, desperate Sarah the time and attention she'd needed.

That was another thing he'd never forgive himself for.

As Jane turned the chaise onto the two-track trail that bisected spring-green birch and aspens, Mannion craned his neck to keep his transfixed gaze on the wreckage of his home as though the charred chimney, half-burned ceiling beams, and mounded ashes were the wreckage of his checkered past and if he stared at them long enough, he would learn the key to his failings and maybe not fail again so miserably in the future.

Jane reached over and placed her gloved hand on his knee. "Joe?"

He turned to her.

"Don't fret. It was just a house. You and Vangie are still alive and she's doing fine."

"You said it was just a house," Mannion said, keeping his gaze ahead now at Del Norte growing before him. "It was my life. Vangie's life."

Jane shook her head. "It was just a house. You're going to build another one."

"I am." Mannion sighed, removed his hat, and brushed dust from the crown. He chased away the shadows he felt nibbling at his consciousness a moment ago and resolved to think more optimistically. "She is doing well, isn't she?"

"After what she went through, she's doing amazingly well."

"Just wish it hadn't happened. That I hadn't--"

"Nope." Again, Jane shook her head. "It's past, Joe. Look ahead."

"I'm trying."

"Maybe I can help," Jane said, as the black trotted into the outskirts of the town, small cabins, houses, stock pens, and chicken coops cropping up along both sides of the trail including the small farm of one of Del Norte's earliest residents, a former fur trapper named Johnson. He was in his eighties now and still supplying hay to the local livery barns. He sat on the leaning front stoop of his age-grayed log cabin, legs crossed, a collie dog sitting beside him. A lean man with thin gray hair and long side-burns, dressed in sack trousers, suspenders, a wool plaid work shirt, and lace-up boots, he was smoking a pipe.

As the chaise passed, Mannion pinched his hat brim to the graybeard. The stoic, taciturn Johnson gave his chin a single, slow dip and continued puffing his pipe. The dog rose quickly as though to chase the carriage, but Johnson placed a spidery, red hand on the collie's head, and it sat back down beside him.

Mannion looked at Jane, one brow arched. "How can you help?"

She glanced at him, half-smiled. "Marry me."

Mannion's jaw dropped. "Why, Jane, are you asking for my hand?"

"No," she said. "I'm demanding it."

When he just looked at her, she said, pulling the carriage up to a locally famous German eatery on First Avenue, "Neither one of us is getting any younger. I'm pushing forty and you're pushing fifty. If anyone can tame you, Joe, it's me."

She gave him a direct, serious look.

Mannion probed her with his cobalt eyes set deep in sun-seasoned sockets. "My God—you're serious!"

"Indeed." She pulled the chaise up in front of Ida Becker's Good Food, a long, low log building with a large shingle over the roof with a coffee pot and a steaming skillet painted to either side of the place's name.

Mannion looked at the humble eatery. "Ida Becker's, eh? This *must* be a special occasion!" He laughed.

Jane gave him a cockeyed smile. "I know it's your favorite."

"Your place is my favorite."

"Well, this is your second favorite." She leaned over and planted an affectionate kiss on his cheek and rubbed it in with her finger. "Think about it. I'd be good for you, Joe."

"What if I don't want taming?"

"You do. You just don't know it yet." Jane gave him a wink then set the brake and wrapped the reins around the handle. "Come on—I'm starving."

Mannion walked around and helped her down. They went inside and were greeted by the cheery, full-hipped German woman, Ingrid "Ida" Becker, who ran the place. There were only a few customers this time of the day— mid-morning. Mannion had slept in after having been up till two A.M trying to run down some rannie who'd robbed a couple of muleskinners. The trail had gone cold a few miles from the scene of the robbery, and he'd ridden back to town exhausted in the moonless dark.

He wasn't a young man anymore.

He and Jane sat down and ordered and just after their food came, Mannion spied movement in the window to his right. He looked that way to see three big men walk past, heading for the front door. Two were bearded. One wore a handlebar mustache with waxed ends. All three were dressed in wool and leather and even in just the quick glimpse Mannion had gotten of them as they'd passed, he'd spied at least two pistols on each.

Their boots thudded on the boardwalk fronting the restaurant, dwindling. They were replaced by the door squawking open. The first man striding through the door had a big, red beard and a pale, fleshy, freckled face with a rosy nose. He wore a broad-brimmed leather hat. He had two Remington revolvers on his hips. A bone-handled bowie knife jutted up from the well of his left boot.

The man stepping through the door behind him was taller and thinner. The dark-brown handlebar mustache trimmed a long, pale face with a long, slender, knife-straight nose and deep-set, pale blue eyes. Cold and flat eyes. He wore nearly all leather except for a red shirt under his black, bull hide vest. He wore a long, black duster over the vest. He, too, wore two pistols but the bulge in the duster likely bespoke a shoulder rig. He also wore a knife behind his right-side hogleg—a long, wooden handled Arkansas toothpick.

The third man in was shorter than the first two but stocky with broad hips and legs the size of tree trunks. Pale blond hair dropped down from his tall, gray Stetson. He, too, had blue eyes and they worked the room over quickly as he entered behind the other two, his gaze sweeping across Mannion and Jane just before he swung around and followed the other two to a table near the door. He wore three pistols, two tied down low on his thick thighs with a third wedged behind his wide, brown belt over his belly.

None of the three said anything as they dragged chairs out and sank into them.

The man with the handlebar mustache glanced at

Mannion quickly then turned away to read the menu placard propped against the sugar dispenser at the end of the table. His pale cheeks colored a little.

Jane had followed Mannion's gaze to the three men. Now she turned back to Joe and arched a brow. "Hmmm," she said then picked up her fork and knife and cut into her ham.

Mannion reached across the table and placed his hand on her wrist. "Honey, if I give the word, hit the floor and hit it fast—all right?" There was enough of a conversation hum in the room as well as noise emanating from the kitchen—dishes clanking together and a well pump squawking as well as food frying—that he wasn't worried the three strangers would overhear him. All three seemed to be pointedly not looking at him, keeping their gazes averted.

That and the quick, furtive looks they'd given him was what had tipped him off that they might be trouble. Not to mention their eyes. Stringbean had had it right. Cold, hard, mean eyes. The young man was honing the instincts of fine lawdog.

Mannion picked up his own fork and knife and cut into his rare sirloin served with a German sausage, sauerkraut, and a heap of fried potatoes well salted, peppered, and buttered. He enjoyed the meal despite the possible trouble on the lurk though his and Jane's conversation had been stymied by the presence of the three obvious toughnuts. Jane was tense. Mannion could see it in her shoulders, in the stiff set of her face, the way she glanced at him meaningfully as they ate.

Was this what she wanted for the rest of her life?

Tense meals?

Mannion had had a target on his back for the past

twenty years, ever since he'd started working in the lawdogging racket. He'd become used to it. Maybe he even fed off it.

Jane led the calmer, more cultured and mannered life of the sophisticated business lady.

She was having second thoughts now, Joe silently opined. What woman in her right mind would not? A meal ruined by the threat of danger...

He couldn't marry her, he realized now. What he'd done to Vangie...what he'd *caused* to be done to Vangie...could not happen to Jane. The fewer people in his life the better. He wouldn't tell her now. He'd wait for the danger to pass.

If it passed...

He calmly finished his meal.

When he'd swabbed the last of the potatoes and the sausage and steak juice from his plate with a baking powder biscuit, he looked up to see Jane regarding him with an ironic half smile. She'd eaten only half her own breakfast. She sat staring at him over the brim of her coffee cup, which she held in her hands up close to her chin, trying to figure out how, with such men present, who may or may not be gunning for Joe, he could be so calm.

Well, I'm used to it, honey...

Mannion started to think the three obvious hardtails were not here for him, after all, and was about to rise and walk over to the lunch counter and pay Ida Becker, who was placing clean plates on a shelf and talking to the big Chinaman who cooked for her while the Chinaman, clad in a white smock and with his long, black hair in a queue, was smoking a loosely rolled wheat paper quirley.

Mannion had just started to slide his chair back when

the broad, stocky gent with pale blond hair threw his arms up above his head, stretching, and said louder than necessary, "Well, gentleman, I do believe it's time to see a man about a horse!"

The other two chuckled with more vigor than the joke warranted.

The stocky gent slid his chair back, rose with a grunt and a belch, turned, and started walking in his heavy-footed gait toward Mannion, who lowered his hand to his lap in case he needed to make a quick draw. As the big man approached Mannion's table, he gave a smile and a cordial nod to Joe, pinched his hat brim to Jane, and continued walking on past their table to the back of the room, where a door let out onto the back where the privy was.

"All right, all right," said the big, red-bearded man with the wide, fleshy face. "I'll pay. *This* time!" He gave the dark-haired man with the waxed mustache a hard look. The dark-haired man's eyes flicked toward Mannion —a very quick, fleeting glance—before he turned to the red-bearded man and smiled.

Mannion sipped his coffee casually, using his left hand, while sliding his right hand across his belly toward the top-break, silver-chased Russian revolver holstered for the cross-draw on his left hip. He took another sip of his coffee as he released the keeper thong from over the Russian's hammer then lay his right hand flat on his thigh. As he did, the big gent slugged the last of his own coffee, rose from his chair, cursed under his breath, and walked toward the counter where Ida Becker was now placing clean glasses on a shelf near the plates.

She was alone. The Chinaman had returned to the kitchen.

"All right, all right," he said in a gruff tone. "What do we owe you, lady? By the way, my potatoes was *cold*!"

He'd just gotten the last word out of his mouth when Mannion yelled, "Jane—*down*!" and leaped from his chair, knocking the chair back behind him where it toppled to the floor with a loud thud just before the Russian in his hand bucked and roared.

CHAPTER 4

MANNION SHOT THE MUSTACHED GENT AT THE TABLE just as the man leaped from his own chair, bringing his pistol up from his hip, his slitted eyes bright with determination.

The Russian roared and then, as Mannion saw Jane throw herself from her chair across the table from him, he dove forward as two more guns blasted, the slugs caroming through the air where his head had been a moment before to smash into the window left of the front door.

The roar of the two blasts rocketed around inside the eatery as Mannion rolled onto his left shoulder and raised the Russian, clicking the hammer back.

BANG! BANG!

The big, red-bearded man gave a girlish scream and fired his own pistol twice wildly around the room as Mannion's slug drilled into his chest and hurled him back over the counter, evoking a German curse from Ida Becker as she, too, flew backward, hurling the glass she'd been holding high in the air before she bounced off the wall behind her and thumped onto the floor.

"*Kill you, Mannion!*" bellowed the blond-headed gent as he came bulling toward Joe from the rear of the room, clicking the hammer of his own aimed Colt back and narrowing one eye as he aimed down the barrel.

BANG! BANG-BANG!

The first report had come from the blond man's Colt, that slug ripping into the seam of Mannion's shirt over his right shoulder before smashing into a chair behind him. The next two explosions came from Mannion's Russian as he fired twice quickly, punching two holes in the blond-headed gent's broad chest and throwing him back through the door behind him, which he'd left open when he'd bounded back into the building just after closing it, gun extended.

Now he fell just outside the door on his back. He gave an enraged yell and, digging the spurred heels of his boots into the ground, arched his back, gave another yell, raised his Colt, and fired a round at the sky.

Then he collapsed, the hand holding the gun dropping to the ground. He shivered, feet quivering, spurs jangling, as he died.

Mannion cocked the Russian again as he swung his arm around and aimed toward the counter. No movement there. He slid his body around on the floor and aimed straight out ahead of him at the man with the handlebar mustache. He was sitting against a ceiling support post, bleeding from the hole in his throat, raising his own hogleg from the floor as he stretched his lips back from his large, square teeth.

Mannion dropped the hammer on him.

The man threw his head up, tensing, closing his mouth but stretching his lips even farther back from his teeth. Blood oozed from the fresh hole in his chest, over his heart. The man blinked his eyes rapidly as he stared at the ceiling, slowly lowering the revolver in his right hand.

"Who sent you?" Mannion yelled.

The man dropped his chin and glared at Joe from the other side of the table he'd been sitting at. His eyes blazed with pain and fury. "You go to hell! Damn you, you killed me!"

"Who sent you!" Mannion shouted once more.

The man continued to glare at him from the other side of the table. Then his lips shaped a leering grin.

Mannion gritted his own teeth and fired his aimed Russian again, drilling a puckered, blue hole in the dead center of the mustached gent's forehead. The man's head snapped back and tipped sideways until his chin rested on his shoulder.

Mannion turned toward Jane. She lay on the floor on the other side of the table they'd both been sitting at.

She wasn't moving. Blood had pooled on the floor beneath her head.

"*Jane!*"

He scrambled to his feet, wincing at his aching joints —when a man pushing fifty throws himself to the floor as though he were thirty, he feels it more than he had when he was thirty—and ran around the table to drop to a knee beside his woman.

"Jane...honey, are you alright?" Of course, she wasn't all right. There was a good bit of blood on the floor beneath her head.

"*Ach du Lieber!*" yelled Ida Becker as she rose from behind the counter and looked around the room.

There were five other customers at two different tables, and they'd all hit the floor and were still down, arms covering their heads, a couple looking in mute exasperation at Mannion.

"Why you have to do that in here, Joe?" Ida Becker cried, fists on her stout hips. "Shoot! Shoot! Shoot! That's all you do!"

Ignoring the woman, Mannion eased Jane onto her back and winced when he saw the notch a bullet had carved across her skull just above her hairline and in nearly the middle of her forehead. Blood oozed from it, glistening in the morning light angling through a near window.

"Dear God," Mannion said, cradling Jane's head in his arms.

Jane winced, stretched her lips back from her teeth. Her eyes half-opened then closed. "J-Joe?"

She raised her right hand and placed it on his arm.

"Going to get you to the sawbones, honey!" Mannion said, picking her up in his arms and straightening.

Just as he turned to the door, his two deputies, String- bean McCallister and the middle-aged, thick-set Rio Waite came in, Stringbean wielding his 1878 Winchester, Rio his double-barreled shotgun.

"What in God's name happened?" Rio said.

"It's them!" Stringbean said, pointing at the man with the handlebar mustache sitting against the wall to the kid's right, his chin on his shoulder. "I knew they was trouble!"

"Unfortunately, you were right, kid!" As Stringbean and Rio made way for the marshal, Mannion said, "Hall that beef over to the office and try to match them up to wanted circulars. I want to know who they are...or *were!*" He glanced at the two deputies over his shoulder. "Better yet—I want to know who *sent them!*"

He stepped out onto the boardwalk, fumbled open the door of the chaise, and eased Jane onto the rear, quilted leather seat.

"*Ach du Lieber!*" Ida Becker yelled behind the lawman. "Who's going to pay for my window? I swear, wherever you go, Joe, trouble follows!"

"He ain't called Bloody Joe for nothin'!" yelled one of the customers, his tone deeply indignant.

Mannion climbed onto the front seat, unwrapped the reins from around the brake handle, released the break, shook the reins over the black's back, and swung the carriage into the street, turning sharply, yelling at a ranch wagon stopped dead ahead of him while the driver and a man standing in the street beside him stared back skeptically at Mannion.

"Get out of the way!" Joe yelled. "Vernon, get that infernal contraption out of my damn way. I got an injured lady here!"

"All right, all right, Marshal!" Vernon said, turning the horse in the traces of his wagon, the box of which was heaped with burlap feeds sacks, sharply right.

The other man ran to get out of the way.

Mannion whipped the black into a full run. He took the corner that let on to Main Street too fast and nearly ended up capsizing the carriage for his haste. The black whinnied with indignation. When he was back on all four wheels, Mannion whipped the reins over the horse's back again.

"*Hy-yahhh, boy!* Get out of the way—injured lady here! Get the hell out of my way, O'Brian—ooops, sorry Mrs. Bjornson, damn near ran you down! Hy-yahh boy! *Hy-yahhh!*"

He took another corner too fast. Again, he nearly overturned the carriage. When he straightened it out, he pulled the horse up to a wooden shingle extending into the street announcing DOCTOR MARCUS P. BOHANNON, MD. The sign was shaped in the form of a hand with a finger pointing up the staircase that ran along the side of the two-story, unpainted, wood frame building. The lower story housed a furniture shop.

The furniture maker also made coffins, which was handy for when things didn't go well upstairs for Doc Bohannon.

The fifty-something, short, portly, gray-haired medico was just then standing on the second-floor landing outside his office, smoking a fat stogie. He hitched his baggy, broadcloth trousers up his broad hips with one hand, gave his head a fateful wag, and said, "I heard the shooting. Had a feeling I'd see you sooner or later, Joe. Good Lord—is that Jane Ford in that chaise?"

"It's Jane, all right, Doc." Mannion wrapped the reins around the brake, stepped out of the carriage, opened the rear door, and saw Jane grimacing and raising a hand to her bloody forehead.

"Good Lord," the medico said again then dropped his stogie over the rail. It plopped to the ground, sparking. He hitched up his trousers and waddled down the steps.

"I got her, Doc," Mannion said, turning to the stairs.

"All right, all right—poor Jane!" Bohannon said and swung around, breathless, his full face mottled red in stark contrast to his thick gray muttonchops. His long, oily, gray hair danced down below his shirt collar.

Everyone in town had a soft spot for Jane Ford. Not only did she run the finest saloon, eatery, gambling parlor, and hurdy gurdy house in town, she was a damn nice woman. Beautiful, educated, and dignified. For the life of them, the town couldn't understand what on God's green earth she was doing with Bloody Joe Mannion. Two people couldn't have been more different.

What they didn't understand was that was the very

reason she'd become attracted to Joe. Just as that was why he'd become attracted to her. Foolish on her part.

Now he might have killed her...

Bohannon shoved the door open and stepped inside, stepping to one side as Mannion carried the groaning Jane through the doorway.

"In there," Bohannon said, gesturing at one of two open doors flanking his cluttered desk. "Take her in there."

Mannion walked around the desk, stepped into the examining room that smelled of camphor and cigar smoke, and lay Jane on a leather cushioned examining table. Bohannon stepped in behind him, rolling up his shirtsleeves.

He looked at Mannion. "Go now, Joe. Let me see to her."

"I can't leave her, Doc," Mannion said, planting his fists on the edge of the table, giving the medico a hard, determined look.

"You have to, Joe. Get out of here. Go get a cup of coffee. I'll send someone for you when I've gotten her cleaned up and been able to evaluate the wound."

"What's to evaluate? She took a bullet that was meant for me, Doc!"

"Get out of here, Joe. I need room to work. I don't need you in here glaring at me and making me nervous. Now *get out of here!*"

Mannion cursed. He swung around and headed for the open doorway. He glanced over his shoulder at Bohannon. "Keep her alive, Doc. Just keep her alive!"

"I'm going to do everything I can. Close the door."

Mannion stepped out, glanced once more at Jane writhing in agony on the examining table, then drew the door closed, letting the latch gently click into place. As he stepped out onto the stairs' top landing, he removed his hat and ran a hand through his hair in frustration, tugging on it, cursing under his breath.

Last time it was Vangie who'd been hurt because of him.

Now Jane...

He was halfway down the steps when a tow-headed boy stepped out from the front of the furniture shop on the street below and was about to pass on the boardwalk before Mannion. He was carrying a box that appeared filled with groceries.

Nine-year-old Harmon Hauffenthistle was an odd-job kid, one of the busiest around, so he was usually carrying something and hustling somewhere. He wore a black wool watch cap, sack trousers, suspenders, and a blue plaid work shirt. His hair was so blond it was almost white, and his clear-skinned, blue-eyed face was deeply tanned.

"Hey, Harmon!" Mannion called.

The boy stopped and gazed up at the lawman descending the stairs. "Awful busy, Marshal."

"Too busy to drive Miss Jane's chaise over to Griggs' Livery for a dollar?"

Mannion stepped down onto the boardwalk before the boy and dug a silver dollar out of the pocket of his black denim pants.

"Heck, no," Harmon said. "Mrs. Benedict's only paying me a dime for hauling her weekly groceries over to her. That old hen can wait."

Mannion tucked the coin in the front pocket of the kid's shirt. "Don't let 'em rob you blind, kid."

"Half the time I walk around with my pockets hangin' out!"

"Set that box in the chaise. You can use it to haul Mrs. Benedict's groceries to her."

"No kiddin'?" Young Harmon brightened as he gazed at the smart-looking chaise hitched to Jane's fine black Morgan.

"Why not? She's not going to be using it again for a while," it pained Mannion to say.

"What happened?" Harmon asked, setting the box in the chaise.

"Took a bullet. It looks bad, kid." Mannion winced and ran his thumb along his jaw as he turned to stare up at the doctor's office. His guts were tight with worry. "And it was my damn fault," he added under his breath.

"Sorry to hear that, Marshal Mannion. Miss Jane's a fine lady. Best tipper in town. I hope she feels better soon."

"Me, too."

Harmon clambered up into the chaise. "Don't worry—I'll take good care of Miss Jane's rig, Marshal"

"Later, Harmon."

Mannion was still staring up at the doctor's office, wondering how Jane was doing, hoping like hell she was still alive.

He started walking north along the boardwalk, eyes down, gray-brown eyebrows stitched. He could hear the late-morning clamor around him but was mainly seeing Jane in his mind's eye with that nasty gash on her forehead, a gut-wrenching look of pain on her lovely face.

Vaguely, as though from far away, a man said to his right, "What happened to her?"

Another man said, "Took a bullet no doubt meant for Mannion."

"Teach her to steer clear of that old hellion. Why doesn't she find herself..." The man, Keel Brandywine, let his voice trail off as Mannion stopped dead in his tracks and turned to him. Several men including Brandywine were standing out front of The Wooden Nickel Saloon, sipping beers and smoking cigarettes. Brandywine's lower jaw dropped when he saw Mannion.

"Uh," the man said. "Uh, sorry, Marsh--"

Mannion cut him off by slamming his clenched right fist against the nub of the man's right cheek. Brandywine screamed, dropped his beer, and flew back through The Wooden Nickel's batwing doors.

Rage burned hot inside Mannion—so hot it was roasting his eyeballs. He cursed and stepped forward, raising his clenched fist again. He was just pushing through the batwings to pick Brandywine up off the floor to give him another tattoo when a young woman's voice yelled above the thud of galloping hooves, "Pa! *Stop, Pa! Pa*—for the love of Pete, *stop!*"

CHAPTER 5

MANNION FROZE.

He turned back through the doors to see Vangie gallop up to the hitchrack fronting The Wooden Nickel, brown hair bouncing on her shoulders, anger cutting deep rungs across her suntanned forehead.

"Pa!" she yelled as she reined in the long-limbed calico mare she'd named Willow. "Good grief!"

"I echo that, Joe," came another admonishing voice behind him. "Good grief!"

He turned to see the Del Norte mayor, the diminutive, suited, and bespectacled Charlie McQueen, stoop down with one other gent and help Brandywine back to his feet. Brandywine glared at Mannion, a red welt growing on his cheek around a half-inch cut just below his left eye. He was tall and slender with neatly combed blond hair and a neatly trimmed mustache.

Mannion had never liked the man. He owned a lumber mill and had mining interests throughout southern Colorado and thought he was the cock of the walk. He stooped down to pick up his green bowler hat and set it on his head. He cast another incriminating glare at Mannion then turned to the mayor, jaws hard as he said, "Why this fool is still wearing a badge in this town is a mystery to me, *Mister Mayor*!"

He turned to walk over to the bar.

McQueen cast his own look of deep frustration at Mannion then set his hand on the taller man's shoulder and said, "Keel, let me buy you a beer."

Brandywine brushed McQueen's hand from his shoulder. "I'll buy my own damn beer!"

"Now you're in trouble again."

Mannion turned to see his daughter gazing up at him with frustration and disappointment in her eyes. That look made Joe feel like a boy who'd tossed a snake through the half-moon in the girls' privy door. But then, what he'd done had been damned childish and he deserved the tongue lashing he was getting.

"They're both popinjays," Mannion said, defensively.

"I know, but Mister Brandywine is a respected businessman around here."

"Like I said..."

"I heard about Jane," Vangie said. "How is she?"

Mannion shrugged. "I don't know. She's up with the doc. He kicked me out of his office."

"Can't blame him," Vangie said, drolly. She placed her hand on his arm. "I heard it was a head wound, Pa."

"It is. A graze but it looks bad. There was a lot of blood."

"Oh, Pa—I'm sorry!" Vangie reached up to wrap her arms around his neck and snug her cheek up taut against his chest.

"So am I, darlin'," Mannion said. "So am I." Her ran his hands down her slender back, returning the hug though he felt self-conscious about such an obvious display of affection in public. He wasn't accustomed to that.

He frowned as he looked down at his daughter. "Say, I do believe this is the first time you've been out on the street like this since..."

He didn't complete the thought. Neither of them made a habit of referring to the previous horrific episode with Whip Helton. Since her recovery, after not speaking for several weeks after the savage ordeal, Vangie had become a virtual recluse, leaving the hotel only to feed and work with her horses. She hadn't ventured into any of the stores or restaurants which there were getting to be more and more of now with Del Norte still growing, more ranchers, miners, and loggers pouring into the area.

Vangie looked at the people passing on the street around them. "You know...I just realized that." She shrugged and looked up at her father. "Didn't even think about it. I just saddled Willow and headed for town after I heard about Jane. Mrs. Dillon told me. She was passing on the way to deliver a baby in the country."

Mrs. Dillon was a midwife who made rounds far and wide.

"I see. Well, don't worry about her, honey. I'll do enough of that for both of us."

"So sorry, Papa. Let me know if there's anything I can do."

"I will. In the meantime, I'm gonna try to find out who those jaspers were who shot her."

"Speaking of worrying," Vangie said, grimacing up at her father. "I worry so about you, Pa. All these men gunning for you all the damn time!" She stomped her boot down on the boardwalk.

"Shh, honey!" Chuckling, Mannion looked around at the passersby, several of whom were giving him and his daughter scandalized looks. "People are gonna think you were raised by wolves."

"I was," Vangie said. "I was raised by a big bad wolf." She hugged Joe again, looking up at him with those deep lines carved across her forehead again. "One who is hunted all the time!"

"Ah, it's not all the time. Just seems like it." Mannion squeezed her. "I'm sorry you worry, honey. I wish you wouldn't. I have a feelin' things are gonna settle down now for a while. They usually do after a dustup."

Mannion turning would-be bushwhackers toe-down usually discouraged others with the same intention. At least, for a while.

"Why don't you go on over to the hotel and lie down for a while?" Mannion suggested. "Make you feel better."

Vangie gave a wan little smile and shook her head. "I did plenty of lying around all winter. And that beautiful roan you brought me isn't going to gentle himself."

"No, that's pretty obvious," Mannion said with a dry chuckle.

"Goodbye, Pa." Vangie rose onto the toes of her boots to plant a kiss on his cheek. "Do be careful...?"

"I will, honey."

Vangie turned and stepped back up onto her mare's back. She reined the horse around and cast Mannion another worried look then touched spurs to the mare's flanks and trotted back in the direction from which she'd come. Mannion cast a look over the batwing doors behind him. Ed Brandywine was standing sideways to the bar at the back of the room, talking to another man and casting an indignant gaze back toward Mannion.

Joe turned away and continued walking, heading to his office which doubled as a jailhouse, the jail part of the building residing in the stone-floored and -walled basement which the locals had dubbed Hotel de Mannion. Most of the rowdies in town had been a guest at one time or another. Some several times. The big shingle hanging from chains beneath the building's porch roof read: JOE MANNION—TOWN MARSHAL.

One night some prankster had climbed up on the porch's railing and added the word "BLOODY" to the left side of the sign in sloppy red paint. Mannion had left it there. He didn't like the nickname, but he'd worn that handle for so many years—he'd acquired it back in Kansas—he'd sort of gotten used to it.

Besides, why let the prankster know he'd gotten under the lawman's collar?

Now as Mannion approached the building, he saw the town undertaker, Marvin Bellringer, sitting in his wagon before the jailhouse's front stoop. Rio Waite and String-bean were standing out there, Stringbean gazing into the wagon box while Rio spoke with Bellringer, a slender, sharp-faced man with close-cropped gray hair and a close-cropped gray mustache. He wore a black frock coat over a work shirt and bib-front overalls. He was smoking a cigarette. His little, yellow mutt sat on the seat beside him.

Rio Waite's black-and-white cat who boasted a black fur bowtie, Buster, stood on the rail fronting the stoop, his back in a hump as he glared at the dog, who pointedly looked away from the threatening feline.

As Mannion approached, Bellringer took a drag from his quirley and, blowing the smoke out through his nostrils, said, "Sorry about Miss Jane, Marshal." He glanced into the bed of his buckboard. "You sure punched their tickets, though."

"You don't recognize 'em, do you, Marvin?"

The undertaker shook his head. "Nah, can't say as I

do. Strangers, seems like to me. Getting to be more an' more of 'em in Del Norte of late."

"Yeah." Mannion studied the three dead men.

"Think someone sicced 'em on you, Marshal?" Stringbean asked.

"I'm betting on it. I don't know 'em. Of course, they might have a beef of their own with me. Maybe I sent a brother to jail. Who knows? I just have a strong hunch someone sent 'em. I want to know who." Mannion looked at Bellringer. "Marvin, set 'em up on planks in front of your place for a few days, will you? Until they start to smell, leastways. Put a sign up. 'If you recognize any one of these men, report to Marshal Joe Mannion.'"

He glanced at Rio. "It's worth a try."

"Could be Helton," Rio said. "He's ruined, I hear. After all his men died right here on Main Street, fightin' for him, no one will work for him."

Garth Helton was the late Whip Helton's father.

"Possibly," Mannion said as Bellringer rode off in the wagon containing the three dead men. "I'll ride out for a powwow. In the meantime, I'm gonna look through some wanted circulars."

He'd just started to turn toward the jailhouse when something on the street caught his eye. He turned back to scrutinize the horseback rider just then angling toward Hotel de Mannion, leading three horses with blanket-wrapped bundles tied across their saddles.

The rider who rode a rangy, handsome cream stallion was a tall, dark-haired man with one piercing green eye set in a deep socket below the broad brim of his black, bullet-crowned hat. A black patch covered his left eye. In fact, he was mostly attired in black save for a white shirt and red and gold wool vest behind his black frock coat.

Longish, coal-black hair hung down from the hat to cover his ears and brush his collar.

A big, silver-chased, pearl-gripped Colt revolver was holstered for the cross-draw on his left hip. A new-model Henry repeating rifle jutted up from a saddle boot.

"Well, I'll be damned," Mannion said.

"What is it, Joe?" the rider said, checking the cream down in front of Mannion. "See a ghost?"

"I do believe I do," Mannion said. "One I never figured I'd see again. If I did, I figured I'd probably have to shoot him."

"Who is this fella, Marshal?" Stringbean asked, standing to Mannion's right. Rio Waite stood on the other side of Stringbean.

Obviously, the newcomer's striking, one-eyed appearance had caught the two deputies' attention as well as their fascination. It didn't hurt that Longshot Hunter Drago was packing a curious cargo across the three spare horses strung out behind him.

"This here is Longshot Hunter Drago," Mannion said.

"No," Rio said, scowling skeptically at the newcomer. "I heard he was dead."

"Dead in prison," Mannion said, staring up at Drago smiling down at him like the cat that ate the canary.

Stringbean looked at Mannion, frowning curiously. "Who's Longshot Hunter Drago?"

"Why, I am, Junior," Drago said. To Mannion, he said, "I don't believe I've yet had the pleasure of getting your deputies' handles, Joe."

Mannion canted his head toward the kid beside him. "This is Stringbean. That's Rio."

He continued to stare skeptically up at the tall man before him, wondering if he really was seeing a ghost.

Drago chuckled. "They thought they killed me, sure

enough. Four big toughs—two white men, including Bruno Sands. You remember Bruno—don't you, Joe? You put him in the federal pen just behind me. The other two was a butt-ugly Mex and a half-breed Apache who once rode with Geronimo. Jumped me, cut out this eye, and cut my throat."

He pulled his foulard tie down to reveal a long, grizzly, knotted red scar stretching for a good ten inches across his neck.

Stringbean gasped.

Rio sucked a sharp breath of revulsion.

Drago was still smiling. "Oh, they thought they killed me, all right. Even the pen surgeon did. They even had me in a pine box and were nailing the lid down when I came to and started thumping against the lid. Scared one of the grave-diggers so bad he made water in his pants!"

"You survived that?" Mannion asked, lifting his chin to indicate the man's scarred neck.

"I did. Don't ask me how. Sprang out of that box spitting up blood. The gravediggers fetched the surgeon and somehow he managed to sew up my neck and save my life." Drago grinned broadly. "Really disappointed the warden."

"I bet it did. You're one son of a bitch, Drago. What are you doing in my town?" Mannion glanced at the three spare horses. "Packing beef, no less."

"Don't worry, Joe." Drago stretched his mustached mouth in a coyote grin and narrowed that one piercing green eye. "I'm not here to kill you...though I do admit to passing one hell of a lot of time behind bars thinking about it."

CHAPTER 6

MANNION WALKED OVER TO ONE OF THE THREE PACK horses and peeled open the bedroll the body was wrapped in to see the sandy-haired head of a dead man in his mid-twenties. He pulled the head up by its hair to get a look at the slack-jawed face with its death-glazed, half-open eyes.

"The not-so-Lucky Brocious," he said, glancing at Stringbean and Rio.

Mannion released the dead man's head. It slapped down against the cream's barrel. Joe looked up at Drago. "Once a killer, always a killer."

"I killed these men in self-defense," Drago said. "And, if I must repeat myself—I'm not here for you, Joe. I did my twelve years." Again, he smiled. "I'm a changed man. I come to Del Norte for purely legitimate reasons." He glanced behind him and hooked a thumb over his left shoulder. "I bought The Three-Legged Dog Saloon."

"Pshaw!" said Rio.

"Sure enough," Drago said. "I don't know what happened, but somehow, after lying on my cot at night fantasizing about killing the man who caused me to be there, I suddenly felt a calm come over me. My anger faded. I no longer hold what happened against you, Joe."

"What happened was I braced you for your involvement in the Meyer County land war in Kansas. They should have hanged you, but on the day of the trial the witnesses who were going to testify against you got cold feet. Never showed up. The judge gave you twelve years for stealing a horse."

"A trumped-up charge. The horse I *appropriated* after mine was shot out from under me had belonged to a dead man."

Mannion shrugged. "The judge had to give you something. He knew what a cold-blooded killer you were. The men who got cold feet were found dead in their bedrolls, throats cut. Everyone knows you hired that done from behind bars."

"It couldn't be proven," Drago said with a shrug.

"You really bought The Three-Legged Dog, Mister Drago?" Stringbean asked, polite as always. Even to a killer.

"I did, indeed, son."

"He's not your son, Drago," Mannion said, chafed by the man's presence as well as by his phony friendly demeanor. Mannion knew him for who he really was—a stone cold killer who shot men in the back from hundreds of yards away and rode off whistling his delight at a job well done. "I want you out of my town or I'll arrest you for the murder of these three punchers. I assume all three rode for Marvin Walsh."

"The so-called murders you mention, Joe, can be explained by the lovely widow lady, Ma Howard, who runs the Beartooth Inn Road Ranch out by the Rio Grande. She witnessed the whole thing and will attest to my innocence in the matter. They tried to ambush me in the privy, of all places to kill a man." Drago smiled. "I don't use privies. They disgust me."

"Don't worry," Mannion said. "I'll check your story."

Drago smiled and pinched his hat brim. "In the meantime, I have a saloon to open. Nice meeting you gentleman. We'll be seeing you around." The killer dropped the reins of the three packhorses, swung the cream around, and rode back out into the street, heading toward The Three-Legged Dog, which had been closed for the past three months, ever since its owner had been killed by a gambler disgruntled at the luck—or lack thereof—he'd been having at the proprietor's craps table.

Mannion stood in silent fury, watching the man negotiate his way across the busy street.

Rio turned to him. "You think he sent that fresh beef in Bellringer's wagon, Joe? Kind of a coincidence he showed up in town right after..."

Mannion shook his head. "Not a chance. If he wants me dead—and I'd bet gold eagles to navy beans he does; a man like that has a long memory—he'd want to have the honors himself."

"I heard of him," Rio said, watching Drago now standing on the boardwalk fronting The Three-Legged Dog, saddlebags slung over his shoulder, unlocking the closed double door. "Didn't know it was you who put him away, though, Marshal."

"It was me, all right. And I'd love to go back in time and do it all over again. He might ride into town with a smile and nice lies, but he's still the devil he always was. He's up to something. And I'm gonna keep one hell of a close eye on him."

"We will, too, Joe. Stringbean an' me."

"I don't know," Stringbean said, hiking a shoulder. "Folks have been known to change, Marshal."

Mannion looked sharply at him. "Don't fall prey to his lies, kid."

Stringbean gave another shrug, this time with both shoulders, and drew his mouth corners down.

Mannion cursed, wheeled, and stomped up the porch steps and into his office. It wasn't even noon yet. What a day.

He slammed the door shut behind him.

———

STRINGBEAN TURNED TO RIO. "THE MARSHAL SURE HAS an awful mad on for that fella."

Rio spat a wad of chaw into the street and stared toward the Three-Legged Dog, its big double doors now closed as Drago was apparently getting the place ready to reopen. "Understandable for a man who's had as many fellas gunnin' for him like them Bellringer just drove off with."

"Hard to believe that Mister Drago was once a cold-blooded killer. I don't know," Stringbean said. "He looked nice enough to me. Maybe he really just does want to open his own saloon and start a new life after spending so long behind bars."

Rio gave a grunt. "I don't know—I reckon it's possible. But let's keep a close on him just the--"

"Henry!" a young woman's voice cut the older deputy off.

"Oh-oh—here comes trouble," Rio muttered as he watched young Molly Hurdstrom step out of a lady's dress store on the opposite side of the street, a parcel in one hand. She stepped onto the edge of the boardwalk and waved with her other hand, a big smile on her pretty, heart-shaped, gray-eyed face as she gazed affectionately at Stringbean.

She was a lovely brunette dressed to the nines in a low-cut, sleeveless yellow dress edged with black lace and with a matching little yellow hat resting atop her pretty head. She wore long, white gloves on her slim, pale arms.

"Oh, go on, Rio," Stringbean said, his full attention on the girl on the other side of the street. He elbowed the older man playfully. "Does that pretty girl over there look like trouble to you?"

"Yes, yes, she does," Rio said, pensively fingering the three days' worth of beard stubble on his chin. "Maybe not her personally, but her family..."

"Her *family*?" Stringbean said. "Why, the Hurdstroms are one of the wealthiest, most upstanding families in Del Norte!" He waved back at the girl and yelled. "Stay there, Molly. I'll come over!"

He didn't want her braving the heavy ranch and mine wagon traffic passing along the street just now as it pretty much did all day in the burgeoning Del Norte. He waited for an ore dray being pulled by a six-hitch team of draft horses to pass then lurched into a jog, vaguely hearing Rio say behind him, "Her family is what I'm talkin' about, kid..."

Stringbean stepped up onto the boardwalk fronting the lady's dress shop and turned to the pretty brunette, beaming. "Hello, Molly. Been a rough day so far, but it's sure better now!"

"I heard about the shooting over at Ida Becker's Café. You weren't involved, were you, Henry?"

"No, no. That was some killers gunnin' for the marshal. The marshal's all right, but Miss Jane took a bullet."

"Oh, Henry—I heard that, too." Molly placed her hand on his arm and looked up at him sadly. Molly was one of the few people in town who called him by his given name. He liked it. At twenty-three, he was getting too old to be called Stringbean anymore. "I'm sorry about Miss Jane. I certainly hope she's going to be all right."

"Yeah—me, too. I guess the doc's with her now."

"This town is just getting absolutely wild!" the girl complained, stomping her foot down angrily. "I do so worry about you!"

"Ah, heck—you don't have to worry about me, Molly. I can take care of myself just fine."

"Oh, I know you can, Henry. But I still worry about you. It's a girl's job to worry about her guy." She gazed up at Stringbean lovingly. Then suddenly she glanced across the street, and her brows knit indignantly. "Tell me, Henry—what is it that Deputy Waite has against me?"

Stringbean turned to look across the street. Rio was no longer staring this way. He was staring south along the street and looking at his pocket watch, probably gauging how much longer it would be until the noon stage rolled into town. It was Rio's job to be at the stage depot to look over the passengers, as, per Marshal Mannion's orders, the law in Del Norte was always on the lookout for troublemakers.

"Figured that out, did you? I'm sorry, Molly. I don't know what's put a bee in his bonnet. He knows how pretty and sweet you are and what a fine family you have."

"Hmm," she said, gazing at Rio again, who was returning his watch to his pocket and was starting to stroll toward the Rio Grand & Company Stage Line. "Just notional, I reckon. Maybe I'll bring you both lunch tomorrow, and he can see what a good cook I am. I bet he's partial to fried chicken."

"He loves it."

"All right, then. That's what I'm gonna do. I have a feeling his attitude toward me will change in a heartbeat after he tastes my milk gravy."

Stringbean chuckled. "I wouldn't count on it too highly, Molly. Like you said, Rio can be notional."

"Well, it's worth a try." She turned her pretty eyes to Stringbean. "Speaking of food, I'd like you to come have dinner with Mother and Father and myself soon."

"Really?"

She'd invited him over for supper a couple of times before but mostly when he went over to the Hurdstroms' impressive house, he and Molly just sat on the porch swing and talked and looked at the stars or took a walk through the trees, always staying in sight of the Hurdstrom house as per her parents' orders.

"Absolutely."

Stringbean thought of something troubling. "Molly... your parents like me, don't they? I mean, they always seem like they do, but..."

"Of course, they do, Henry." Again, she placed her hand on his arm. "How could you ever doubt it?"

"I don't know—I guess it's just that..."

Stringbean looked down at the deputy town marshal's badge on his shirt. His job was humble. At least, in contrast to Molly's familys' work. They ran a prestigious freighting business. Stringbean lived a humble life, just renting a room in a local boarding house. He'd saved a little money, but Molly's parents likely expected her to find a young man with a better job. And with better blood than Stringbean's, which, he had to humbly admit, would not be all that hard to do.

His family had owned a little shotgun ranch in Oklahoma. That's where Stringbean had fallen in love with horses and had started his career of gentling them for himself and his father and other local ranchers.

Now he looked at Molly's hurt face with knit brows and pouting lips and said, "Ah, heck. I'm sorry, Molly. I know your folks wouldn't mind what I did for a living as long as I liked you and you liked me."

"Henry, don't you know by now, after all these months together?" she asked, brows still stitched. "My feelings have gone a lot farther than that."

Stringbean smiled the biggest smile he'd ever smiled. "You don't know how much I like hearing that, Miss Molly."

She glanced around to make sure no one was overhearing their private conversation. Then she canted her head to one side. "Is the feeling mutual, Henry McAllister?"

He looked around self-consciously then ran his hand down her slender arm, enjoying the sensation of her smooth flesh against his own. "Of course, it is. I reckon I thought you knew."

"I think I did, but I still like hearing you say it."

"I love you, Miss Molly."

Her face brightened. "I like the sound of that. See you Wednesday night?"

"Wednesday night, it is," Stringbean said, feeling as though he were riding a flying carpet.

She winked, swung around, and trotted off to her buggy waiting nearby, the mare in the traces craning her head around to regard the two lovers dubiously. Maybe even a little forebodingly.

CHAPTER 7

R

IO

 W

AITE

 TOOK HIS TIME STROLLING TOWARD THE
Rio Grande & Company Stage Line office. The stage was
due, but it was hardly ever on time, as it was rugged
country up here in the foothills of the San Juan Mountains, with the Sawatch Range humping up like vast gray
boulders to the north and the dramatic Sangre de
Christos looming in the southeast.

Rio was halfway to the station and had just nodded to
a Chinese café owner standing out having a smoke and a
cup of coffee when he heard the unmistakable thunder of
the stage to the north. He could hear the drumming of
the six-horse hitch and the rattling of the large, iron-shod
wheels and hear Lyle Horton, the jehu, bellowing at his
team and cracking the blacksnake over their backs.

Rio stepped into the street and saw the horses and
coach rising up out of the rolling, sage-stippled hills,
threading its way between two rocky dikes and then
following the trail as it straightened out and headed
straight for Del Norte. The horses jostling and pitching.
Portly Lyle sitting on the right side of the driver's seat.
His shotgunner, Magnus Haroldson sitting to Lyle's right,

Magnus holding his double-barreled shotgun across his thighs. Both men had their bandannas drawn up over their noses.

Rio winced, seeing the stage rocking and pitching behind the galloping hitch.

Neither Magnus nor Lyle were young men anymore. They were closer to Rio's age, fifty-six, and Rio could imagine what that contraption would do to his backside if he ever dared driving on or riding shotgun for one. Those drivers' boot seats might be leather padded, but no amount of padding took the pain out of them—not when your backside was over half a century old.

The stage came thundering into town, and the good citizens of Del Norte and cow punchers and muleskinners and the drivers of ranch and mine supply wagons all hurried out of the way, cursing and shaking their fists and making old Lyle Horton laugh uproariously. He did love a show, Lyle did. Fortunately, or unfortunately, he had a reputation for hoorahing the town with his bucking and rocking Concord, so as soon as the good folks—and not so good folks—of Del Norte heard the thunder of the stage's approach, they hustled to clear the street.

Even the dogs scampered quickly into breaks between business buildings or under raised boardwalks to lay with their chins on their paws, mewling.

Rio gained the boardwalk fronting the long, white-frame, clapboard-sided office of the Rio Grande & Company Stage Line just as the guffawing jehu leaned back in his seat, tugging on the reins, the wheelers, the leaders, and the two big swing team animals in the middle of the hitch skidding to dusty halts, gray froth spraying off their withers. Rio kept back against the front of the office building so he wouldn't get hit with any of that horse sweat.

When the horses were all stopped and snorting and tossing their heads and blowing, Rio stepped forward and glared up at Horton and said, "Lyle, you just love bein' a son of a bitch—don't you?"

Loud guffaws issued down from the driver's boot.

The shotgunner, gray-bearded and blue-eyed Magnus Haroldson just grinned and shook his head. He pulled down his blue, polka-dotted bandanna.

"Good Lord!" came a voice from the near side of the coach. Rio turned to see a dandy with a red walrus mustache and glinting spectacles poke his head out the window right of the door. "I've never been so assaulted sitting down in my entire life!" He turned his head and lifted his chin to yell up at the boot. "I did not pay five dollars and seven bits to be sick to my stomach the whole darn trip!"

That only made the jehu—a big-gutted man with a red beard liberally streaked with gray—laugh all the harder.

"Nope," Rio said, chuckling as he regarded the dandy. "No one does."

As Lyle and Magnus climbed gingerly down from the boot on the carriage's side—the shotgunner first and the jehu following close behind—the door opened and the dandy stepped out, wincing and rubbing his backside. Behind him came two men Rio took to be gamblers and if the third wasn't a whiskey drummer with his customary cheap suit, ratty bowler, and two big carpet bags bulging with what were likely samples of coffin varnish, Rio was no judge of men.

He was a judge of women, however. The one the whiskey drummer turned to extend a hand to and help out of the carriage was eye-catching, indeed. She was even more eye catching when her eyes caught Rio's and, as she stepped down onto the boardwalk beside the carriage, smiled brightly and said, "Well, I *thought* I recognized that raspy bass!"

Her lovely cheeks dimpled. "Though I don't believe I've heard it in over twenty years!" she added.

Rio fumbled his hat off his head and held it down by his side. "Before my very eyes," he muttered, eyes widening in shock. "Antonia? *Antonia Greer*—is that *you?*"

"The one and only, my dear man," she said as Rio stepped slowly toward her, his knees quaking so badly he was afraid he'd stumble and fall in a heap.

She was as lovely as she'd been the last time he'd seen her, and that had been when she'd been in her mid-twenties--twenty years ago. Of course, she'd aged. But some women aged in a way that their beauty was seasoned by time, in a way that takes all that raw beauty of youth and smooths it out and accentuates it and adds soul and personality to it.

Certainly, her brown eyes were larger, brighter, and more direct than they'd been twenty years ago. Her face was nicely, delicately sculpted, with a long, fine nose and proud chin framed by straight, firm jaws. She was still a strawberry blonde. Of course, the blonde probably mostly came from a bottle these days, but Rio wasn't complaining. Her bust, accentuated by the deep purple, low-cut gown she wore with a lacy black shawl around her shoulders, and with a matching purple picture hat pinned to the large bun atop her head, was exquisite, indeed. She filled out the corset better than he remembered, and his aging loins couldn't help giving a warm, little tug at that.

Antonia Greer must have caught the straying of her former lover's gaze and the flush in his craggy, fleshy, most unhandsome cheeks. She laughed bawdily, showing her still-fine teeth framed by plump, red lips.

Rio's self-consciousness grew even keener. He knew what he looked like; he tried not to look too hard, but he shaved in a looking glass two or three times a week on the porch of his humble cabin flanking Hotel de Mannion, with Buster watching skeptically from the porch rail, and there was no denying that while Rio had never been a handsome man, he was decidedly less handsome now. And gone to tallow, as well, he not so vaguely became self-conscious enough of that he darted a glance from her smiling, knowing eyes to his own middle that was pushing out his hickory shirt so that the buckle of his gun belt was damn near facing the ground.

Not only that, but a lower button of his shirt had come open, revealing his wash worn longhandle top peeking out from behind it. There appeared even a small hole in the undershirt. Lordy be—was that his sandy-colored belly hair poking out, as well, curling against his most unappealing, fish-belly white tallow?

Why, oh, why had he not taken a proper look at himself and pulled himself together a little better before wandering over here only to run into the only woman in his depraved and lonely life he'd ever loved?

A raging beauty even pushing forty! No. More years had passed than he could comprehend. She must be pushing forty-five! She was ten years younger than he, but he looked a good twenty older than she...

Here he stood in all his beastliness. And he'd even stolen a look at her bosoms!

Ugly as well as uncouth!

As though she were reading his mind, she stepped up close to him, her eyes both amused and affectionate. She raised her slender, long-fingered hands, sandwiched his face between them, leaned in close to him and, pressing those ripe breasts against his chest, planted a long, lingering, soft kiss on his lips.

Rio's ticker lurched and chugged.

The top of his head felt hot.

His knees were shaking. Did she notice?

She pulled her head away slowly. "How've you been, my darling man? Fancy meeting you here in Del Norte..."

"I've been...I've been." He grinned with embarrassment. "You know me—I'm the same old me. Just a little fatter and uglier."

"Oh, hush. I've turned into a slattern!" She held her arms out to her sides. "Look at me!"

"A slattern! Ha!"

Toni had always been proud of her beauty. She'd revealed that pride through her self-deprecation. She knew what she looked like in a mirror, and she knew what she looked like in a man's eyes, and she was not humbled by either of them, indeed.

And why should she be?

"What are you doing here in Del Norte, Toni? Just passing through?"

"I suppose you could say that, but I'll be here for a while. I'm performing at the Spider Web. For the next month, in fact."

"You're still performing, then?"

"Yes." She frowned suddenly, turned her lovely head a little to one side. "Why—shouldn't I be at my age?"

"Oh, God, no, woman. That's not what I meant!" Here he was, still putting his foot in his mouth even after twenty years. Just like old times.

She smiled. "We'll have to get together, Rio. We have a lot of catching up to do—you and me."

"We certainly do, we certainly do." Rio heard the hesitation in his voice.

She drew her mouth corners down and frowned again, this time suspiciously. "You're not still mad at me, are you, Rio?"

"Oh, hell, no." Rio chuckled.

No, he wasn't angry. He was, however, broken-hearted. He had been for the past twenty years though of course those wounds do tend themselves after a while. He didn't think of her every day and every night but every other day and every other night. He'd tumbled for her back in Nacogdoches, when he'd run a small saloon and moonlit as a night marshal. She'd sung and danced in his saloon, and he'd taken her out eating and dancing and for long buggy rides in the country.

He'd tumbled for her and by the sweet way she'd made love with him, he'd thought she'd tumbled for him. They'd spent four months together. She'd sung and danced in other saloons in addition to his, and in one of these she'd met a gambler named Brent Price. He was the one she'd tumbled for, and they'd ended up leaving together, heading for Yuma by an early morning stage.

Toni had been up front about her love for Price with Rio. She hadn't cheated on him. Still, that night she'd told him that she and Price were heading out for other opportunities in their respective fields, he'd aged ten years.

Maybe that's why he felt so old now. Even older than his years.

The kicker in the whole deal was that he'd felt foolish. How could he have ever thought a girl like the long-legged, high-kicking Antonia Greer, looking killer in her little black dance outfits and high-heeled shoes, with her lustrous blonde hair and glinting brown eyes, could have ever fallen for the likes of Rio Waite?

"Shall I have your bags sent over to the San Juan, Miss Price?" The voice had come from the half-breed porter who worked for the stage line.

Rio whipped an astonished look at the man, lower jaw hanging. Then he turned to Toni. "Price...?"

"Oh. Yes. I'm sorry, Rio. I should have corrected you," Toni said. "Brent and I married. He died three years ago."

It was as though some strong hand reached up from inside Rio's chest to pull his tongue down his throat. He croaked, "I...I...see..."

Toni turned her pretty face and luminous eyes to the big half-breed, Kenny Two Owls, who wore a suit two sizes too small for his length of bone. "That would be wonderful, thank you." She frowned at Rio curiously. "Where is the San Juan, if I may ask?"

"Just across the street," Rio said, sort of half finding his tongue again. "The street's busy. I'll walk you." He shrugged. "If you like, Toni?"

"Maybe we can have a drink?" Toni suggested. "You know—to cut the dust." She smiled.

"I could have a cup of coffee," Rio said.

He turned and offered her his arm.

"Thank you, kind sir."

She took his arm. They stepped off the boardwalk together and started across the street.

What might have been...

CHAPTER 8

THREE DAYS LATER, MANNION REINED HIS PRIZED BAY Stallion, Red, to a halt atop a low divide in the broken bluff country of the San Juan Range. Pines and cedars rose, laying long shadows across the greening spring grass and mountain sage around him.

He'd spied movement through the trees before him and down in a bowl below also stippled with evergreens and aspens. He reached back to fish his field glasses from a saddlebag pouch and removed them from their baize-lined case.

Through the two spheres of magnified vision, he saw a rider loping a horse nearly directly away from him, climbing the next rise. The man wore a black vest and a high-crowned cream hat. The horse was coal black with one white stocking. Horse and rider topped the next rise then disappeared down the other side.

Then there was only the blue arch of the flawless, high-country sky.

Mannion lowered the glasses, frowning. Probably a cow puncher looking for spring calves. Joe had seen many cow-calf pairs on his ride out from town. No other punchers, though.

An old, time-sharpened apprehension ran a cold finger down his spine.

He returned the glasses to the saddlebag pouch then booted Red ahead slowly and dropped down the declivity, keeping a sharp eye on the terrain ahead. He leaned forward to loosen his Yellowboy rifle in the saddle scabbard jutting up ahead of his right knee, within an easy grab, if needed.

It was often needed.

He let Red choose his own path down the hill, weaving around standing trees as well as deadfalls. When he reached the bottom of the slope, he checked Red down and looked around again, carefully, pricking his ears, listening.

No sounds but the breeze in the tree crowns, the occasional thudding of pine cones tumbling to the ground, and the chittering of a distant squirrel.

Red lurched a little, as though with a sudden start, and looked around, twitching his ears and whickering quietly, finally turning his head to stare ahead toward the opposite slope and a little to the right. Mannion could feel the horse's muscles expanding and contracting beneath the saddle. The horse continued to stare in the same direction, lifting his long snout and sniffing the breeze.

"What is it, boy?" Mannion whispered.

He couldn't hear or see anything over that way, but that didn't mean anything. Red had a good sniffer, and he was obviously scenting something. Could just be a deer. Maybe a cow. Might even be a bear out of recent hibernation and preying on the young calves that had dropped only a month ago, sating its long pent-up hunger.

Only one way to find out.

Mannion clucked. Red continued forward, hooves thudding softly against the soft floor of the forest.

As horse and rider rode across the crease between slopes then started up the rise, Mannion reached forward, slid the Yellowboy from its scabbard, quietly levered a round into the action, off-cocked the hammer, and rested the barrel across his saddlebow. His back grew taut with edginess. He, too, sensed trouble but all he had to base it on, besides gut instinct, was Red.

Was the black-vested rider he'd seen a few minutes ago stalking him? Possibly sent by the same man or men who'd sent the three in town?

Mannion rode up to within a few yards of the crest of the rise, stopped Red, and swung down from the saddle. He doffed his hat, hooked it over the horn, and then walked, crouching, to the crest of the rise, dropping down behind a rock a little larger than a gravestone and fronted by a shrub. He peered over the rock and the shrub.

Beyond lay another crease between hills much like the one he'd just crossed except at the bottom of this one a creek muttered in a stony bed sheathed in aspens and brush. Another pine- and aspen-stippled rise rose beyond the creek, capped with several large granite outcroppings, some twice again as tall as the pines and aspens growing up along their base.

This was good bear hunting country. Mannion and Vangie had hunted here just off the open range the thuggish, territorial Garth Helton had always considered his own. There were lots of places up in those rocks for bruins to hole up come fall when they were getting ready for that long-winter's snooze. They could fill up on water in the creek and on the wild berries growing on each bank.

Those rocks made for plenty of places for a bush-whacker to hole up, too.

Mannion returned to his horse, donned his hat, mounted Red, and continued up and over the rise. Again, he looked around carefully, keeping an eye on Red, as well. If trouble was imminent, the horse would likely know before Mannion would.

The bay splashed across the creek and followed a game trail up the bank through the brush. On several shrubs were the white blossoms of cranberry and service-berry, both of which Vangie picked for pies in the fall. Red continued following the game path up the slope, angling slightly from left to right, then right to left. Just as the horse turned onto the second switchback, Mannion lowered his head to pass beneath a low pine bough.

As he did, he heard the sizzle of a bullet and then the hard thump as it tore into the bough he'd just ducked to avoid.

The thump was followed by the sharp bark of a rifle.

Mannion cursed as he swung his right leg over the horn and dropped straight down to the ground, landing flat-footed. Red was whickering and dancing, having been as startled by the sudden assault as Mannion was. Joe slammed the Yellowboy's barrel across Red's neck and yelled, "Git out of here, hoss!" and threw himself to the ground to his left.

The bay didn't need to be told twice.

Red gave a loud whinny, swung hard right, and took off running across the belly of the slope, dragging his reins.

Belly down on the ground, Mannion stared up the

slope and right to see the breech of a rifle flash in the sunshine as a man worked the cocking lever. It was the black-vested rider in the cream hat, all right. He knelt on a ledge near the top of a large outcropping. Just as he raised the rifle to his cheek and began to bring the barrel to bear on his target once, more, Mannion, aiming quickly, triggered the Yellowboy.

He'd aimed too quickly.

The round hammered rock dust from the side of the outcropping to the right of his target. At least, it caused the bushwhacker to throw his next round wild. As the bullet plumed forest duff three feet to Mannion's left, Joe racked another round, fired, racked another round, and fired again. Both rounds cut the air where the shooter had been kneeling before he'd quickly thrown himself to his left, out of the notch he'd been kneeling in.

Mannion racked another round, snugged his cheek up against the stock, and aimed up at the outcropping, his heart thudding angrily. "Where are you, you gutless slime?"

The barrel of the man's rifle appeared but before he could get it leveled, Mannion fired. His bullet tore through the brim of the man's tall, cream hat, blowing it off his head. The man pulled back again quickly. As he did, Mannion heard him give a startled grunt.

Again, Joe cocked the Yellowboy and, still belly down on the ground, aimed up the slope at the giant rock. His heart hammered so hard it made the rifle jerk. His jaws were like stone, his teeth gritted. Rage consumed him, sent a hot fire rolling through every inch of him.

He hated bushwackers more than anything.

"Who are you, you yellow-livered dog?" he shouted up at the rock.

No response.

"Show yourself!" Mannion shouted again. "If you want me dead, the least you can do is face me!"

Still nothing.

Distantly, hooves drummed.

"*Damn you!*" Mannion hurried to his feet and took off running up the slope, spurs chinging, breathing hard, holding the Yellowboy up high across his chest.

The thudding hooves were dwindling gradually. It was a tough, uphill run for a man Joe's age, one who rarely walked much less ran. He was so angry, however, that he gained the crest of the ridge at the left side of the outcropping the bushwhacker had fired from in only a couple of minutes. His knees feeling like putty, he ran along the edge of the outcropping until he could see down the other side of the steep slope.

He got there just in time to see the black-vested, cream-hatted SOB gain the crest of the next ridge and disappear down the other side. The thudding of the black's hooves faded quickly to silence.

Joe cursed and spat the copper taste of exhaustion from his mouth. He ran his sleeve across his lips and then through the sweat on his forehead and stared in the direction the bushwhacker had disappeared. There was nothing more frustrating than an ambush.

And not being able to catch the lowly dog who'd flung the lead at you from cover. Not being able to kill him. Leastways, not being able to kill him *after* you'd found out who'd sent him or had learned the nature of his grudge.

Nah, he'd been sent, Joe thought. *Just like the three in Ida Becker's café.*

It would be too much of a coincidence for two parties of men harboring grudges to come after him in such a short window of time.

Helton?

Joe had ridden out here to find out that very thing.

Likely Helton.

Last fall, Mannion had let the old rancher live after the dustup on the Main Street of Del Norte, but Helton's son and his men were dead. Since then, his reputation had gone south and he hadn't been able to replenish his payroll. He likely held Mannion responsible for that. He'd likely chewed on it for so long—over the long, cold winter—that he couldn't help himself anymore but to send killers...

Joe wheeled and, fingering fresh cartridges from his shell belt and punching them through his Yellowboy's loading gate, tramped back down the hill. Once he'd whistled for Red and mounted up, slipping the rifle back in its scabbard, he looked around to get his bearings then continued his journey southwest—toward Helton's Spur Ranch.

———

HE DIDN'T SEE MANY BEEVES ON HELTON LAND.

When he'd followed the trail that led to the Spur headquarters and had reined up atop the last hill and looked down, he was a little surprised to see how shabby the place had become. The big house sat on a hill to the right of the barns, stables, and corrals. All the buildings including the house appeared shabby and in disrepair.

Damned quiet down there, too. Mannion saw only two old cowpunchers sitting atop one of the headquarters' three corrals, inspecting three horses that were munching hay from a crib at the two old-timer's feet. Gray hair shone beneath the brims of their Stetsons. Their faces were deeply browned.

They were likely long-time waddies who likely hadn't been able to get work elsewhere, so they'd come to work for Helton though about all they were capable of doing anymore was sitting on the corral and watching horses eat. They were turning their heads toward each other and their mouths were moving, chinning about the old days, maybe horses and women they'd once known.

Speaking of horses, the three in the corral with the old men were the only three Mannion could see on the place. Helton might have sold the others to keep the Spur. Mannion had heard that after the trouble Whip had gotten into and then getting crossways with the entire town of Del Norte by threatening to burn it to the ground if Mannion didn't release his son from jail, Garth had lost most of his business partners. Considering the man unpredictable in the least and likely off his nut, they'd pulled their proverbial irons out of his metaphoric fire, leaving him high, dry, and cash poor.

"Yep, likely harboring one hell of a grudge," Mannion muttered to himself and booted Red on down the trail and through the portal announcing the Helton name with the Spur brand burned into each side of it.

He crossed the yard to the house, reined up near the broad steps climbing to the broad front porch that needed a fresh coat of paint. Shrubs and flowers in the yard around the house were as unkempt as the rest of the place.

Mannion swung down from Red's back, mounted the steps and stopped about halfway up. Sitting before him was none other than Garth Helton himself—a big, balding, craggy-faced man, unshaven and appearing at least ten years older than he had the last time Mannion had seen him. The man appeared to have been as badly neglected as his headquarters.

He sat in a pushchair; he had a big, striped wool blanket draped across his shrunken body. His head was tipped to one side. He was snoring, lifting his chin slightly with each inhalation. Sound asleep.

Or so he appeared.

Mannion climbed another two steps and stopped when Helton suddenly turned his face to him. The rancher opened his eyes and gave a wolfish smile. He lifted one corner of the blanket to reveal the double maws of a shotgun yawning at Joe.

Mannion winced at the ratcheting clicks of two hammers being cocked.

CHAPTER 9

"I could do it," Helton said, that wolfish grin in place. "I could do it right here an' now. Blow the famous Bloody Joe Mannion to hell an' gone!"

"*In*famous would be a more accurate word. And you sure could. In fact, go ahead and do it." Mannion raised his arms in supplication. "I deserve nothing less for being so stupid—waltzing right into a rattlesnake den!"

Helton seemed to consider it, narrowing his eyes till deep lines spoked out around them. His face was paler than Mannion remembered. In fact, the last time he'd seen the man, last fall, it had been saddle-leather brown. Now it looked pasty and sickly, and the several days' worth of beard stubble was entirely gray.

There were two more ratcheting clicks as Helton eased the hammers back down into their cradles.

"Nah," he said, pulling the sawed-off out from under the blanket. It was an old Richards coach gun with a leather lanyard and Damascus steel barrels. He set it on a table beside him on which rested several medicine bottles, a half-empty whiskey bottle, a shot glass, a large open folding knife, and a peeled, half-eaten apple. The peel lay like a coiled red rattler beside the knife. "What'd be the point at this late date?"

Mannion studied him curiously. More than a little surprised that he hadn't been blown out of his boots. He tried to study it through, but his mind became a nest of confusion. It obviously shone on his face.

Helton laughed suddenly, lifting his head and pounding the arms of the push chair with his open palms. "You thought I was gonna do it. *Hah!*"

He guffawed raucously, delightedly.

"Why didn't you?" While glad he was still kicking—for Vangie's sake if not his own--Mannion was a little offended. Had he been so wrong about who wanted him dead?

Helton guffawed some more, pounded the chair arms once more, then sobered slightly. His eyes were bright with humor and probably with the medicine and Irish whiskey on the table beside him. He shrugged a shoulder. "Like I said, what--?"

"Pa?" The girl's voice cut him off.

Mannion turned to see Helton's daughter, Landry, step out of the house, a big, shaggy dog following close on her heels, which were bare. Her feet were bare and dirty. She wore a plain day dress. When the dog saw Mannion, it lunged out from behind the girl, hackles raised, growling, barking, and showing its teeth.

Landry leaned down quickly and grabbed the dog by its rope collar, pulling him back.

"No, Ivanhoe!" she said, laughing. She was a pretty, young blonde roughly Vangie's age. An odd one, like Vangie. Not a pack animal. More like a forest sprite in the company of her dog. Mannion had seen her out on the range before, she and the dog playing like children. "It's impolite to bark at the guests!" she admonished the dog, who sat contritely down but mewled, keeping its defensive eyes on Mannion. "We get few enough as it is."

Joe removed his hat. "Hello, there, Miss Helton." He'd never spoken to her before, just seen her from a distance. He wasn't sure how he even knew her name. "I'm Joe Mannion."

"Oh, I know who you are, Marshal Mannion." Landry glanced at her father with a slightly sheepish smile before returning her gaze to their guest. "I've heard your name bandied around here a lot. I hear everything."

"She eavesdrops," Helton said, rolling his eyes then looking down at the girl's feet. "And simply refuses to wear shoes!" He raised then dropped his hands back down to the chair arms in defeat. "Oh, well. I don't have any men around here anymore. At least not *young* men." He gazed off down the hill and across the yard at the corral. "Those two are too old to count. They'd never catch her even if they worked up the energy to chase her."

He croaked out a laugh.

"I like Burt and Tobias, Pa," Landry said, frowning as though hurt. "They know everything there is to know about horses. Ivanhoe even likes them. They're real sweet to both of us."

Helton looked at Mannion and sighed as though he were embarrassed by the girl's innocent nature, so different from his own and that of his son. He shook his head and drew his mouth corners down.

"If I'd know you had company, I would have brought some tea. Ma's asleep."

"I'm sure she is."

Landry wheeled and started for the door. "I will bring some tea and cake!"

Helton turned in his chair to yell at her back, "Just coffee!"

"Just coffee, then!" came the girl's tart reply as she retreated into the lodge, the dog following close behind her but turning its head to cast Mannion another suspicious glance.

Mannion looked at Helton. "This wasn't exactly a social call."

"Oh, I know." Helton turned his head to indicate a wicker chair on the porch to his right. "But since you're here, you might as well make it one." He scowled with what appeared genuine disappointment and longing at his old enemy. "You know, aside from those two down there, I haven't seen another man's face on this place in damn near five months?"

Mannion walked over and sat in the chair, half-facing Helton. He held his hat down between his knees, absently tossing and turning it as he regarded the push chair. "Why the wheels?"

Helton stared off over the porch rail but touched a thumb to his chest. "Ticker."

"I hadn't heard."

"I told the doc not to tell anyone." Helton glanced at Mannion. "You know, it's not easy for a man like me to have tumbled so far."

"I didn't do it to you."

"No, I know very well who did it to me." Helton looked at Mannion again, pointedly. "I didn't kill you, did I?"

Mannion looked down at his hat.

"And I didn't send those men to kill you, either," Helton said, that wolfish smile returning to his chapped mouth.

Mannion frowned. "How did you know?"

"Why else would you be here? To check on my welfare? The father of the son who burned your house, savaged your daughter?"

Mannion had no idea how to respond to that. Could Garth Helton actually have spent the winter recounting his past and coming to honest terms with who he was. Or had been?

Had he changed?

Mannion almost thought he might have, but he couldn't quite wrap his mind around the possibility. He'd known the fiery, old rancher too long. The man who hanged rustlers and left them where he'd hanged them as a warning to others. Maybe being so close to death—and old Garth certainly did look close to death—had caused him to take stock of himself, what his life had been about. And to regret some things.

Landry brought coffee in two china cups on a silver tray and set one on the table beside her father, and one on the table beside Mannion.

"Probably kind of strong. It's been on the range since morning. Ma likes her coffee all day long—good and hot and black." Landry gave Mannion a fetching smile then wheeled and skipped back into the house, batting the silver tray against her thigh. The dog was waiting for her in the doorway. As she brushed past him, lightly running her fingers along his back, the dog wheeled and followed her inside.

"That's not true," Helton said, staring again over the porch rail and out toward his mostly empty pastures. "Landry just wants her to prefer coffee."

"I know what she prefers," Mannion said.

"Yes, most around here do. Berenice came from the East and never liked it out here, but her father made her stay here. He and I were business partners. He wanted his daughter and me to raise a whole passel of kids out here, and to make this the biggest ranch in southern Arizona for many generations to come. The only problem with that is it was an arranged marriage. No love on either side. She took to drink while I took to my herds, my men, and my account books. It didn't help that she was crazy to start with."

He twirled an arthritic finger in the air by his ear.

"And you probably weren't much help with that."

Helton looked at him, held his gaze for nearly half a minute with a probing, conspiratorial one of his own. "You know something about that—don't you, Joe?"

Mannion looked down at his hat again. "Sarah hanged herself from a tree in our backyard. Back in Kansas."

"I heard."

"Of course."

Helton gave a weak smile. "Two mossyhorns like ourselves...cock of the damn walks; me at one time, anyway...we got no secrets. Folks plunder our pasts for any and all weakness."

"I have plenty."

"So do I." Helton chuckled dryly as he stared out at his holdings again. "So do I..." He looked at Mannion again. "But, being enemies, we know each other almost as well as we know our best friends—don't we, Joe? Leastways, if either of us had a best friend."

"I suppose that's true," Mannion said with an ironic laugh of his own, still staring down at his hat. He had no idea why he was having a heart to heart with Garth Helton, but here he was. He wasn't sure why he wasn't leaving.

"Look at that out there," Helton said, raising a spidery hand straight out from his shoulder and waving it slowly. "Range is damn near empty."

"You sell 'em off?"

"Some. 'Bout half. Rustlers got most of the others—horses as well as cattle. Hell, I can hear 'em while I lay in bed at night. Here 'em whistling and calling 'Come, bossy! Come, bossy! Here little dogie!' I hear 'em laughing as they run off my stock." Helton looked at Mannion. "The surrounding ranchers, nesters, farmers—hell, they're picking my bones."

Mannion just stared back at him. He was almost uncomfortable with how sorry the man was now. The old hellion was spilling his broken heart to the man who had broken him though it was also true that Helton had broken himself.

"I can't get anyone but those two graybeards down there to work for me. When I lost my men in town, I lost my reputation. I lost respect. Hell, I lost my *self-respect*." He frowned, truly befuddled. "How could I let you do that to me, Joe?"

"You should have let your son stand trial."

Helton smiled, shook his head. "Wasn't in me."

"No, I know. You had to fight. Just as I did. To the damn near death."

Helton looked at him again, pointedly, genuinely befuddled. "What is it about us, Joe?"

"Fear."

Helton frowned. "Really?"

"Yep. Fear of looking weak. Fear that if we look weak, the younger wolves—and there's getting to be quite a few of those now, at our ages—will gang up on us, beat the hell out of us, turn us out of the pack. At least out of the *head* of the pack."

"And we'd hate that more than anything—wouldn't we?"

"Yes."

"And here I am," Helton said with a heavy sigh.

"You should've let me kill him," Mannion said after he'd taken a sip of his coffee. "You should've let me take him out of this house, take him out there onto your range, and put a bullet in his head. He deserved that. But you didn't do that. And now look where you are."

"You're wrong, Joe."

Mannion arched a brow at him.

Helton thumbed himself in the chest again and stared off over his range. "I'm the one who should have done that."

Mannion looked down at his hat again.

They sat sipping their coffee for a time then Helton said, "Your daughter. How is she?"

"She's better. I caught a wild stallion for her. I think gentling it will do wonders for her."

"The blue roan?"

"Yep."

"Good!" Helton smiled. "Still, hard to think of a wild creature like that tamed."

"I know. But he'd be dead if I hadn't caught him."

Helton looked at him again. "Would that be so bad?"

Mannion gave a knowing smile and took another sip of his coffee.

Helton threw back the last of his own coffee then said, "Tell me, Joe—why in hell did you let me live, anyway? Back in Del Norte. After the dustup."

Mannion was about to answer when bare feet slapped inside the house and then the door opened and Landry Helton came out wearing a knit shawl about her shoulders and a big straw hat on her head, her blond hair jostling about her shoulders. She held a folded burlap sack under her arm. Her dog, Ivanhoe, was leaping excitedly up against her, barking raucously.

"Goodbye, Papa. I'll be back soon. I'm going out grubbing for mushrooms. I want to add them to the roast tonight." She paused to give her father an affectionate grin. "I do know how much you love your mushrooms with your beef."

"Sauteed in brandy!" Helton said.

"Sauteed in brandy!" Landry echoed him. She pinched the frayed brim of her hat at Mannion. "Good day, Marshal Mannion. I think Pa has enjoyed your visit. Do come again!"

With that, she dashed barefoot down the porch steps, Ivanhoe leaping up against her with the sheer joy and excitement of living and going out on another outing with his favorite person in the world.

He and Helton watched the girl skip off across the yard and head up the side of a pine-stippled mountain, the shaggy dog rushing off ahead of her to chase a rabbit. They watched her until she and the dog were gone.

Then Helton glanced at Mannion, pressed his lips together, and nodded.

CHAPTER 10

EVANGELINE MANNION TRIPPED THE LATCH ON THE stable door, opened the door, poked her head inside, and said, "Good morning, Willow! Good morning, Jack!"

As was his custom, her handsome buckskin gelding, Jack, kicked his stall and loosed a high-pitched whinny in greeting. Willow snorted and bucked a little, making the straw in her stall crackle, hanging her head over the stable door and turning toward Vangie, the horse's brown eyes glinting in the mid-morning light. Jack thrust his own head over his own stable door and nodded it vigorously.

Vangie smiled.

She enjoyed this morning ritual.

Leaving the door open behind her, she stepped inside and called, "Hello there, Cochise!"

That was the name she'd given the stallion, who was in his own stall two stalls down from Jack, on the right side of the stable alley. Vangie thought the name fitting, for the blue roan was as wild as the wildest Indian. She'd heard that Chief Cochise, even though he'd died ten years ago on the Chiricahua Reservation in Arizona

Territory, had remained wild at heart for his entire life. While at some point she wanted to be able to ride her Cochise without being bucked off, Vangie wanted the handsome stallion to remain wild at heart forever.

She went inside and greeted both Willow and Jack, kissing their snouts and nuzzling their ears, whispering to each how much she loved them, and then set to work feeding and watering both and turning them out into the regular corral. She intended to take Willow on a ride. She and the mare each needed to rid themselves of some stable green leftover from the long winter. Tomorrow, she'd ride Jack.

This day was for the ladies.

She smiled at the notion as she went back into the stable and greeted the stallion.

He stood, big and strong in silhouette against the buttery light angling in through the stable's sashed windows, regarding her coldly, his head held proudly, defiantly high.

She was able to rope him and lead him around now though it was often a struggle. He tried to break loose whenever he sensed a loosening of her grip on the rope. In the morning, Cochise was usually more subdued and so looked forward to being free of the stable that he walked relatively agreeably to the round corral, though he yearningly eyed the wild open spaces stretching all the way to the Sawatch Mountains in the north.

The last thing Vangie wanted to do was to have him rip his halter rope out of her hand and head back to the tall and uncut he'd come from. Of course, he'd be happier there. But there he'd likely die from a rancher's bullet. The sad truth was that this country was no longer as wild as the stallion was. This country either gentled or killed wild things.

Vangie hated that about it. But there it was.

She watered and fed a bait of oats to the bronc then, nervously, the halter rope wrapped tightly around her gloved right hand, led him over to the gentling corral. When she got him safely inside and the gate closed and locked, she breathed a sigh of relief then forked hay into the crib so he could eat at his leisure. He rarely ate in front of her when he was in the corral. It was as though he didn't want to give her the satisfaction of knowing that he had to depend on a human for his survival. Or maybe he was telling her that he'd eat hay only when he could crop the grass himself.

"That's all right, Cochise," Vangie said, smiling at the bronc through the corral poles. "I don't blame you a bit. You be good today. I'm going to take a ride, but I'll be back in a couple of hours, and we'll get to back to work."

As though in response, the big stallion backed away from her a couple of feet and angrily pawed the dirt with his right front hoof then lifted his head high again and gave it a defiant shake. He nickered deep in his chest. Vangie hoped her father and Stringbean had built the corral high enough to keep the bronc inside. She knew it was stout enough, but just barely.

A handsome, defiant creature was Cochise. He reminded Vangie a little of her handsome, defiant father...

Vangie bridled and saddled the gentle Willow, kissed Jack goodbye, mounted up, and galloped off to the north, hearing Jack give a lonely whinny behind her. Jack's whinny was followed by the forlorn whinny of the stallion. Vangie winced and closed her eyes. He wanted to ride this way, too, but not with some nettling human on his back.

She knew he was watching her. She didn't look back. She didn't want to see him.

She felt guilty.

She and Willow rode through open country for two miles then descended into the valley of Paradise Creek. They crossed the creek, rode up the opposite ridge, and followed an old Indian trail into a rugged badlands area—one canyon after another, a long, twisting gash in the earth cut eons ago by some ancient river.

The sandstone walls on either side of the cut brightly shone here and there with pictographs painted by the ancients. Vangie's father had shown her these when they'd first come to this country from Kansas; he'd introduced the country to her by riding with her out into the high and rocky reaches beyond the stifling confines of Del Norte. They hunted out here together every fall.

Vangie knew that her pa tried to spend as much time with her as he could because he felt guilty for not having spent enough time with her mother when Sarah Mannion had gone through a "hard time," as her father had called it, in the days and weeks after Vangie had been born.

But Vangie liked to ride alone out here, too. She wasn't sure why. She supposed she was an odd girl, hardly ever keeping company with other girls or boys her own age. She preferred to be by herself or with her horses. She felt more comfortable alone.

However, she hadn't ridden this far out away from Del Norte since the horror she'd gone through last fall. She suddenly grew aware of that now as she rode along the lip of another deep canyon—the canyon on one side, a dense forest of spruce and firs on her left. Realizing that chicken flesh had risen across her shoulders, beneath the short denim jacket and wool plaid shirt she wore with suspenders, she reined in suddenly and hipped around in her saddle to look behind her.

Seconds ago, she'd glimpsed something in the corner of her right eye.

Not an unnatural shape. More like a human shape. More like a *horse and rider* shape.

Was someone following her?

Vangie's heart quickened.

She reined Willow around and rode a good fifty yards back the way she'd come, looking around carefully. Seeing no sign of anyone, she suddenly laughed and heaved a deep sigh of relief.

Just nerves. She'd suddenly realized how far away she was from home and then she'd imagined someone following her, that was all it was.

Just nerves. The only way to get rid of those was to confront them head-on. That's what Pa had told her. Though what Bloody Joe Mannion knew about nerves, Vangie had no idea. She doubted her father had ever been nervous in his life.

She smiled as she reined Willow around again and continued following the ancient trail between the canyon and the steep, forested mountain wall. After several minutes, the trail left the wall and cut through a relatively flat stretch of open terrain. Vangie heard voices and the bawling of cattle to her right.

Again, she reined in sharply, heart thudding. She felt relief again when she saw three drovers a good hundred yards away, herding cows and calves down a gentle ridge toward a valley. They were twirling loops over their heads and whistling and laughing as they herded their "beef on the hoof," likely getting ready for spring branding.

One of the three punchers, a tall man with a black hat, green shirt, red neckerchief, and with the obligatory batwing chaps, turned his head toward Vangie. He smiled then removed his hat and waved it. Vangie waved back a little stiffly. She was glad when the three punchers and their cattle disappeared behind a knoll, still heading for the valley a good distance away from her now.

Glad to be alone again, she nudged Willow ahead and reined up twenty minutes later at the lip of yet another canyon. This was her own secret chasm. That's how she thought of it, anyway. She followed its lip toward the prattling sound of a falls then stopped.

The falls lay just ahead. A creek came down a stone trough to drop over a steep ridge and splash into the canyon nearly directly below Vangie, forming a wide, dark, inviting pool.

Vangie called it Lost Canyon because she'd never seen any sign of anyone else visiting here. Except the ancient peoples who'd once called this area home, of course. She'd found pieces of broken pottery and charred animal bones from ancient fires as well as pictographs painted on the canyon walls portraying stick figures enjoying the falls and the creek.

She stared down at the pool, cream and silver where the falls tumbled into it, dark as ink way back to where the pool spilled over a stone trough to form a stream farther off down the canyon. The water looked inviting. Vangie used to come out here to swim. It was a very private place. She hadn't ridden out here, though, since...

Well, since last fall.

Maybe it was time she started swimming here again.

She looked around. What was there to be afraid of?

Nothing. Still, she felt afraid. She felt vulnerable way out here, so far from home.

But that was silly. She was safer out here where she

was alone than she was at home. After all, it had been at home the bad thing had happened.

Besides, you have to face what you fear head on. Take the bull by the horns.

Vangie chewed her lower lip then reined Willow around and rode back along the canyon lip until she found the trail down the steep ridge wall. She put the mare down the trail, leaning far back in the saddle, holding the reins up high against her chest. Once in the canyon, Vangie booted the mare over to where the falls tumbled down from the ridge and into the pool and dismounted.

The mare put its head down and glowered and switched its tail at the ripples the falls sent out across the pool. Vangie dropped the reins, ground-reining the well-trained horse, and, crossing her arms, looked around cautiously. She looked around the falls then followed the creek as it rippled on down the canyon in its rock- and shrub-lined trough, angling sharply to the left about seventy yards downstream.

She was fearful. That was silly. There was nothing here to fear.

The water was refreshing. What's more, every time she'd swum here, she'd always felt so good and relaxed afterwards. She shouldn't deny that to herself because of fear.

"Okay, girl," she said to the mare idly cropping the dry brown grass growing up from the base of the near ridge. "Time to have some nice, relaxing fun all the way out here in Lost Canyon. No one else out here, right?"

She looked around as she shrugged out of her jacket, slid the suspenders down her arms, and began unbuttoning her shirt. "Just you and me." A hawk gave its ratcheting cry from high in the sky above the canyon.

"Oh, and the hawk. Hawks are nothing to fear—right, girl?"

The horse kept munching grass and idly swishing her tail.

Vangie kicked out of her boots as she removed the shirt and then reached down to grab the hem of her chemise and lift it up over her head, catching it in her hair, which she wore down around her shoulders today. She dropped the chemise where she'd dropped her jacket and shirt and then sat down on a rock to strip out of her tight, blue denims.

She peeled the pantalettes down her legs and then slid her socks down her feet.

Naked, she crossed her arms on her breasts, looked around once more, chewing her bottom lip, fighting her fear. Finally, she walked over to the edge of the pool, dipped a toe to gauge the temperature. She winced. It was cold this time of the year, but you didn't notice so much once you got in. Besides, the cold mountain water was bracing.

So, holding her arms straight out to her sides, she stepped into the pool.

The water inched up her long-legged body. Higher and higher, it climbed until she threw her arms straight out before her, sucked a deep breath, and dove forward into the cool, black pool. She swam deep, the cool water deliciously numbing her skin. She looked at the sandy-bottom rising toward her, the sand ribbed from the currents, so she did not see the three riders ride up to the edge of the canyon and stare down at the pool under the surface of which the pretty girl they'd seen earlier had disappeared.

CHAPTER 11

VANGIE SURFACED, BLOWING WATER, SWABBING IT FROM her eyes.

She turned to see the mare staring up the ridge, tail arched. Just then, a rock tumbled down from the top, bouncing off the side of the ridge until it bounced once more, off a red bulge of sandstone, and plopped into the water five feet in front of Vangie.

She gasped and looked toward the lip of the ridge.

Nothing above the canyon but the shaggy, blue-green forest climbing the mountain above

What had cast the rock into the canyon?

Treading water, shivering from the cold and from another onslaught of sudden fear, Vangie stared up the canyon wall. The mare turned her head to regard her dubiously.

"What is it, girl?" Vangie asked. "What did you see up there?"

The horse merely gave its tail a single swish then looked up the ridge once more.

"You saw something—didn't you?" Vangie asked She heard the tremor in her voice.

She jerked with a start when a rider suddenly appeared, turning a big, brown horse onto the trail that descended the canyon wall--the same trail that Vangie and Willow had taken. Another rider and then another followed the first, who wore a black hat, green shirt, and red neckerchief. He was the puncher who'd waved at her.

Vangie continued treading water, heart hammering, as she watched in horror the three men descend the ridge wall, their chins down so that their hat brims menacingly concealed their eyes.

Vangie shifted her frantic gaze to the mare. Her father made her carry a Winchester carbine with her everywhere. It jutted up from the scabbard strapped to Willow's saddle.

Again, she looked at the men descending the ridge.

Could she make it to the carbine before they reached her?

That she was what they were coming down here for there could be no doubt. After last fall, she'd come to know men all too well.

They were halfway down the ridge now.

The lead rider lifted his head. The broad, black brim of his hat rose to reveal his eyes. They were very dark, and they were smiling in a typically male, goatish, threatening way. So was his mouth, which was mantled by a thick, black mustache.

"No!" Vangie barked, angrily. Angry at herself for merely staying here in the water when she should be swimming to shore and retrieving the Winchester.

Her own angry bark sparked her into motion.

She lunged forward, swimming hard, taking long, water consuming strokes, kicking her feet fiercely, propelling herself forward. She didn't look at the men directly now. She was too intent on trying to save herself.

But as she neared the side of the pool, she could see in the periphery of her vision that they were on the canyon floor now and booting their horses into fast trots.

One gave a whoop.

The last man—thick-set and red-haired—yowled and said, "*Look* at that filly!"

Then, as Vangie climbed up out of the pool and ran toward the mare, who had turned to face the newcomers, fortunately putting the Winchester on the side nearest Vangie, the second man—short and sandy-haired—yelled, "Look at 'em jiggle!"

The first man, in the black hat and with the dark eyes and mustache, put his horse ahead quickly then skidded to a stop ten feet from Vangie just as she pulled the Winchester out of its scabbard and turned to him, furiously, frantically levering a round into the action.

"Get out of here!" she screamed, raising the rifle which she was handy with. Still, it suddenly weighed as much as a wagon wheel. So heavy she was having trouble wielding it.

She was having trouble keeping it raised, and her hands were shaking so that the rifle shook like a leaf on a windblown tree.

"Oh, come on, little girl," said the black-mustached man, who appeared in his mid- to late-twenties. "We just seen you swimmin' an' wanted to come watch."

"You sure are purty," said the short, sandy-haired rider, swinging around to Vangie's left.

The mare gave a frightened whinny, reared, wheeled, and went trotting over to stand by the falls behind Vangie, snorting and rippling her withers.

Vangie crouched over the carbine so that the rear stock was pressed against her breasts, concealing them somewhat. She pivoted on her hips, swinging the rifle from right to left and back again, trying to keep all three men covered. They all had oily expressions on their faces and were ogling her, thoroughly enjoying terrorizing her.

She wanted in the worst way to punch a bullet through the black mustached man's chest. He was the one inching closest to her, holding his reins in one hand, holding his other hand up to Vangie as though in supplication. She drew her index finger back against the trigger but she just couldn't draw it back far enough to fire the rifle.

"Get away," she said through gritted teeth. "Get away —all of you! I'm warning--"

"Hyahh!" The red-haired man suddenly spurred his horse forward, ramming it into Vangie's left hip and shoulder.

She screamed and fired the rifle into the pool as she tumbled to the stone-hard ground and rolled.

And then all three closed on her, laughing and whooping and hollering.

"I'm first," yelled the black-mustached gent. "I seen her first—I get to *have her* first!"

Vangie looked up at him in horror just as he started to swing his right foot over his saddle horn. He'd just gotten his right boot over the horn when the back of his head suddenly went spewing off over the rear end and tail of his horse. His hat flew off. His upper torso sagged backwards; Vangie saw his eyes roll so far up into his head that all she could see were the whites.

Her mind had not yet caught up to her eyes when a rifle blast rocketed around the canyon.

"What the *hell?*" said the red-headed puncher, hipping around in his saddle to stare up the ridge behind him.

He gave a loud grunt as he was punched sideways in his saddle, the center of his back opening up with a fist-sized hole and spewing viscera down his stirrup fender and onto the ground.

The echo of the next blast had not died before the third man—the short sandy-haired puncher, stared up the ridge, snapping his eyes wide and throwing up both gloved hands, palms out. "*No!*" he pleaded.

A half-second later, he was punched back and sideways in his saddle.

He rolled down the side of his suddenly screaming, pitching horse to strike the ground to Vangie's right. "No!" he cried again, climbing to his knees and clamping his left hand over his right shoulder from which blood was oozing. "We was just funnin' with her's all!"

He scrambled to his feet, grunting and mewling, and, hatless, long sandy hair dancing on his shoulders, he went running down along the side of the pool and then leaped over the slight ledge over which the pool overflowed before it dropped to feed the creek running down canyon. He ran as though drunk, keeping his hand clamped over the bloody wound in his shoulder, batwing chaps flapping about his denim-clad legs.

As Vangie watched in hang-jawed shock, the man's head exploded.

He ran a few more stumbling steps before staggering to the right and dropping face down in the creek where he jerked as he died.

Vangie swung her head around to gaze up the ridge. A tall, slender man sat a fine cream stallion on the ridge's lip. He held a rifle in his hands. He was just then turning his head to look from the man he'd just killed to Vangie. He was a striking figure. He wore a long, black leather duster over a black, three-piece suit with a red and gold, gold-buttoned vest. He wore a black leather patch over his left eye.

Long, coal-black hair hung straight down from the bullet-crowned, broad-brimmed hat he wore.

He set the rifle on his thigh, barrel up, reined the cream away from the edge of the ridge and showed his teeth as he clucked to the fine animal. He and the horse disappeared from view before reappearing again where the trail dropped down into the canyon. The man reined the cream onto the trail and rode down slowly, leaning back in the saddle, his gloved left hand wrapped around the stock of the pretty, brass breeched Henry rifle resting barrel up on his thigh.

Pulling herself out of her shock, Vangie rose and, holding one arm across her breasts, walked over to her clothes. Casting cautious glances toward the man riding slowly toward her, taking his time, keeping his head down, the brim of his hat hiding his eyes, she started dressing. She was still a little wet so it wasn't an easy chore, but she did it quickly, shivering from both the cold water and from fear.

She had everything except her boots on and was buttoning her shirt as the man and the cream dropped the last few feet down the trail to the bottom of the canyon. Slowly, his one-eyed face expressionless, the man rode toward Vangie, the cream's hooves clacking on the canyon's stone floor.

The man's lone eye was a strangely luminous green.

Vangie's heart was still racing. She wasn't sure if she had anything to fear from this stranger or not. Maybe he'd killed the others because he wanted her to himself. He was older, however. Much older, though there wasn't a strand of gray in his hair or in his thick, black mustache. His face was handsome but craggy in a way that reminded Vangie of her father's face, though Joe's hair was about half silver as was his mustache. She thought the stranger and her father were probably around the same age, though.

The stranger's face remained menacingly expression-less as he reined up fifteen feet away from Vangie, canted his head a little to one side, and arched the brow over that lone, green eye. "Are you all right, Miss?"

"I've been better." Vangie buttoned the last button on her shirt, hearing her voice tremble. Quickly, she stuffed the tails of the shirt down into the waistband of her denims. She glanced around at the dead men in revulsion. She turned to the newcomer. "I do appreciate the help. If you hadn't come along..."

She didn't want to think about what had been about to happen to her.

Just like before.

But of course, she did. She was visualizing that other time, matching it to this one though she tried not to. She'd thought she'd made it through all that—the gut-wrenching fear and sleepless nights. The ache in her belly, no appetite, dreams in which she'd heard men laughing and howling and herself screaming...

Would they all be back?

"Do you mind if I light?"

Vangie frowned at the stranger. "Do I mind...?"

"If I step down from my saddle?"

A dam broke inside of Vangie when she realized what the man was asking and why he was asking it—because, obviously, she feared him just as right now she feared every other man in the world. She stepped back and to one side and raised the back of her right hand to her mouth, sucking a long, deep breath and releasing it in a shrill, trembling sob.

She half-sat on a rock and wailed into the back of her hand.

"Here, here."

The man shoved the Henry rifle into its black, leather scabbard then swung down from his saddle. He removed his duster and walked slowly over to Vangie, who did not fear him now, for some reason. Because of the question he'd asked her, maybe. It had removed the threat she'd naturally felt in him because he, like the dead three, was male.

He said, "Let me just wrap this around your shoulders, young lady," the man said, gently, and gently, slowly, wrapped the leather duster around her shoulders. "You look very cold."

"Thank you," Vangie said, through another sob, unable to quell the terror oozing out of every pore of her and being given voice by the uncontrolled sobs. "I am very cold!"

"I'll build us a fire," the man said. "Make us a pot of coffee. Make you feel better."

Vangie just wanted to climb onto her horse and head for home, but she felt like she'd felt a few minutes ago, when she'd been lying naked on the ground—immobile. As unable to move as a stone. She was almost afraid to turn her head one way or the other, as though fearing what she might see there. Her terror was the wild roan galloping inside her, making her heart continue to pound.

She watched, shaking, as the man gathered chunks of driftwood left by spring floods when the falls and the creek it created was a torrent. He arranged rocks into a ring and set about building a fire, starting with tinder. When he had a couple of fledgling flames going and was leaning low, holding the black hat in his hand, to blow on the flames, he glanced over at Vangie, who was no longer sobbing but still trembling.

"What's your name, child?" he asked.

Vangie drew a deep breath, cleared her throat. "V-Vangie," she said. "Evangeline Mannion."

The man looked surprised. Then a smile quirked the corners of his long, thin mouth. "You don't say?"

Vangie frowned. "What's yours?"

"Drago. *Longshot* Hunter Drago." That one mesmerizing green eye narrowed as he smiled warmly at Vangie. "Pleased to make your acquaintance, Miss Mannion. I know your father. We go back a ways—me an' Bloody Joe."

He smiled more broadly and winked.

CHAPTER 12

When Longshot Hunter Drago had a good fire going and had hung his coffee pot from an iron tripod to cook it, Vangie found the fire so warmly appealing, leaching the chill as well as the terror out of her bones, that she finally came down off her rock and sat on one nearer the fire.

She leaned forward and wrapped her arms around her knees. She looked at Drago on the other side of the fire where he absently prodded the burning wood with a willow stick.

"Are you...or *were* you...a lawman, Mister Drago?" He wasn't currently wearing a badge that Vangie could see.

"Me? Nah, nah," Drago said, glancing up at her with his green eye.

"I thought maybe that was how you knew my father."

"Nope. But your father and I go back a ways." He gave a wry chuckle.

"Were you friends?"

"Your father—well, I'm not sure how he sees us."

"My father can be rather, um..." Vangie hugged her knees more tightly, feeling much better now, physically calmer, as well as safe. Drago had hauled away the bodies so she could no longer see them and could instead enjoy the fire and her and Hunter Drago's conversation in peace. "My father can be rather stubborn, narrow in his way of seeing things."

"I can honestly say I've never known a more stubborn man than Joe Mannion."

"Bloody Joe," Vangie said with an affectionate smile.

She glanced at Drago. She saw a strange, dark light in that lone eye now, suddenly, as he stared across the fire at her. Just as suddenly, her suspicions were aroused. Her thoughts returned to her feeling of having been followed when she'd been riding along the edge of the canyon earlier, believing she'd spied someone in the corner of her eye.

Fear returned, making her heart hiccup once more.

"What are you doing out here, Mister Drago? If you don't mind me asking."

"Honey, a pretty girl like you can ask me anything she wants." Drago flashed her a warm smile. The warmth touched his lone eye again, which calmed her again, at least a little. "I reopened The Three-Legged-Dog Saloon in town. The place has a small kitchen and I'd like to serve game. Always been partial to venison and elk and... well, you see, I haven't had the opportunity to enjoy any of that in quite a few years. Bear, too. Nothing like a pan of bear liver fried with wild onions or the tenderloins— two long cylinders of muscle that run beneath the ribs. You eat that, you'll think you died and gone to heaven!"

"I see," Vangie said, nodding but continuing to study the man closely, suspiciously. "You know...back along the trail I had the sense someone was behind me."

"Probably me," Drago said. "I don't recollect seein' you, though." He offered another warm smile. "And I'm sure I would have remembered." He looked at her point-edly, concern suddenly flashing in that jade eye. "Oh, don't worry, honey. I'm no threat to you. I may not always have been a civilized man, thus the 'Longshot' moniker, but I'm civilized now. Through and through. And you know who I have to blame for that?"

"Who's that?"

"Your father."

Vangie frowned, genuinely curious.

"He put me in prison a little over twelve years ago."

"He did?" Vangie slapped a hand to her chest in shock. "That's how you knew my father?"

"Rest easy, honey," Drago said, chuckling as he used a stick to remove the boiling pot from the tripod. "I give thanks every day for Bloody Joe Mannion. Him throwin' me in prison is how I found the Lord...and a better way of life. A different way of lookin' at things, you might say. The world is a kinder, gentler place for me now."

Drago reached into his coffee pouch sitting with its mouth open beside him and tossed a fistful of Arbuckles into the pot. He used a leather swatch to return the lid to the pot then hung the pot over the fire once more.

He absently brushed the swatch against his knee as he stared into the flames and said, "Before prison, I was a dark man. A soulless, unhappy man. I was a killer. I not only didn't *mind* killing, I *enjoyed* killing." He cast his gaze across the fire at Vangie. "Now, you probably can't fathom a man thinking that way. No, you couldn't in a million years. Your soul is sweet. But that's how I thought, sure enough. It was an awful way to live, and you don't even realize it. You don't know the happiness you're missing out on. Dark. Oh, God—so dark!"

A sheen grew in his eye. A tear dribbled down his cheek as he poked again at the fire with the stick. "Sorry,

sorry," he said, thickly, self-consciously, and brushed the tear from his cheek with his gloved right hand. "I lost so many good years." He looked at Vangie again. "You know what I mean? Too many wasted years, and we get only so many, honey."

Vangie felt her renewed suspicions and fear leeching away as the others had done. As she stared across the fire at this suddenly emotional man—a man who just a minute ago she never would have suspected capable of feeling such emotion—the warmth of a vague affection and sympathy touched her. She could imagine all the darkness that must be part and parcel of such a life as that he'd described. She could imagine it because in the depths of her own horror, she'd been able to imagine that darkness behind the grinning faces of her howling attackers—back last fall and here again today.

How empty such souls must be. How constantly desperate.

"How I do go on," Drago said, removing the pot from the fire once more and setting it on a rock. He poured a little water into the pot from his canteen to settle the grounds.

He dug out a couple of fire-scorched, white-speckled black cups from his war bag and used the swatch to fill each with the piping hot brew onto the surface of which a couple of gray ashes from the fire floated. He rose and handed one across the fire to Vangie.

"Be careful with that, honey. It's hot."

"I got it," Vangie said, wincing against the burn as she took the cup in both hands. "Thank you." She set the cup down on her thigh and blew on it and glanced once more across the fire at Drago, who suddenly appeared deep in thought now, brow ridged, as he stared into the fire, holding his coffee cup in both of his gloved hands.

Suddenly, he smiled as he looked at her again. "Enough of the darkness talk. The past is buried. I can't do anything about it now. My spirit is light now. Light as angels' wings. I came here to settle down and build a business and a life. A *good* life. The Lord's life. I'm not perfect. No, no, no. Far from it! But I do try. I know I may be too old to start a family, but I'd still like to find a good woman and settle down. Have someone to warm my feet in my old age. Someone to say goodbye to when —well, you know..."

"At the end," Vangie said, understanding though she'd never yet felt that impulse herself. To settle down with a husband. She was too happy with her solitary life with her horses. But now, talking with Drago, she felt the glimmer of a notion that maybe that one day would change.

Maybe it *should* change.

After all, she didn't want to spend her entire life alone, did she? Her pa wasn't going to live forever.

"Well, I'm glad Pa did that for you, Mister Drago." Vangie gave a dry chuckle. "I have to admit there aren't too many folks who feel that way about my father."

Drago sipped his coffee, swallowed, and said, "Please, call me Hunter."

"All right," Vangie said with a smile. "Hunter it is. I'm Vangie."

Drago stood and thrust his hand across the fire at her. "Pleased to make your acquaintance, Miss Vangie."

Vangie laughed, stood, and shook the man's hand, a little surprised to feel the stiffness of fear gone from her limbs. "The pleasure is all mine, Hunter." She glanced off to where he'd hauled the bodies of the men he'd killed. "For obvious reasons."

Drago threw back the last of his coffee. "Well, what

do you see we ride back to town together, Vangie?" He smiled. "Get you back to your pa?"

"Sounds good, Hunter. Under the circumstances I would more than welcome a trail companion though I vow not to let what happened here today bother me for long."

"Oh, it won't, it won't. You have a strength in you, Vangie. I can see that. It'll take you far."

"I think so, too, Hunter."

Drago took the cups over to the pool to rinse them out. "Let's get you home." He glanced over his shoulder at the girl. "Can't wait to see the expression on Bloody Joe's face when he sees who his daughter is riding back to town with!"

Vangie laughed.

———

MANNION PUSHED THROUGH THE BATWINGS OF THE San Juan Hotel & Saloon and stopped dead in his tracks, scowling.

Just ahead of him, Jane Ford was setting drinks down on a table manned by three Del Norte businessmen, from the tray she held on the flat of her left hand. She looked damn near as beautiful as she always did, dressed to the nines as she was, her curly red hair pinned atop her head. She would have looked every bit as beautiful as always if not for the wide white bandage wrapped around the top of her head, over the bullet burn she'd taken because she'd been fool enough to breakfast with Joe himself.

Also, she was paler than usual and still a bit drawn, which was no surprise. She'd lost a lot of blood that fateful day, had left most of it on the floor of the indignant Ida Becker's Good Food. The doctor had ordered

Jane to stay in bed for at least two weeks and to not return to work for a good month.

Well, it had only been *three days* since she'd taken the bullet meant for Mannion.

As she lowered the tray and turned away from the businessmen's table with her trademark fetching smile, Joe marched up to her and somehow managed to keep his voice down: "Good Lord, woman, are you *trying* to kill yourself?"

"Oh, Joe, please," Jane said, returning his scowl. "I can't lay around in bed. I was going mad. Besides, I have a business to run!"

"Jane, you were down for only two days!"

"Two and a half. The doctor said it was a relatively minor wound and the only problem was that the scalp, when cut, bleeds something awful. So, I lost some blood. I have it all back now from all that soup you forced down my throat, and I am going back to work." She fingered the heavy, padded bandage. "If only I didn't have to wear this. Doesn't go with anything else in my wardrobe despite my best efforts to find something."

She smiled and rose up on the toes of her high-heeled shoes to plant a kiss on Mannion's cheek. "Please, don't worry about me."

"Well, I do worry, Jane, dammit."

"I'm ready for a break. Join me for a cup of coffee?"

"If it'll help get you off your feet, of course, I will." Mannion took the tray out of her hand and pulled out a chair from the nearest table. "You sit down. I'll fetch the mud."

"Oh, Joe," Jane chuckled.

"Don't 'Oh, Joe,' me, Miss Ford—damned stubborn redhead!"

With that he strode around behind the bar, set the

tray down, and continued through a swing door into the kitchen and filled two stone mugs with coffee from a pot steaming on the warming rack of the big range manned by Jane's Mexican cook, Guillermo Apodaca, and his wife, Pilar.

Guillermo glanced at the steaming cups sitting on the food preparation table littered with the makings of what would likely be a savory rabbit stew for later in the evening. "I take it one of those is for Miss Jane, Senor Joe?"

"Indeed," Mannion said. "Anything to get her off her feet."

"I tried to convince her to stay in bed," Guillermo said, opening an airtight tin of beans. "But you know Miss Jane."

Pilar was stirring a pot of soup on the range and slowly shaking her head in silent disapproval.

"Yes, I do know Miss Jane," Mannion said, picking up the two mugs and heading for the door. "All too well sometimes!"

He pushed back through the swing door, walked out from around the bar, and set both mugs down on the table at which Jane was sitting. She was leaning forward, elbows on the table, gently kneading her temples with the tips of her fingers.

"See, there?" Mannion reprimanded her, taking a seat across the table from her and brushing his fist disgustedly across his thick mustache. "You've gone and overdone it, haven't you?"

"Not at all, Joe," Jane said. "Just a little tension is all. Carlton Sprague is late with those hogs I ordered, and the Santini wedding is the day after tomorrow." Carlton Sprague was a local pig farmer and Omar Santini was a wealthy Italian mine owner soon to become one of Del

Norte's former most eligible bachelors. A leggy dance hall singer from Leadville had stolen his heart and would no doubt soon have most of his money, as well.

At least, that was Mannion's customary cynical view.

Joe drew a deep breath and studied Jane with concern as he blew ripples on his black coffee and sipped it.

She smiled wanly as she reached across the table and wrapped her right hand around his left wrist. "I'm fine, Joe. Really. I need something to get up for in the morning, even if it's dealing with one pain in the backside after another."

Mannion returned her wan smile.

"Speaking of weddings," Jane said, suddenly frowning at him. "You've decided not to marry me, haven't you?"

Mannion was saved from having to answer when Stringbean McCallister pushed through the heavy oak batwings and strode up to Joe's and Jane's table. "Uh... Marshal Mannion?"

"What is it, Stringbean?"

Stringbean had a constipated look on his long face. He canted his head toward the batwings, half-turning his body, and said, "You're uh...you're uh..."

"*Yes*, Stringbean?" Jane said, annoyed at having her and Joe's conversation interrupted at such an inopportune time.

To Mannion, Stringbean said, "You're gonna want to come out and take a look at this, I think. At who just rode into town, I mean. And who's ridin' with her!"

CHAPTER 13

"'AT WHO'S RIDIN' *WITH* HER'?" MANNION SAID, echoing his young deputy and gazing curiously across the table at Jane.

He rose from his chair and followed Stringbean across the room to the batwings. Stringbean pushed slowly through the louvred doors then stepped to one side, making way for his boss. Joe stepped through the doors and Jane followed him, both gazing curiously into the street still busy and dusty now at nearly five o'clock in the afternoon.

"Good God!" Mannion said when he saw who Stringbean was looking at--none other than Joe's precious daughter riding side by side with Longshot Hunter Drago, angling toward the San Juan. Drago had three more packhorses trailing behind him, outfitted very similarly to the three he'd trailed into town when he'd first come to Del Norte.

"*What in holy blazes!*" Mannion fairly roared, rage engulfing him.

"Joe!" Jane cried as Mannion bolted forward, running down the San Juan's porch steps and into the street. "You son of a bitch!" he bellowed as he reached up and grabbed Drago by both coat lapels. "*How dare you?*"

"Hold on, Joe!" Drago cried.

"Pa, no!" Vangie yelled.

Too late. Mannion pulled the tall man off his horse.

"*Joe!*" the killer yelled as he flew down the side of the cream and landed in the street, dust wafting around him.

Drago groaned.

"Pa, please—it's not what you think!" Vangie cried, leaping from her saddle.

"I know him better than you do," Mannion bellowed. "It's exactly what I think!"

He crouched and pulled Drago up off the street. The man was grimacing, shaking his head as though to clear the cobwebs. He held up one hand in beseeching to Mannion. "Joe, please—I ran into her by accident!"

Mannion brought his clenched right fist up from his waist and smashed it against Drago's jaw. The killer flew back into the street, his cream and the packhorses, which were tied together, side-stepping nervously.

"Pa!" Vangie cried again, running up to her father and grabbing his right arm. "*He saved my life!*"

Mannion only vaguely heard the girl beneath the churning of the fury mills inside his head and beneath his heart. He brushed Vangie aside as he again crouched to pick the tall, lean gunman up out of the dirt with a fierce grunt.

"If I ever catch you within a city block of my daughter again, Drago, I'll kill you!"

Again, Joe slammed his fist into the killer's face—this time opening a cut beneath his eye patch. Drago gave an indignant groan as he stumbled farther back into the street where, as he struck and rolled, he came to within three feet of being run over by the six-hitch team of mules pulling an ore dray.

The driver bellowed and laughed. "Bloody Joe's at it again, folks! Puts on a good show every time!" The driver continued to bellow as he cracked the blacksnake over his team's backs and rolled on down the street to the south

Drago lay on his belly in the dirt and ground horse manure, pressing the palms of his hands into the dirt, trying to lever himself to his feet. He was breathing hard. His black hair was dirty and badly mussed.

Mannion walked up to him, preparing to deliver a vicious kick to the man's side.

"Pa!" Vangie cried again.

That stopped Joe. He glanced behind him to see Vangie standing behind him, sobbing, pressing the heels of her hands to her temples in misery.

"You don't understand who that is, daughter!" Mannion bellowed, pointing down at the writhing, black-clad killer. "He's the devil himself, and he's not here in Del Norte by coincidence, either!"

Mannion stepped forward and rammed the pointed toe of his right boot into Drago's ribs.

"*Ohh!*" the killer cried, rolling onto his back and clutching his injured side.

"Will someone please stop that man!" came a man's shout behind Mannion. Joe recognized Mayor Charlie McQueen's voice.

Joe was about to reach down and pull Drago up out of the dirt once more but then two men came up behind him and grabbed his arms.

"Joe, stop!" Rio Waite yelled, holding his right arm. "He's done, Joe. He's finished. You beat on him anymore, you'll kill him!"

"Please, Marshal!" Stringbean urged, standing on Joe's left side, clutching Joe's other arm and regarding his boss with no little pleading. "It's over. You done kicked he stuffing out that fella—both ends, purely!"

Rage still searing through his bones, Mannion looked down at Drago. The killer stared up at him with phony beseeching. Mannion could see the light of mockery in the man's lone eye.

Oh, he was in pain, all right. That part was genuine. But he was loving every bit of it. Mannion knew he'd walked into the man's trap, but he hadn't been able to help himself. Seeing Vangie riding with that cold-blooded killer was like seeing a baby being taken from its crib in the middle of the night by a wildcat that had slipped in through an open window.

"Please, Joe," the killer urged, grimacing painfully. "I'm finished. Really. And, for what's it's worth...if it'll make you feel better...I do apologize." He raised both hands, palm up. "I didn't touch a hair on her head—I promise. I wouldn't. I *couldn't!*"

"You malicious cur!" Mannion barked down at him, lurching forward but being firmly held by his two deputies. "I know what you're up to. Don't think I don't!"

"Marshal Mannion!" The dapper, bespectacled Charlie McQueen walked up to Joe. His head came up only to Joe's shoulder, so the man had to lift his immaculately bearded chin to look up at him, his eyes glinting with deep indignation. "Your daughter says this man saved her from those three men slung over their saddles. I looked them over. They're Delvin Potter's men, and, knowing their reputations—as you do—I don't doubt one but that they'd attack a young lady they found alone in the mountains."

"It's true, Pa," Vangie put in, walking up to stand

beside the mayor. Tears streaked her cheeks and deep sadness and frustration shown in her eyes. "They attacked me. I thought I was alone. Hunter shot them before they could finish what they started."

"*Hunter?*" Mannion said, his voice pitched with disdain.

"Listen to your daughter, for God sakes, Marshal," McQueen urged. "He saved her life." He pointed at Drago playing the injured lamb in the street before them. "And this is how you thank him!"

"For God sakes," came another man's voice. "What in tarnation is going on here, Joe?"

Doc Willoughby pushed through the small crowd that had gathered and brushed past Stringbean to crouch down over Drago, who lay breathing like a landed fish, lips stretched back from his teeth. The doctor glowered up at Mannion and said, "Christalmighty—why are you trying to kill the owner of the Three-Legged Dog, Joe? He's a respected businessman." He looked down at Drago. "Easy, Mister Drago. Take it easy. I'm going to check and see if you have any broken bones, and then we'll get you over to my office."

The sawbones glanced up at Mannion once more, shaking his head in disgust. "For *Godsakes!*"

Touched with chagrin, but only just a little, Mannion turned to Vangie. He wasn't quite sure what to say. Again, she'd been attacked. *This time Longshot had saved her?*

What was Drago doing anywhere Vangie was?

That hadn't been an accident. Not anymore than Drago's presence in Del Norte's was an accident. How could he get that across to her? And to everyone else in the town?

He cleared his throat to speak but Vangie merely stared up at him in disgust then swung around suddenly, marched up the hotel's front porch steps, and disappeared inside. Vangie had marched past Jane, who stood at the bottom of the steps, regarding Joe with the same expression Vangie had. Slowly, she, too, shook her head in disdain then swung around and headed back into the hotel.

Mannion stood numb as a stone until he realized there was no one around him anymore. While he'd been staring at the hotel's front louvred doors, Drago had been lifted up off the street and carried over to the doctor's office for tending. Rio Waite and Stringbean were gone. Charlie McQueen was gone. Most of the crowd had dispersed. Those remaining regarded him as though he were some escaped circus lion.

Mannion spat to one side, brushed the bloody knuckles of his right first against his pants, then headed up the street in the direction of his office.

Rage still burned in him. Not as hotly as before. It was tempered by a deep frustration.

There was a wolf in the fold here in Del Norte, and he was the only one who knew it. The other citizens stood with the wolf.

Which meant they were the most vulnerable sheep of all.

———

AROUND SIX O'CLOCK THAT NIGHT, STRINGBEAN McCallister turned his coyote dun, Banjo, onto the trail that led up to the Hurdstrom house just outside of town on the north side, in a pretty grove of aspens near Hatchet Creek. He always felt a little strange heading for the Hurdstrom house. He liked Molly a whole lot—no, he loved Molly a whole lot—but her family was so far removed from his humble upbringing in Oklahoma, that he felt out of place here in her stately digs.

On the other hand, he was both humbled and proud that Molly's parents hadn't objected to her seeing this lowly deputy town marshal. He didn't know what he'd do if they suddenly didn't want him coming by anymore. His life would be a right empty, lonely one without Miss Molly in it.

He looked down at the spray of pansies he held in his gloved right hand. He'd bought the freshly cut flowers from Miss Eugenia Day's Flower Shop on 4th Avenue in Del Norte. They'd cost him a pretty penny—seventy-five scents for eight of them wrapped in purple tissue paper—but they were worth every penny. Pansies were Molly's favorite.

As he approached the two-story brick house with a white-columned portico off the right side, that feeling of strangeness grew inside him again. To the left of the portico, on the gravel driveway, sat a fancy-looking carriage with two fine, white horses sanding in the traces. The carriage looked much like a Concord coach only it was painted white, trimmed in dark red, and was tricked out with fancy brass fittings and high, red wheels. Green velvet curtains hung over the windows. Over the door was scrolled in ornate lettering: McClarksville & Company Mines. On the door was a gold 'M' in a black circle.

As Stringbean rode up beside the carriage, he saw that the driver's boot was painted red, as well. The seat itself was upholstered in quilted red leather.

It was the sort of contraption that Stringbean imagined a governor would be carted around in. Or, hell, maybe even the President himself.

Cold fingers of apprehension danced across the back

of the deputy's neck.

The Hurdstroms had visitors. Had he gotten the day mixed up? No, he was sure that Molly had invited him over for supper Wednesday evening.

He sat the dun staring at the front door on the other side of the portico, chewing his bottom lip. Should he knock on the door or turn Banjo around and ride away?

He couldn't leave. He'd promised Molly he'd come today, so despite his fears and awkwardness, he was going to climb down out of the saddle, firm up his spine, and walk over and knock on the door, by God.

He swung down, tied Banjo at the hitchrack, stepped between the white columns, and crossed the stone-paved portico to the big, carved front door with a knocker in the shape of a lion's paw. He lifted his hand to use the knocker but stopped when he heard the hum of jovial conversation issuing from the other side of the door.

Men laughing.

Glasses and bottles rattled together.

Stringbean frowned. Shyness, fear gripped him.

He couldn't give into it. His girl was on the other side of the door. What kind of man would he be if he turned tail and ran when he'd promised her he'd be here now?

He lifted his hand, which shook slightly, and wrapped the knocker against its brass plate three times, wincing a little with each loud knock.

The knocks silenced the conversation on the other side of the door.

"Who in the world could that be?" a man's voice said. Stringbean recognized Mr. Hurdstrom's voice.

Footsteps rose, growing louder as someone approached the door.

Stringbean felt like dropping the flowers and turning tail, but he stood his ground, by God.

CHAPTER 14

ANOTHER SET OF FOOTSTEPS ROSE, THESE SOFTER THAN
the first.

Molly's voice said, "I'll get it, Pa."

"Oh," said Mr. Hurdstrom. "Yes, I suppose you
should. Hurry, though, dear. We don't want to keep Adam
and his father waiting."

The heavier footsteps drifted away. The lighter ones
grew louder until the door latch clicked, the door
opened, and Molly stepped out onto the step beside
Stringbean, drawing the door closed behind her.

She was always a vision, but tonight she was dressed
in a way Stringbean had never seen her dressed before.
To absolute immaculate perfection in a frilly silk and
taffeta gown the color of a cloudless sky at midmorning.
Her hair was immaculately coifed, much of it gathered
into a French braid behind her head and held in place by
a silver clip. She smelled like rose water and cherries.
Over her bare shoulders was a white silk shawl thin as a
moth's wings.

"Molly," Stringbean said, unable to keep his eyes from

roaming over her creamy skin and stunning figure. "I've never...I've never..."

"Seen me dressed this way? No, you wouldn't. I mean, I don't make it a habit. My mother bought me this frock in Denver...back when she and Pa first got the idea that I might be..." Molly's expression grew pensive, sad, and she looked away briefly, her lovely cheeks flushing a little with emotion.

"That you might be what?"

She looked up at him, desperation in her eyes. "Look, Henry, I should have told you this long ago. I guess I didn't want to think about it...or believe it. But..."

"But what, Molly? That carriage over there. I got a feeling a young man came in it, didn't he?"

"Yes. And his father. Malcom and Adam McClarksville and a friend of Adam's rode up from Denver. Malcolm McClarksville is one of my father's business partners. They both got to thinking what a wonderful idea it might be if Adam and I..."

Suddenly, Stringbean's heart was breaking as he said, "Got hitched?"

Molly looked up at Stringbean. "Believe me, Henry, I've been fighting the idea tooth and nail for a long time. Adam has been in college, so my parents haven't brought him up to me in over a year. Then, well, Adam and his father and Adam's friend, A.J. Lamb, just suddenly showed up a couple of hours ago." She gave a weak smile. "Said they wanted it to be a surprise. I have a feeling that after supper Adam and I will go outside on the porch and sit in the swing, and he'll propose to me."

Stringbean let out a long, deeply held breath. "I see." He poked his hat brim up off his forehead. He was beginning to understand what Rio had been warning him about.

To Molly, he said, "I suppose you'll say yes." He glanced at the opulent carriage. "They must be real moneyed folks, the McClarksvilles."

"Well, Mister McClarksville owns two railroads and he's going to run for territorial governor of Colorado. I guess he lives in Denver half the year. That's why he has my father eating out of his hand. My parents see me marrying Adam as a business decision. They're practically bursting at the seams in there."

"I suppose they are."

"That's why I'm not sure..."

"Not sure what?"

Molly looked up at Stringbean with a near frantic expression. "That's why I'm not sure how I'm going to tell them I turned down Adam's request for my hand."

"You are?" Stringbean asked in shock. "I mean...that's what you're gonna do, Molly? You're gonna turn him down?"

"I don't love him. How can I marry a man I don't love?"

"I...I..."

"Henry." Molly took the flowers out of his hand and smiled up at him. "You're the one that I--"

The door latch clicked and the door suddenly opened, and there was the tall, bearded, severely handsome Mr. Hurdstrom, dressed in an immaculate black suit with a burgungy vest and black tie, glaring at Molly and her visitor. He looked at Stringbean and said crisply, "I'm sorry if there's been a misunderstanding, Mister McCallister. But my daughter will no longer be able to see you. Come, Molly, our guests are waiting," he added in a taut, anxious air.

He grabbed Molly's arm and pulled her inside, saying to Stringbean, "I truly am sorry, Deputy. You are a good man. I've enjoyed our conversations. But you're just not the man for our Molly. I hope you didn't think you were. Good night, sir."

He closed the door but not before Molly cast a haunted look back through the opening at Stringbean. Stringbean turned away, heart thudding, not quite believing what he'd just heard and witnessed. The door opened behind him, and his flowers came flying out to land on the stone floor of the portico beyond him and to his right. The light, purple paper tore and the flowers scattered.

The door closed behind Stringbean.

He walked over and stared down at the flowers. A deep bitterness was seeping through him. Bitterness and rage. He glanced back at the door that Mr. Hurdsville had so rudely slammed in his face, as though he were no more than a stray dog howling on the stoop for scraps. He looked down at the flowers again then gave them an angry kick, scattering them far and wide.

"You can go to hell!" he said to the closed door.

He stomped over, untied his dun's reins from the hitchrack, and swung up into the saddle. He looked at the door again and said, "Go to hell, you popinjay!" Then he booted the dun into a gallop and didn't slow even a little until he reined up in front of Hotel de Manion ten minutes later.

Rio Waite was kicked back in a chair on the front stoop, boots crossed on the rail before him, battered hat tipped far up on his forehead. His big greener was leaning against the wall behind him. Buster was sitting on his lap, lapping cream from a small tin saucer resting on Rio's bulging belly.

"Whoa! Whoa! Where's the fire? Shall I ring the bell for the bucket brigade?" Rio queried in jest.

"You were right, Rio," Stringbean said, tossing his reins over the hitchrack. "I'm sorry I doubted you."

"Oh, hell," Rio said, instantly realizing the score.

It had been Stringbean's night to work but Rio had traded shifts with him so Stringbean could have supper over at the Hurdstrom house.

"What happened?"

Stringbean loosed the dun's saddle cinch then walked up onto the stoop. "What you figured would happen. Right down to Hurdstrom slammin' the dang door in my face!"

"Ah, hell, kid," Rio said, glowering up at the younger deputy.

Stringbean said, "Why don't you go home? I got plenty of time to pull my own shift now."

"Maybe you need to go get drunk. Find yourself a sweet li'l doxie, Stringbean. One who'll curl your toes and erase your memory."

Stringbean sat angrily down in the hide bottom chair to the left of Rio as well as the open office door flanking him. "Nothin's gonna erase my memory." He shook his head. "Dang, that was humliatin'. He even threw my flowers out the door!"

"He did?"

"Sure did."

"Uppity son of a buck," Rio said.

"You called it."

"Never liked that man myself. Rides around in that leather buggy of his with his chin in the air." Rio dropped Buster to the porch floor and set the now-empty pan onto the porch rail beside him then rose from his chair, the wood creaking with his shifting weight. "Well, if you're gonna sit up all night an' stew you might as well get paid for it. Me?" He grinned and pulled his hat down lower on his forehead. "I'm gonna go a-courtin'."

Stringbean looked up at him in surprise. "You are?"

"You watch me." Rio winked. "I still got a little romance left in these old bones. Later."

"Later, Rio," Stringbean said, chuckling until he remembered that sad, desperate look Molly had given him right before her father had slammed the door in his face.

He sat back in his chair and crossed his arms on his chest, fuming.

———

STRINGBEAN TOOK SEVERAL RIDES AROUND THE TOWN. All was relatively quiet, it being a weeknight, though now with Del Norte having grown so much so fast in the two years Stringbean had been deputy, you just never knew when or where trouble would erupt.

By ten o'clock, he'd only had to break up a skirmish between two Chinese miners who'd been about to beat each other's brains out with shovels out front of the Come One, Come All hurdy gurdy house on third street, and shoot a skunk lurking around one of the livery barns and was believed to be rabid.

He returned to the jailhouse, beefed up the fire in the stove, and set a half-full pot of coffee to warm. He'd just blown a dead fly out of his tin cup when running footsteps sounded in the otherwise quiet street fronting Hotel de Manion. He'd left the door open to the cool, spring night air, so when he turned to it, he saw the tow-headed Harmon Hauffenthistle run up the porch steps, the nine-year-old's suntanned face red with anxiety beneath the brim of his black watch cap.

"Stringbean, where's the Marshal?"

"I ain't seen him since this mornin'."

"Since he punched the lights of poor ol' Mr. Drago, ya mean?" Young Harmon enjoyed a fight as much as any healthy, red-blooded nine-year-old, but that had obviously been hard to watch even for him.

"Yeah, I reckon that's what I mean." Stringbean turned to face the boy and hitched his cartridge belt and old-model Colt revolver up higher on his lean hips. "What's happening, Harmon? Did Mrs. Bjornson's cat fall into that old well again? You know, I told her she needs to cover that blame hole. I'm sick to heck of havin' to--"

"No, that ain't it." Harmon wagged his head. "Miss Jane sent for you. She was hopin' the marshal wasn't here...after this mornin', I reckon. She said to fetch you or Rio. Since it's you here..."

"Would you get to the point, Harmon? I was hopin' to enjoy my coffee in peace and then try to take a little nap."

"Gee, what's got your drawers in such a twist, Stringbean?"

"Never mind. Get on with it, Harmon. What does Miss Jane need me for?" Stringbean sipped his mud.

"Dusty Wallace and Dwight Beauchamp are givin' each other the wooly eyeball in the San Juan." Harmon gave a knowing grin. "You know what about, too, I bet —he-he."

"Ah, heck—not them two again!"

Dusty Wallace and Dwight Beauchamp were cow punchers who once rode for the same brand. They'd once been friends until Beauchamp had married a pretty former whore they'd both been fond of. That was when the rancher who'd hired them both fired Beauchamp to keep the peace in the bunkhouse.

Now Beauchamp and his wife, the former Sally Little Boy, a pretty half-breed girl, had their own shotgun ranch in the San Juans. Word around Del Norte had it that Beauchamp's having married Sally hadn't kept Sally and Dusty Wallace from trysting in an isolated mountain cabin on occasion.

It sounded like Beauchamp might have found out where that cabin was and what exactly was going on in there...

Harmon snickered. "Miss Jane's worried they're gonna get drunk an' get in a dustup and break the place apart like they *almost* done last time over at the Wooden Nickel. She wants you to go over and settle 'em down. She said you're good at that—at keepin' a lid on trouble." The boy grinned and winked, again with meaning. "Unlike one town marshal we both know."

Again, Harmon snickered.

"I wish you'd quit havin' so much fun at the marshal's expense, Harmon. And what're you doin' up this late? Isn't it past your bedtime?"

Harmon shrugged as he pulled an apple out of his coat pocket and rubbed it on his coat sleeve. "Ah, heck, I always skin out a window after Ma an' Pa start sawin' logs, an' come uptown. Someone always needs me for somethin', and I raise my rates after seven. I can always use the extra cash, don't ya know. Me, I got ambitions."

He bit into his apple and chewed.

"All right, all right," Stringbean said, reluctantly setting his freshly poured coffee on the marshal's cluttered desk. "I'll go over an' see if I can't keep a lid on them two. Miss Jane's right. If anyone can do it, I can..."

Besides, he could use the distraction.

He kept remembering that door slamming in his face.

CHAPTER 15

"You wait out here, Harmon," Stringbean told the boy as he climbed the broad steps of the San Juan's front veranda. "This is no place for boys out beyond their bedtimes."

The place was hopping as it usually was even on weeknights between ten and midnight. Stringbean could hear the muffled roar of jovial conversation beyond the batwings, smell the cigarette and cigar smoke and the perfume of Miss Jane's lovely doxies—the prettiest, most professional girls in any hurdy-gurdy house in the southern Territory.

"To hell with that," Harmon said, defiantly following Stringbean through the batwings. "One of the girls might need an errand run, and I'm here to run it for her for the right jingle or a swallow of beer!"

Stringbean sighed as he stopped just inside the batwings and looked around. Miss Jane caught his eye right away. She was standing at one of the tables ahead and to Stringbean's right, chinning with several men in business suits and crisp Stetsons on the table before them. Out of towners. Impressive looking men in their forties with mustaches and neatly combed hair. Likely men looking to buy or sell cattle or horses, as Del Norte and the area around it had become a lucrative market over the past few years. The men were looking at Jane with the twinkle of male appreciation in their eyes. Even wearing the bandage around her head, albeit a much smaller one than before, and one that matched the color of her dress, Miss Jane was a sight to behold, that was for sure.

Even Stringbean could see that.

"If you'll excuse me, gentlemen," Jane told the men before her, her gaze on Stringbean, a smile stretching her red lips. "I have some business to take care of."

Jane walked over in that graceful way of hers, the light from the wagon wheel chandeliers glinting in her eyes as well as off the pearl choker encircling her fine, long neck. The eyes of the men she'd been speaking with followed her brashly. She wore her hair partway down tonight, and she had several decorative, jewel-encrusted pins in it. They, too, glinted in the light from the lanterns and chandeliers.

"Hello, Stringbean," Miss Jane said as she approached. She glanced at young Harmon. "Thank you for fetching him, Harmon." She glanced at the clock over the door then frowned down at the boy. "I didn't realize how late it was. Shouldn't you be in..."

Jane let her voice trail off as Harmon, who'd apparently caught someone else's attention, snugged his watch cap down tighter on his head and headed deeper into the drinking hall. Sure enough, Stringbean saw one of Jane's girls hooking a finger at the boy, summoning him for some chore—maybe hauling out a night vase or fetching coal for the brazier in the girl's room.

"Quite the little businessman," Jane remarked.

"You're tellin' me," Stringbean said with a chuckle. "You having trouble with Dusty and Beauchamp again, Miss Jane?"

"Not yet but they're spoiling for a fight." Jane looked toward the bar. "They're bellied up to the mahogany."

Stringbean picked out the two men at the bar. Dusty Wallace stood near the bar's left end, Dwight Beauchamp stood near the middle. There were roughly five men between them, maybe a dozen all together standing at the bar under a roiling, blue cloud of tobacco smoke. Dusty and Beauchamp were both hunched over drinks.

Each man had a bottle of whiskey and a schooner of beer before him. Each was attired in typical drover's garb, the mustached Dusty with a ragged black Stetson tipped back off his forehead. Beauchamp was bigger and broader than Dusty, and clean-shaven. His cream Stetson sat on the bar near his drinks. Just as Stringbean glanced at the man who'd given up the life of the thirty-a-month-and-found puncher for the life of the small rancher with a wife and possibly kids on the way, Beauchamp slid the right flap of his black denim jacket back behind the Schofield revolver holstered on his right hip.

"Oh, boy," Stringbean said, poking his own hat up onto his forehead. "Don't tell me it's come to this."

"Each man has one hell of a mad on," Jane said. "I saw it as soon as they saw each other. I'd have Edgar kick them both out, but I'm afraid it might only set them off." Edgar O'Malley was one of Jane's bouncers constantly patrolling the San Juan. "You seem to have a lighter touch, Stringbean. Could you go over and talk to them before they start swapping lead and someone *really* gets hurt?"

"Of course, Miss Jane," Stringbean said. He sighed and headed toward the bar with its elaborate back bar and glistening, leaded mirror bearing the San Juan's 'S' and 'J' initials in large, fancy gold leaf lettering. He saw that the two men were staring into the mirror before them, giving each other the wooly eyeball.

Stringbean almost chuckled. Imagine two grown men acting like schoolboys over a woman. But then again, he sort of felt like a schoolboy over Miss Molly, didn't he?

Thinking of her was like a dog's sharp nip. He shook his head to clear it.

Still, he saw that door slamming in his face again.

He walked up to Dusty Wallace, leaned forward, and spoke quietly into the man's right ear. "Pull your horns in or I'll pull them in *for* you. Miss Jane won't put up with what you go got goin' on between you and Beauchamp."

It was almost as though he'd heard someone else say it. The rough tone hadn't been like him at all. But then, he wasn't feeling like himself.

Dusty had just started to turn an incredulous look toward him when Stringbean walked along the bar and stopped before Dwight Beauchamp, who must have seen him stop and talk to Dusty in the back bar mirror, because Beauchamp was turning toward him now with a look of deep incredulity on his sunburned, cattleman's features.

"If you can't keep your hand off that hogleg"—he suddenly realized he was reaching forward and pulling the man's Schofield revolver from its holster—"I'll hold onto it for you until you're ready to leave town." He'd said the words in a taut, menacing voice that hadn't been his at all. But it *had* been his. Where it had come from, he had no idea.

Beauchamp jerked forward, the glower of sudden rage twisting his features. "Stringbean, you give me that consarned gun back right--"

Stringbean's jaw hardened as he swung the man's gun back behind his right shoulder, shifting his grip till he was holding it by the steel frame. He swung the butt in a blurred arc until it smashed against Beauchamp's left cheek.

"*Oh!*" The man flew sideways against the bar, the men to either side of him yelling their surprise and making way.

"*Stringbean!*"

Stringbean turned to see Dusty Wallace standing six feet away from him, glaring at him. Wallace jerked forward, grimacing as he swung his clenched right fist toward Stringbean's face. Stringbean ducked the blow easily, heard the swish of the man's fist in the air where his head had just been. Stringbean straightened and rammed Beauchamp's Schofield into Dusty's solar plexus.

The air rushed out of Dusty's lungs in a loud, raking roar. The drover jackknifed sharply, closing both arms over his belly and striking the varnished floor on his knees. He lowered his head as though in prayer, making deep, guttural strangling sounds as he tried to work air back past his temporarily mangled solar plexus.

Stringbean stepped back and looked at each man in turn, first Beauchamp who stood leaning back against the bar, a look of exasperation and shock on his face as he held a hand over his bloody left cheek, and then to Dusty still down on his knees as though trying to get right with his maker and his maker wasn't having it.

"If you two wanna kill each other, then do it outside the city limits. I won't put up with it in town!"

With that, Stringbean clicked open the Schofield's loading gate, held the gun up by his right shoulder, turned it upside down, and slowly turned the wheel. Each of the five loads slipped out of its chamber to clank onto the floor around Stringbean's boots. Once the gun was empty, he slipped it back into Beauchamp's holster, snapped the keeper thong over the hammer, and gave the man a twisted look as he said, "Git out of here. Both of you!"

Beauchamp just blinked as he stared at Stringbean for the next fifteen seconds. He stumbled forward, picked up his hat, set it on his head, and crouched over Dusty. "Here, Dusty," he said. "Let me help you to your feet. Let's get the hell out of here." He grimaced at the deputy. "Stringbean's gone plumb loco!"

"Oh, Lordy, Lordy, Lordy," Dusty said as his friend helped him to his feet after crouching and setting Dusty's hat on his head.

Both men cast Stringbean one more disbelieving look before they turned and, Beauchamp snaking his left arm around Dusty's waist, led him through the tables and around the men and working girls who'd walked up near the bar to give their disbelieving gazes to the formerly timid young star-wearer. It was then that Stringbean realized that the entire saloon had gone as silent as graveyard at midnight.

All eyes were on him, lower jaws hanging.

Jane Ford stepped aside to let Dusty and Dwight Beauchamp pass as they headed for the batwings. She strode briskly forward and stopped in front of Stringbean. She cast him a befuddled, skeptical, arch-browed gaze. "Drink?"

Suddenly self-conscious, Stringbean ran his palms down his shirt. "I, uh...I, uh..."

Jane glanced at the bar tender who stood frozen behind the bar, the apron's startled, round-faced gaze also on the wiry young deputy. "Hal--brandy."

Hal sighed and turned to a back bar shelf. "Comin' right up, Miss Jane."

Hal set the bottle and two brandy snifters on a silver tray and slid the tray across the bar to Jane. Jane took the tray and glanced over her shoulder at Stringbean, one brow arched commandingly.

He followed her through the room, meandering around tables. Conversations were just now beginning to pick up again though incredulous glances kept being cast Stringbean's way. He stopped suddenly when he saw young Harmon Hauffenthistle standing near the batwings, holding a white enamel thunder mug by its wire handle, and staring in red-cheeked, wide-eyed shock toward the deputy.

Slowly, the boy shook his head at Stringbean then swung around and pushed out through the batwings.

Someone gave a short, high-pitched whistle.

Stringbean turned to see Jane sitting at a table near the entrance to the Bear Den, the room beyond an arched doorway housing her gambling layout. All conversation had gone quiet in there, too, though it sounded like the roulette wheel was starting to spin again and the craps dice were being thrown. Men were stumbling backward from the arched doorway, beers or whiskey shots in their fists as they, too, regarded Stringbean in hushed astonishment.

Stringbean's cheeks were warm with chagrin.

"Never mind them," Jane said, splashing brandy into each glass and setting one in front of Stringbean. "They've just never seen a wolf break its chain before." She raised her glass to her red lips and widened her eyes. "It's a little startling."

She threw back a good half of the glass in one fell swoop then splashed more brandy into the snifter.

"S-sorry about that, Miss Jane." Stringbean help-lessly, confusedly shook his head. "I honestly don't know..."

Jane regarded him levelly over the rim of her freshly replenished snifter. "If I'd wanted him to come, I'd have sent for him."

There was no doubting whom she meant by "him."

"I know."

"On the plus side, you very well might have made them friends again. Nothing like having a common enemy. *Still...*"

"I know."

"Where did that come from?"

Stringbean hiked a shoulder. "I got no idea."

"Yes, you do. All that anger. It was suddenly like *his* anger. Where did it come from? I know where it comes from in Joe. He hates himself."

Stringbean frowned in surprise at her.

"Long story," Jane said. "Come on—out with it, deputy. I demand to know at the risk of getting pistol whipped." She gave a husky, ironic laugh.

"Oh, Miss Jane, I never would--"

"Where did it come from?"

Stringbean gave a deep sigh. He looked down at his glass. He winced a little in revulsion. He wasn't much of a drinker. Just a beer now and then. He didn't imbibe in the hard stuff. He didn't like the way it burned going down or how light-headed and downright silly it made him feel.

The occasional beer was enough.

"Go on," Jane prodded him. "Drink up. It's a good stress reliever and truth teller, brandy. Especially the good Spanish stuff. It's my contention the New World never would have been discovered without it."

"All right." Reluctantly, Stringbean picked up the glass and sipped.

"Come on, come on—more than that."

Stringbean said, "Can't we just leave it at 'sorry' and let me go about my business? I'm on duty, Miss Jane."

"Not until we've chatted. You might think he's your boss. But being the redhead here, I'm your boss." She smiled at that. She had one fetching smile, Miss Jane did. A fella couldn't tell her no. Of course, she knew that.

"All right, all right." Stringbean drank down half the glass.

He set the glass back down on the table and pressed his hands palm down as though to steady himself in a hold of a clipper ship in stormy seas. "Whew!"

He ran the back of a hand across his mouth and looked across the table at her. "You know Miss Molly Hurdstrom?"

"Your sweetheart, of course."

"Don't think she's my sweetheart anymore."

"Oh."

"Her folks want her to marry into a rich family. Tonight, I got their front door slammed in my face."

"Ahh..."

Jane reached across the table and wrapped her hands around his wrists.

"At ease, cowboy. We all make mistakes. She's yours."

"She says she don't want to marry him. She says she loves me."

"Then she won't. It's as simple as that. If she can't buck her family and marries someone she doesn't love as opposed to someone she does, then she's not right for you, anyway."

Stringbean looked across the table at her. Wanly, he smiled. "I wish it was as simple as that."

Jane sighed and sat back in her chair. She turned her brandy glass on the table with her thumb and index finger. "Me, too, Deputy. Me, too."

"Marshal Mannion?"

"Yep."

"You let me know if I'm talkin' out of school, but are you two gonna get hitched, Miss Jane?"

She looked from her glass to Stringbean. "No."

"I see."

"After what he showed me he was capable of today, I no longer wish to marry him. I thought I could. I love him. Probably always will. I'm a sucker for big, handsome, temperamental reprobates like Joe." Slowly, she shook her head. "I'm not a girl anymore. I'm older, and I've had enough. I want a *nice* man. A man who can keep his wolf on its leash." She smiled. "I want a man who thinks of me first instead of himself."

CHAPTER 16

LATER THAT NIGHT, STRINGBEAN WAS MAKING HIS midnight rounds, looking around cautiously, on the lookout for trouble.

It was good dark now, and it was his job to make sure no businesses got robbed under cover of darkness. There'd been a few backdoor break-ins lately. He was about to cross the night-shrouded, star-capped, nearly deserted Main Street and check the rear door of a gun shop that had recently been robbed when a soft whistle sounded from ahead.

He saw a smallish, silhouetted figure, touched partly by the orange light of a still-burning oil pot, step out of a break between a grocery shop and a Chinese laundry, and beckon to him.

"Henry! Here!" came the hiss.

Stringbean frowned in surprise. The only one who called him by his given name was Molly. He continued walking ahead, quickening his pace.

What in holy blazes was she doing out this late? Del Norte was not safe after dark for anyone, much less a seventeen-year-old girl.

"Molly!" he hissed as he approached the girl standing on the covered awning of the grocery shop, beside a rain barrel. She wore a black, hooded cape over a simple, dark-colored day dress. "You shouldn't be out--"

She pressed two fingers to his lips. "Henry, I had to see you!"

"But Molly--!"

Again, she pressed two fingers to his lips. "Henry, all hell broke loose at my house tonight. I rebuffed Adam's proposal. Let's just say it didn't go over well at all. Father sent me to my room as though I were a little girl being punished for not cleaning her plate. I slipped out a window after everyone had stopped arguing downstairs and gone to sleep. I *had* to see you!"

"Oh, Lord, Molly—I'm so sorry. But it's dangerous out here at--"

"Henry, I think they're going to send me away!"

Stringbean frowned. "Send you away? Where?"

"It's a long story." Molly squeezed his arm. "But you *must* believe me!"

"Look, Molly, it sounds like emotions were running a little high tonight, is all."

"A *little high*? Adam is furious. And he's nothing but a thug. When I turned him down, he called me a slattern— right in front of everybody. His father is furious, as well. The McClarksvilles are not used to *not* getting their way. I'm afraid I've driven a wedge between him and Father. For that I'm sorry, but I cannot marry a man I not only do not love but detest!"

"Your parents seem like reasonable folk to me, Molly. I'm sure everything will cool down tomorrow, and your parents will understand your feelings about the whole thing. They'll come to an understanding."

"I think I might have to run away, Henry," Molly said

in a high, hushed, exasperated voice. "I'm *afraid!* My parents—they'll send me away. They've done it before."

"I don't understand."

Molly hugged herself and shivered as though deeply chilled. "Let me just say that the place they sent me to was a very bad place, indeed!"

Stringbean wrapped his arm around her shoulders. "Come on back to the jailhouse. We'll talk about it there."

Molly nodded.

Together they headed up the street in the direction of the Hotel de Manion.

They'd just started up the porch steps when Stringbean stopped. He'd left the lamp turned up, and now he thought he'd seen a shadow slide across the window left of the door. He released the girl's hand.

"Molly, you wait here."

"What is it?" she whispered.

"Not sure."

Alone, Stringbean continued up the porch steps. He slowly crossed the porch, not letting his spurs jingle. He unsnapped the keeper thong from over the trigger of the Colt tied down on his right thigh, tripped the door's latch, slowly shoved it open. He took one step into the office, then another.

Ahead and on his right, the door to the basement cell block was open. A lamp burned at the bottom of the wooden stairs, casting a watery glow through the opening.

That didn't make sense. He'd released the only two prisoners—a pair of Scandinavian mule skinners who'd torn up a hurdy-gurdy house in an argument over one of the girls three days ago—that morning. He and the marshal and Rio always kept the door closed. Unless

Harmon was cleaning down there, which Stringbean knew he wasn't. Late as it was, the boy was working over at Miss Jane's place.

There was a light thumping on the stairs, making Stringbean's heart quicken.

Buster strode into the open doorway and sat down—the silhouette of a large, fluffy cat sitting there in the doorway backed by the light washing up from the bottom of the steps. He curled his tail around him and lifted the tip, rattlesnake like, in warning.

The cat moaned deep in his throat.

Sliding his Colt from its holster, Stringbean turned to the cat. "Buster? What is it, boy?"

He'd barely gotten the last word out, barely gotten the Colt out of its holster before a shadow moved in the corner of his left eye. He'd just started to turn that way when the shadow moved again, growing larger before him. And then he saw the narrowed, dark eyes and the cap of short curly, red hair sitting atop a large, square skull, and the fist coming up in a blur of fast motion.

Stringbean grunted and dropped the Colt, heard it thump to the floor, as he staggered forward, head reeling from the vicious blow. He twisted around, getting his boots set beneath him, to face the front of the office just as another man-shaped shadow stepped into the open cellblock door, kicking Buster down the stairs, saying, "Out of the way, cat!"

Buster gave an indignant *meow!*

The man burst through the doorway—as big and thick in silhouette as the other man—and then they were both on Stringbean, one holding him from behind while the other pummeled his face and belly with two large, brutal fists.

"Believe me, you scrawny tin star, you're messing

with the wrong man's girl!" barked the man hammering his fists mercilessly and artfully into Stringbean's face and belly while the other man held him in a vice-like grip.

"*Adam, stop it!*" Stringbean heard Molly scream beneath the bells of agony tolling in his ears.

The man hammering Stringbean stopped suddenly and whipped around.

"Molly—put that gun down, you whore!"

Molly screamed and squeezed her eyes shut as the gun she was holding in outstretched hands flashed and roared.

The man who'd been pummeling Stringbean flew back against the wall to Stringbean's right, groaning. He looked down, and his eyes widened at the blood oozing from the dead-center of his chest.

"Whoah!" he cried, casting his frantic, exasperated gaze at Molly. "You...you killed me, you whore!"

She screamed again as she ratcheted the hammer back and fired again, the gun sounding like a cannon blast in the tight confines.

The man called Adam grunted and looked down in horror at the second hole in his chest. He stood against the wall for a time, back arched, grinding his heels into the floor. Then, as though he were a marionette whose strings were suddenly cut, he dropped to the floor in a quivering heap.

At the same time, the man who'd been holding Stringbean suddenly released him. Stringbean dropped to the floor and lay writhing, blood oozing from his nose and mouth. Through half-open lids, he saw Molly staring down in shock at the man she'd shot. Her mouth formed a dark oval. Her face was framed by her long, mussed hair dangling down over her shoulders. Smoke curled from the barrel of the Colt as she slowly lowered it straight down in front of her.

The man who'd been holding Stringbean, in his late teens, early twenties, and with longish curly, brown hair, was of average height but was broad and muscular. He wore a tailored three-piece suit with gold cufflinks, a burgundy vest and black tie He moved around to String-bean's left.

He looked at the man on the floor to Stringbean's right, and said, "Oh, my God!" He turned to Molly. "*You murderin' devil!*"

He sidestepped around her, cautiously, and ran out the jailhouse's open door and into the night, feet thudding loudly on the stoop. Running foot thuds dwindled into the darkness.

Then the only sounds were the murmur of men's incredulous voices from out on the street.

The air through the open door was cold against Stringbean's battered face, his cut lips.

He lifted his head and looked at Molly. She looked at the smoking Colt in her hands. She stared in shock at the big, red-headed man, also in his early twenties, lying crumpled on the floor to Stringbean's right.

"Oh, my God," she said in a strangled voice. "What have I done?"

Stringbean swallowed some blood on his tongue, cleared his throat. "M-Molly...?"

Molly opened her hands. The Colt struck the floor with a thud. She ran forward, dropped to her knees beside Stringbean. "My God—*Henry*! Are you all right, Henry? My *God!*"

"What...what in holy blazes...?" Stringbean croaked out. He looked at the man piled up on the flood beside him. He, too, wore an immaculate, three-piece suit with a black necktie and gold cufflinks. A gold timepiece had fallen out of his vest pocket and lay on the jailhouse's scarred wooden floor. An 'A' and an 'M' were engraved in the dimpled, gold-washed casing.

Stringbean cleared his throat again. "That's...that's...?"

"Adam."

Stringbean sat up, drawing one leg beneath the other one, and turned to face the large, square-shouldered, chiseled-faced young man lying in a pool of his own blood. "Lordy be...Lordy be..." His brain was foggy, and the room was pitching ever so gently around him. In the beating, he'd gotten his marbles scrambled.

Tears rolled down Molly's cheeks, glinting gold in the watery light of the lantern hanging from a wire in the middle of the room.

"What have I done?" she muttered. "What have I done?"

"It'll be all right, Molly," Stringbean said, hearing more men's questioning voice out on the street fronting the jailhouse.

She gazed dazedly at the dead man. "They'll send me away now for sure."

"You were just tryin' to--"

"No, they'll send me away."

Stringbean placed his hands on her shoulders. "Honey, that's crazy talk. You're just dazed. Believe me, I understand." He shook his own head as though to clear it.

Molly shuttled her stricken gaze from the dead man to Stringbean. "You don't understand, Henry. You have to get me out of here. Out of Del Norte." She shook her head slowly. "I can't go back to that place!"

"Stringbean, everything all right in there?" a man called from out in the street.

Stringbean turned to the open doorway to see the

silhouettes of several men gathered in the street fronting the porch steps. "Everything's under control, fellas! Go on about your business, now!"

Stringbean turned to Molly. "Don't worry, honey. I'll tell 'em. I'll tell 'em what happened. Why..."

She shook her head. "You don't understand, Henry. If you don't get me out of town, they'll send me away again."

"Where?"

"Get me out of here, and I'll tell you." Molly stomped her foot down hard. "We have to hurry. My father and Mister McClarksville will be here soon!"

"All right, all right." Stringbean knew he should not what he was about to do, but he could not help himself. The terror in the girl's eyes was real.

Slowly, wincing against the pain in every fiber, he rose to his feet. He pulled the towel off the nail over the washstand and ran it gently across his torn lips and bloody nose.

"You stay here. I'll be right back."

He moved to the door, stepped out onto the stoop, and drew the door closed behind him. Several men were still lingering on the street fronting the jailhouse. A small crowd of men also stood outside two saloons on opposite sides of the street from each other—the Three-Legged Dog on the right, the Wooden Nickel on the left.

"Everything all right over there, Stringbean?" a man called from in front of the Wooden Nickel.

Stringbean held up a hand palm out. "Everything's under control, fellas. Everything's fine. Go on about your business, now!"

He looked around, wondering where Marshal Mannion was. Normally, hearing gunfire from over at his suite of rooms at the San Juan, he'd be over here by now.

Stringbean had hoped he'd see him. He'd know what to
do. Stringbean knew his own plan was wrong, that he was
letting his heart steer him from the straight and narrow,
but only Marshal Mannion could convince him of that.

He called, "Anyone seen Marshal Mannion?"

The men nearby and gathered on both sides of the
street glanced at each other, shrugged. "Ain't seen him,"
one man called from out front of the Three-Legged Dog.

A man from in front of the Wooden Nickel said, "I
see him ride out on Ol' Red several hours ago. Looked
plumb disagreeable."

"Even for him," added the man standing beside the
man who'd just spoken.

Men on both sides of the street chuckled or laughed.

"I see," Stringbean said with some disappointment.

When the marshal was in a foul mood, he often
saddled Red and tried riding it out of himself. Just now
he was probably trying to ride out his frustration over
what had happened earlier with Longshot Hunter Drago.
"I'll fill him in later, then. Like I said, everything's under
control here, you men. Go on back inside and have
another drink!"

As the curious onlookers shuffled away, Stringbean
looked around for Rio Waite.

The older deputy lived in an old, abandoned
prospector's cabin behind the jailhouse. If he'd been
home, he would have heard the shooting, which meant
he was probably still 'a-courtin',' as he'd called it earlier.
With neither the Marshal nor Rio around, Stringbean
had to make his own decision. He knew his decision
was the wrong one, but he had no choice but to
make it.

For the terrified girl inside the jailhouse.

He walked down into the street and tightened Banjo's

saddle cinch then walked back up onto the porch and entered the jailhouse.

Molly stood before him, looking anxious. Stringbean glanced at the young man lying dead behind her. Somehow, he'd hoped that when he'd reentered the jailhouse, the dead man would be gone. That what had happened— Molly shooting him—had only been a nightmare and maybe Stringbean would wake up then and find it a bright, brand-new day and Molly had not killed the man who'd earlier asked for her hand to save Stringbean's hide.

"I'm going to get you out of here," Stringbean said. "I know a place. You'll be safe there until I can talk to Marshal Mannion, tell him how it was—that you shot Adam to save my life."

"Thank you, Henry," Molly said, her thin voice quavering.

"Here." He pulled a striped blanket coat off a wall peg, slipped it over her shoulders. "Gonna be cold where we're goin'. You'll need this."

Molly shoved her arms into the coat's sleeves. When she had the coat on, she glanced over her shoulder at the dead man, and shuddered.

"Come on, honey," Stringbean said, giving her hand a squeeze.

Molly nodded.

Stringbean opened the door, led her across the porch and into the street on the dun's left side. He glanced over the gelding at the saloons, relieved to see that the boardwalks fronting each were now vacant. He climbed into the leather then reached down for Molly's hand, freed the stirrup for her, then swung her up onto the dun behind him.

"You alright?" Stringbean asked her.

"No. Just get me out of here, please, Henry."

He'd meant was she comfortable. He hated the forlorn tenor of her voice as he reined the dun out into the street then booted into a trot to the south. He knew that he and the girl were likely being watched from behind saloon windows, but there was nothing to be done about that. He'd ride back to town later and explain the situation to Marshal Mannion. He had no idea what he and the marshal would do about it, but he'd tell the marshal, anyway.

There'd be no hiding what had happened.

But he could hide Molly to protect her for now, to make her feel safe, to rid the terror from her eyes for at least the time being. And that's just what he was going to do.

At the edge of town, he booted the dun into a rocking lope, glad there was a three-quarter moon to steer by. Where he was headed was rugged country, and the route he'd chosen was even more rugged than his regular route.

He didn't want to be trailed.

For now, not even by Marshal Mannion.

Lordy, what a sneak he'd become.

CHAPTER 17

Mánnion rode into town around midnight.

When he'd ridden out a few hours earlier, leaving Rio in charge while Stringbean enjoyed supper with his gal's folks, he'd meant only to be gone an hour or so. The ride had started out as a wool-gathering mission. He feared he'd lost his lady as well as his daughter. He'd taken the mid-day meal at the San Juan, and both women had refused to speak to him, so he'd eaten alone in the main drinking haul and grown more and more morose.

He'd decided to take an hour off, leave Rio in charge, and do the whole town a favor and ride out and blow off some of his mad.

But then Red had thrown a shoe and he'd had to lead the horse to a little shotgun ranch—a three mile walk in boots built for toeing stirrups—where he'd used the rancher's forge and bellows to shape and nail in place a new shoe. Those several frustrating hours had done nothing to blow his mad off. But then, a mere horseback ride in the country wasn't going to do that.

The only thing that was going to blow his mad off was

putting a bullet through the head of Longshot Hunter Drago. Nothing short of that would do.

He rode down Main Street lit here and there by light emanating from the windows of those saloons still open at this hour. Most were but, it being a weeknight, they all seemed rather subdued. He heard some lazy piano music issuing from the All-Nighter as he passed the shabby place, frequented mostly by Indians, half-breeds, and the trashiest whites, on his right.

"Long damn day, Red," Mannion said as he leaned forward to give the bay's left wither an appreciative pat. "Sorry about that."

The horse raised its head and gave an affectionate wicker. That made the lawman feel better. Odd how something so simple as a horse's affection could do more for a man than a three-hour ride in the country. He couldn't let anyone know, however. He had a reputation to keep up. When a rough-and-tumble town tamer loses his reputation, which he'd damn near done two summers ago when he'd been outdrawn right here on Main Street and had taken a bullet in the leg, he might very well get shot out of the privy during his morning's constitutional. That had happened to the town marshal Mannion had first worked for back in Kansas over twenty years ago now.

Somehow, you had to keep your reputation as well as your women, and that could be one helluva tightrope act.

He'd give it another go tomorrow.

In the meantime, he'd head for the jailhouse, kick Rio loose, and take over for the man. It had been a long afternoon and evening, but Mannion doubted he'd sleep, so he might as well man the jailhouse and walk the streets. Maybe he'd catch whoever had robbed one of the gun shops a few weeks back.

He rode another block and began to hear raised voices. They seemed to be issuing from the direction of the jailhouse. He cast his gaze that way to see a large crowd gathered out front of Hotel de Manion.

"I tell you that young devil killed my son, and I'm sending riders after him whether you like or not!" one man shouted.

Mannion recognized Rio Waite's voice: "I'm tellin' you not to take the law into your own hands, McClarksville You leave this mess up to me and the marshal. He should be back soon!"

"Oh, go to hell!" yelled a third man whom Mannion now saw standing on the porch with Rio, all three silhouetted against the open office door flanking them. Both men were taller and leaner and straighter than the thick, lumpy Rio. The third man raised his voice even louder to yell into the crowd of on-lookers before the jailhouse: "I need a good dozen men to ride after the deputy who kidnapped my daughter and bring Molly back safely to me. Thirty dollars per man as long as you bring her back before dawn. That's more than you'd make in a whole month out on the rage!"

A celebratory roar rose from the crowd, several men throwing their arms up.

Mannion booted Red up before the jailhouse and shouted above the din, "What in holy blazes is going on here?"

Rio turned to him and yelled, "Hell, Joe—I'm so glad you're back!" He hurried down the porch steps and pushed, cursing and gritting his teeth, through the crowd of a good twenty, twenty-five men gathered before the jailhouse. Mannion could smell the stench of beer, booze, and tobacco on them.

As the deputy approached Mannion, the lawman said, "What's going on here, Rio?"

"Big damn mess, Joe. There was shootin' over here to the jailhouse. Fellas over to the Three-Legged Dog and the Wooden Nickel heard a girl scream. A few minutes later, they seen Stringbean and Molly Hurdstrom galloping out of town like ol' Banjo had Mexican firecrackers tied to his tail! A few came over after Stringbean and the girl were gone and found a young man dead on the jailhouse floor!"

"My son!" yelled one of the two men on the stoop. Mannion now recognized Ralph Hurdstorm. He did not recognize the other man—a big fella with a ginger-colored walrus mustache and thick muttonchops. He appeared, like Hurdstrom, somewhere in his forties and dressed, like the impeccably attired Hurdstrom, in a tailored, pin-striped suit.

He shoved his thick arm and pointing finger at Mannion. "Your deputy murdered my son, Marshal Mannion, and Hurdstrom and I are sending a posse out for him!"

A man in the crowd rose onto the toes of his boots and yelled, "I can't believe Stringbean could murder any man in cold blood, but, hell, for that kind of money, I'll drag him an' the girl back for you!"

Mannion cursed as he swung down from the saddle. "Everybody, hang on! Nobody's riding out after anybody much less my deputy!" He pushed through the crowd, Rio on his heels, and climbed the porch steps to stand before Hurdstrom and the fancily attired stranger. "Now, what are you saying happened here tonight?"

The stranger half-turned to jut his pointing finger through the jailhouse door, his flesh face swollen and red with fury. "Your deputy murdered my son!"

Mannion shuttled his gaze through the jailhouse's open door. Sure enough, a body did, indeed, appear to be piled up at the back of the room. "All right," he muttered. "Just hold on."

Mannion stepped through the door and walked over to see a young man clad in a three-piece suit lying on his side in a pool of blood. He'd been shot twice in the chest. He was in his early twenties, square-jawed and with broad, pale face under a cap of curly, copper-red hair. A few red pimples shone on his forehead.

Mannion heard a hoarse intake of air and turned to see the fancily attired stranger standing to his right, raising his fist to his face, pressing the back of it against his mouth. Tears wells in his eyes, rolled down his cheeks.

"Your son, eh?" Mannion said.

The man nodded.

"What's he doing here, and why do you think my deputy shot him?"

Hurdstrom was standing to Mannion's left. He turned his head to one side and yelled, "A.J.! Come in here!"

Footsteps thumped on the porch steps, then on the porch, and Mannion turned to see another young man, clad similarly to the one on the floor, in a three-piece suit with red foulard tie and checked waistcoat, step through the door, removing the brown bowler on his head. He was maybe six feet, square-jawed, with longish, wavy, chestnut-colored hair curling down over his ears. Like the one on the floor, he was broad-shouldered, muscular.

To Mannion, Hurdstrom said, "This is Adam's friend, A.J. They met at Yale where they are both enrolled." He looked at the young man who'd taken three steps into the room before stopping. "A.J., tell Marshal Mannion what happened here tonight."

"Yes, sir, Mister Hurdstrom." A.J. switched his gaze to

Mannion and said, "Marshal" and gave a polite nod. He ran his tongue across his thick lips and said, "Adam and I —we accompanied Miss Molly over here earlier. Sh-she, uh, she'd accepted the hand of Adam but was anxious about telling the deputy. You know—of breaking his heart. So, Adam and I—we offered to accompany her. You know, to give her, you know..."

"To support her," McClarksville said.

"Let him tell it," Mannion said.

"Go ahead, son," Hurdsville prompted the young man.

A.J. took one more step forward, licked his lips again, and said, "We accompanied Miss Molly over here to support her while she told the deputy that their relationship was over, because she'd accepted Adam's hand in marriage. We waited outside but when we heard them arguing...or, rather, the deputy yelling at Molly...we came inside. Well, one thing led to another, and the deputy was shouting and calling Molly—well, certain names a gentleman doesn't repeat. We tried to reason with the man—Adam and me—but he just started getting madder and madder until he hauled off and shot Adam in that fit of rage he was in!"

Again, the young man licked his lips and continued: "The deputy grabbed Molly, put his gun to her head, and told me to leave or he'd kill her. So, I ran to get Mister Hurdsville and Mister McClarksville but by the time we got back, the deputy and Molly were gone."

Rio Waite was moving slowly into the room. He stopped beside A.J. and looked at Mannion, slowly wagging his head. "That ain't Stringbean. He'd never do such a thing. Never seen him in a rage. Not even close."

"Neither have I," Mannion said, turning to A.J. "I don't believe a word of—"

"Joe," came a woman's voice from the doorway.

He turned to see Jane standing there, a black shawl about her shoulders, a grave expression on her face. "Can I speak to you?"

Mannion and Rio shared curious glances then Joe walked to the door and followed Jane out onto the stoop. The crowd was still milling around in front of the jailhouse. Mannion turned to them and said, "You men, get the hell out of here now. No one will be going after my deputy and that girl. Either get back to the saloons or go home and sleep it off!"

Grumbling, the crowd slowly dispersed.

When the last man was gone, Mannion turned to Jane. "What is it?"

"Stringbean had a mad on tonight. Nothing like I'd ever seen before. He braced Dusty Wallace and Dwight Beauchamp something awful at the San Juan earlier. His sour mood was due to the Hurdstroms treating him so shabbily at their place earlier. When he got there for supper"—she canted her head to indicate the open door of the office—"the McClarksvilles were there."

"What're you saying?" Mannion said. "You can't possibly think--"

"I'm just telling you what I saw, that's all. A side of Stringbean I'd never seen before. That's all I'm saying. I just thought you should know."

Mannion nodded slowly. "All right."

"I have to get back," Jane said, and walked down the steps, into the street, and started back in the direction of the San Juan.

Mannion stepped back into the office doorway, jerked his chin at Rio, who stepped up to him. "Get this mess cleaned up. I'm going after Stringbean."

"All right, Joe."

"Which direction did he and the girl head?"

"The men on the street said south."

"All right."

"Joe." Rio grabbed his arm.

Mannion turned back to him.

Rio stepped up close and said quietly, rolling his eyes to indicate the three men in the room behind him. "They're lyin'."

"Probably."

Mannion turned and walked out to where Red stood ground reined. Joe grabbed the horse's reins, climbed into the leather, and said, "Sorry, Red. The night just got a little longer."

He put the mount into a lope down the now nearly deserted street to the south.

"Trouble, Joe?" sounded a voice to his right.

He reined in Red to see Hunter Drago standing outside the Three-Legged Dog, smoking a long, black cheroot. The man gazed at him through that lone, whimsically narrowed eye of his. Drago raised the cigarette to his lips and drew on it, the coal glowing bright orange.

Mannion merely grunted, angrily flaring his nostrils, and booted Red into gallop down the street.

CHAPTER 18

AT THE SOUTH EDGE OF TOWN, MANNION WAS ABLE TO pick the relatively fresh prints of Stringbean's dun out of the maze of other hoof and wheel prints that had scored the trail throughout the day. There was a moon, and Mannion was a good tracker, so he had no trouble following the prints until, roughly two miles southwest of Del Norte, they suddenly disappeared.

"What the hell?"

Mannion dismounted and closely scrutinized the trail.

He gave a grim smile.

Stringbean was shrewd. Mannion was shrewder. He saw where Stringbean had rubbed out the prints where he'd swung the dun off the trail. A few feet to the right of the trail lay the aspen branch to which green leaves still clung that Stringbean had used to cleanse his sign. The green leaves were torn and dusty.

The prints continued into the sage, the dun and its two riders heading west into rugged country.

"Hmm," Mannion said, gazing in that direction, the bright moon dimming the stars that hung over the high, indigo ridges. "I do believe I know where you're going, kid."

Stringbean was likely heading for the old trapper's cabin he once lived in when he'd been working as an itinerant horse gentler, roaming from ranch to ranch but heading back every night to his own place. Once when Mannion and his young deputy had been out here hunting the gang that had robbed the local stage line, Stringbean had pointed out the cabin as he and Mannion had ridden along the lip of the canyon in which the shack sat.

At the base of Coyote Rock, if Joe remembered correctly.

He remembered where it was, all right. He had a feeling Stringbean was hoping he didn't. Obviously, the kid had skinned out of town not wanting to be followed.

But could Stringbean possibly be guilty of murder and kidnapping?

Not the Stringbean Mannion knew.

Joe shook his head as he climbed back onto Red's back.

He clucked Red across the night-cloaked, moonlit country to the west.

Ninety minutes later, with the moon hanging low in the western sky, Mannion reined Red to a halt atop a timbered knoll. Coyote Rock thrust itself high against the sky to the southwest, blotting out more than a few stars and most of the moonlight angling down around both sides of the rock.

Mannion had reached his destination. He was glad. With the moon on the wane, it was getting too dark for safe traveling. He didn't need Red breaking an ankle and setting his rider afoot out here. He'd been set afoot once already today. Once was enough.

Besides, he prized the big horse. They'd ghosted many an owlhoot trail together. He far preferred horses over humans. Except for Vangie and Jane, of course.

Mannion ground-reined Red then, while he didn't want to believe he'd need it, he slid the Yellowboy from the saddle sheath. He turned to stare down through the pines and firs toward the cabin sitting in the canyon below, fronting a narrow creek that glistened like a snake's skin in the moonlight. Rocks along the creek shone pale in that same light.

The cabin was a hunched, square box with a brush roof. It was flanked by a small corral and tumbledown stable.

Weak, umber light flickered in the cracks between the vertical planks of the shutters over the cabin's two front windows. Pale wood smoke unfurled from the large fieldstone chimney crawling up the cabin's right wall.

"Time to find out what in holy blazes is going on," Mannion muttered to himself. He patted the bay's rump. "You stay, boy."

Red swished his tail in acknowledgement of the order.

Mannion set off down the knoll, meandering around the trees and stepping over or around deadfalls and blow-downs. He moved quietly but wasn't too worried about the crunching of his footsteps, for the creek was muttering behind the cabin. That would likely cover the sounds of his approach.

At the bottom of the knoll, he continued straight on up to the cabin without hesitating.

He stopped ten feet from the door. Voices sounded inside. Stringbean's and the girl's. The girl was sobbing.

Mannion stepped forward, tripped the latch, thrust the door open, and stepped inside.

The girl screamed and jerked to her feet from where she'd been sitting on the other side of the long table seven feet from the door. Stringbean rose with a started yell. He twisted around to face Mannion, got his feet entangled, and fell to the hardpacked earthen floor, taking his chair down with him. He had his hand on the walnut grips of the old Colt holstered on his right thigh.

"Keep it right there, killer," Mannion said. He planted the Yellowboy's butt plate on his hip and aimed the barrel at the ceiling.

Stringbean blinked up in shock at his boss. He'd gotten the Colt half out of its holster and left it there.

"Marshal!"

Mannion took another step into the cabin and kicked the door closed behind him. "You should've barred that if you didn't want company."

"Didn't realize anybody was shadowin' us," Stringbean said, his cheeks flushed with chagrin.

"You should've taken the time to know."

Mannion took another step forward and set his rifle down, leaning it against the table. He removed his hat and ran a big hand through his hair. He glanced at the girl standing on the other side of the table from him, one hand closed across her mouth in wide-eyed shock. A sheen of tears glittered in her gray eyes in which the light of the lantern on the table glistened.

"I reckon you might've been a little distracted. From what happened in town I'd say you do have something to be distracted about." Mannion extended his hand to Stringbean, helped the young deputy to his feet. "Good Lord, what happened to your face, kid?"

One eye was swollen and the young deputy's lips were torn and bloody. He had several cuts on his cheeks.

"Long story," Stringbean said. "I was gonna tell you all about it, Marshal. I just wanted to get Molly safe first, away from town."

"How is she not safe in town?"

"Like I said," Stringbean said. "Long story."

Mannion tossed his hat onto a peg by the door and kicked out a chair. "I got all the time in the world." He looked at Molly who had lowered her hand from her mouth but continued staring at him with a stricken expression. "Why don't you have a seat, honey?"

She didn't look all that happy to see him. Most kidnapping victims would.

He glanced at the fireplace to his right. A coffee pot sat on the front of the hearth, the fire dancing in the grate behind it. He walked around the table, pulled a tin coffee cup down from a shelf littered with mouse droppings, blew the dust out of it, and set it on the table before the chair he'd dragged out. He grabbed a leather swatch from the table and went over and picked up the coffee pot.

Stringbean and Molly each had a cup on the table. Stringbean's was empty. The girl's was three-quarters full. Mannion filled Stringbean's cup, topped off Molly's, then filled his own. The aroma filled the air over the table. In spite of the hellish day it had been, Mannion's mouth still watered at the smell of fresh-brewed Arbuckles.

"Nothin' like a nice cup of mud at the tail end of a long day," he said. "Been a long one for me." He returned the pot to the hearth and strode back to the table. "For you two, too, looks like." He looked at the girl. "Go on—have a seat, honey." He looked at Stringbean. "You, too, killer."

He blew on his coffee and sipped.

Stringbean and Molly shared an incredulous look. Stringbean walked around the table and held the chair for the girl. She sank into it and he shyly but gentlemanly slid it forward. He moved back around the table, righted his chair, and sat down in it. Mannion sat down in his own chair and looked at Stringbean, who leaned forward, hooking his arms around his steaming coffee cup.

He frowned at Mannion. "Killer?"

Before Joe could speak, Molly said, "I shot the man in your office, Marshal Mannion." She looked down at her hands and added, "He proposed to me tonight."

"Ahh." Mannion lifted his cup, blew on the coffee, sipped, and set the cup back down on the table. He kept his gaze on the girl. "You couldn't have just turned him down?"

He didn't mean it as a joke or even to sound ironic.

"He wasn't taking no for an answer," Stringbean said.

"Is that who gave you those nice tattoos on your face?" Mannion asked him. "The dead fella?"

"Him and his friend," Molly said. "A.J. Lamb. They jumped Henry in the jailhouse." She turned to Stringbean. "They were beating him terribly. I picked up Stringbean's gun and shot Adam. He called me a..." She let her voice trail off, shook her head. "I'd never fired a gun before, but it was as though I had. As soon as I picked up that gun, I knew exactly what to do."

To Mannion, Stringbean said, "If she hadn't shot 'im, Marshal, I'd be dead meat. They were really givin' it to me."

"That's not how they're tellin' it," Mannion said.

Stringbean and Molly looked at each other again.

Stringbean turned to Mannion. "How're they tellin' it?"

"They got you down as a cold-blooded killer, son. They say you went into a jealous rage when Molly and Adam professed their love for each other. You started yelling and shot Adam twice through the heart." He turned to Molly. "That wasn't how it happened, little lady?"

"God no!" Molly leaned forward against the table and tapped her thumbs against her chest. "It was *me!*"

"So A.J. Lamb's a liar," Mannion said.

"Obviously," Molly said. "I know why, too."

"Why?" Both Mannion and Stringbean said at the same time.

"Because of what a scandal it would be if I, the daughter of Mister McClarksville's important business partner and future running mate when he runs for Territorial governor, had shot his son. No, no. So much less damaging it would be if his son was shot by a jealous beau. This way they'll keep the story out of the Eastern papers and me out of jail. They'll just send me away to the Sisters of Calvary Home for Wayward girls...like they did before."

Now it was Mannion's and Stringbean's turn to share an incredulous look.

Stringbean turned to her, reached across the table, and took one of her hands in both of his. "Why'd they send you there before, Molly? I mean...if you don't mind me askin'..."

"I don't mind," Molly said. "Though you're not gonna like what you hear, Henry." She drew a deep breath and stared down at her coffee cup. "Two years ago, my father hired a Ute man and his half-breed boy, Joel, to drive one of his freight wagons. I was working in the office after school. Joel and I fell in love."

She lifted her eyes from her coffee and shifted her direct gaze to Stringbean, her cheeks turning red with embarrassment. "My father caught us together in one of the wagon barns. Oh, we weren't doing anything bad! I'd just brought Joel some fried chicken and pickled eggs, and we were sitting together, holding hands. But I guess I had some straw in my hair and my dress looked a little rumpled."

She looked across the table at Mannion. "That was all it took. Joel and his father were fired, and I was sent away to learn a lesson. Spent three months there. Horrid place run by brutal, vile nuns!"

She set her hands palm up on the table. Several pink scars ran across them.

Stringbean groaned.

"That's nothing," Molly said. "You should see the ones on my back."

She turned to Mannion again, drew another deep breath. "My father and Mr. McClarksville are capable of awful things, Marshal Mannion. Neither one made it to their respective stations in life by behaving the way they'd have liked for me to behave. My father has shut out many business competitors by violent means, and Mister McClarksville, the same. I've heard them talking when I was sweeping out the office. They have high political ambitions—both of them. They'll do all they can to convince you...to convince everyone...that Henry shot McClarksville's son, not me."

Mannion took another sip of his coffee, nodded.

"I'm not worried about it," he said, casually.

He'd no sooner said it that Red gave a shrill, warning whinny from the knoll Mannion had left him on.

Instantly, Joe leaned forward and blew out the lamp on the table before him, casting the cabin in darkness relieved by only the orange flames dancing in the hearth.

The light had no sooner gone out than something thudded loudly into the shutter covering the window to Mannion's right. The bullet screeched over the table and thumped into the wall to Mannion's left just as the rifle that had fired it barked loudly.

Molly screamed.

Another bullet punched through the shutter in the front wall behind Mannion.

"*Down!*" he shouted.

At the same time, Stringbean yelled, "*Molly!*" and threw himself over the table and into the girl, knocking her straight back to the floor and covering her body with his. His back was peppered with wood chunks and slivers from the shredded shutters. Mannion threw himself down as all hell broke loose outside—a sudden cacophony of screeching gunfire sending bullets buzzing about the cabin like wasps around a hive.

He grabbed the Yellowboy, crawled to the window on his right through which bullets continued to whine through the now all-but-obliterated shutter. He waited for a lull in the shooting then thrust the Yellowboy's barrel out the window and fired off three quick rounds toward where he'd seen the flashes of one of the rifles rocketing lead into the cabin.

He pulled the Yellowboy down, pressed his back against the wall.

The thudding of several sets of hooves rose, dwindling rapidly into the distance.

He looked over to where he could see Stringbean still lying atop the sobbing Molly.

"You two stay here," Mannion said. "I'm going after them!"

"You got it, Marshal," Stringbean said.

Mannion opened the cabin's front door but paused before stepping out, not sure all three—at least, he thought there'd been three—shooters were gone. When no more shots came, he went out, closed the door behind him and walked straight out away from the cabin, placing two fingers between his lips and whistling.

Hooves thudded and then Red's silhouette took shape before Mannion, galloping down the rise, weaving among the trees, reins bouncing along the ground behind him. There was enough light in the east now that Mannion thought he could track the three shooters, who, according to the hoof thuds, had galloped off to the west.

"Good boy," Mannion greeted the horse, grabbing the reins and swinging up into the leather.

He booted the stallion west along the two-track trail that threaded the bottom of the canyon the shack sat in. He needed to find out who the bushwhackers were and put them out of commission so they couldn't bushwhack him again.

If it was only he they were after, that was.

They might've been after Stringbean, as well. If Hurdstrom had sent them, he'd sent the wrong men. They'd probably been drunk and thrown caution to the wind and opened up on the cabin despite Hurdstrom's daughter being inside. From the quality of man that Mannion had seen in front of the jailhouse earlier, he didn't doubt it if that had been the case one bit.

On the other hand, maybe Hurdstrom didn't really care if his daughter died. What trouble she'd cause him...

Could the man actually be that evil? Mannion wouldn't know. Until tonight, he'd never exchanged two words with the man.

He followed the trail up a low rise. He was nearly to

the top of the rise when he reined Red up suddenly and gazed off the trail's left side, frowning. Hoof thuds sounded over that way, beyond a rocky bluff studded with pines and cedars. A single rider moving fast to the north.

The thuds dwindled and then the only sounds were the morning piping of birds.

"One rider, eh?" Mannion muttered to himself, pensively smoothing his mustache with his gloved thumb and index finger. "That leaves the other two—doesn't it?"

They could be waiting for him on the other side of the rise. They'd probably scouted their backtrail and knew he was on it. The single rider might have circled back around to finish what he and the other two had started at the cabin. Mannion hoped Stringbean had his guard up.

He swung down from Red's back, walked a little farther up the rise then doffed his hat, got down on hands and knees, and crawled until he could edge a look over the top of the rise and down the other side. Down there in the murky blue shadows, two boulders like two giant dominoes leaned against each other along the trail's right side. If someone was going to affect a bushwhack down there, from behind those rocks would be the place to affect it.

Joe crabbed several feet back down the rise, rose, set his hat on his head, and led Red off the trail and tied him to a pine branch.

Ahead, the shoulder of the rise continued climbing into Ponderosa pines. Mannion shucked the Yellowboy from its sheath and started climbing. Soon he was in the pines. He switched course, heading up and over the rise to the west and started down the other side. He couldn't see the boulders along the trail from here. It was still too dark though it was growing lighter quickly, and the pines blocked his view. But he knew they were beneath him and maybe sixty or seventy yards off to his left.

He continued straight down the decline, moving as quickly as he could in the rocky terrain rendered more dangerous in the murky light by deadfalls and blow-downs. At the bottom of the rise, he continued walking west, keeping to the trees and rocks that screened his passage from anyone lurking around the trail. When he'd walked maybe twenty yards, he switched direction again and headed toward the trail, walking slowly and quietly, keeping his ears skinned.

He stopped suddenly.

He'd heard what had sounded like a man's low voice. It had come from the other side of a large spruce just ahead on his left.

He took another step, another. The spruce slid back behind him, revealing the backsides of the two boulders he'd seen from the top of the rise. It also revealed two men squatting along the right side of the nearest of the two boulders, near the pale ribbon of two-track trail. Each held a rifle.

Mannion could smell the rancid sweat and alcohol on both.

He said quietly, "Don't turn around. I have you dead to rights."

They both croaked out startled grunts and, rising, swung toward him, swinging the Winchesters in their hands, as well.

Mannion cursed as the Yellowboy spoke twice quickly, the ejected cartridges clattering onto the rocks at his boots. Both men jerked back against the boulder they'd been hiding behind, dropped their rifles, and collapsed.

Mannion had wanted to take them alive. Dead men couldn't tell him who'd sent them.

He walked forward through his own wafting powder smoke and looked at each man in turn, having to kick the second man onto his back to get a look at his bearded face. He recognized them both. Local misfits. Nothing special about them. He hadn't seen them in the crowd fronting the jailhouse earlier, but they could have been sent by anyone who'd found them in one of the local watering holes —those that catered to the lowliest of the Del Norte lowlifes.

Remembering hearing the galloping hoof thuds of the third man, he stepped onto the trail and quickened his pace as he headed up the rise.

The sun was just rising above the horizon ahead of him as he galloped down the last hill and saw Stringbean's old cabin hunched in the hollow below. His heart thudded when he saw a man wearing a low-crowed cream hat and wielding a rifle step up to the door and kick it in with a crunching thud.

"*Stringbean, look out!*" Mannion shouted.

As the man stepped into the cabin, disappearing from Mannion's view, a rifle spoke twice.

"Ah, hell!" Joe said as he and Red made a beeline for the cabin.

Dread was a cold stone in his belly as he reined Red up in front of the cabin. He was just about to leap down from the stallion's back when the man in the cream hat reemerged from the open doorway, staggering. His face was twisted into a pained grimace. Blood bibbed his hickory shirt and the brown vest he wore over it.

"Ah, hell!" he said as he dropped the rifle.

He took one more step, dropped to his knees and then to his face, doing nothing to break his fall.

"Thank God!" Mannion said.

Stringbean appeared in the doorway, his own smoking Winchester in his hands.

He looked at Mannion. "You didn't think I'd fall for that old trick—did ya, Marshal?"

He grinned, his busted lips glistening in the buttery morning sunshine.

CHAPTER 19

"Well, Buster," Rio said to the cat curled up on his lap at Hotel de Mannion. "Been a long night. Might be time fer a nap."

Buster purred, licked his paw, and cleaned behind his right ear.

Rio yawned and set his boots on the desk before him, crossing his ankles. He yawned again and leaned back in the chair, crossing his arms on his chest. He closed his eyes.

"Knock-knock."

Rio and Buster jerked with sudden starts. Rio was surprised that he'd been able to draw his holstered Remington so quickly and click the hammer back, aiming straight out over the desk. He hadn't realized he'd ever been that fast...nor still was.

The figure in the doorway, however, was no owlhoot gunning for his head. It was none other than the beautiful, blonde-headed, brown eyed Miss Antonia Greer.

Or Price, as was the case now, since she'd run off with and had married the gambler, Brent Price, leaving Rio heartbroken in Nacogdoches twenty years ago...

"Whoa!" Toni said, holding her hands up, palms out. "Easy, there, Wyatt Earp! This isn't an assassination attempt!"

"Toni!" Rio looked at the cocked gun in his hand, lowered the barrel, and eased the hammer down safely. "Sorry about that."

"My, you're fast with that thing!" Toni chuckling uneasily as well as admiringly as she walked into the jailhouse.

She wore a fancy brown knit cape with the hood down. Beneath she wore the fine, red gown edged in white lace that she'd worn earlier when Rio, having been relieved by Stringbean, had gone over to the Spider Web to watch her sing and dance—which she still did every bit as fetchingly as she had twenty years before. When she'd been performing earlier, she'd worn her hair up but now it hung straight down over her shoulders and glistened in the lantern light from a recent brushing.

Rio felt his cheeks warm as he dropped Buster to the floor and rose from the chair, returning the hogleg to its sheath. "Just noticed that myself," he said, chuckling with genuine pride. He might have been old and lumpy but he was fast, by God! "Imagine!"

"Not hard to imagine at all, Rio. Why, you're a seasoned lawman."

"Seasoned, yes," Rio said, coming around the desk, moving awkwardly with Buster rubbing up against his boots, jealous of the attention his master was suddenly giving this strange woman. Rio clucked and shook his head. "Never made it above deputy, though. Just never quite had what it takes, I reckon."

"Listen to how you sell yourself short, Rio," Toni said, moving up to him and sweeping a stray lock of his thinning hair back over his nearly bald pate. "I won't listen to it. You've lived a life to be proud of."

"Think so?"

"I know so."

"Well, thank you, for that, Toni," he said, daring to plant a tender kiss on her cheek since she'd done the same to him a few times since she'd first ridden in on the stage though their time together had been otherwise chaste. "I do appreciate the good accounting." He chuckled again, self-consciously. "What are you doing here? I figured you'd be in bed by now. It's nearly dawn."

"When I went back to the hotel, I heard about the trouble that had occurred over here. I wanted to come over and make sure you were all right."

"Oh, sure, sure—I'm all right," Rio said, glancing over his shoulder at the faint blood stain remaining after the dead kid's body had been hauled away by the undertaker under the close scrutiny of the man's mucky-muck father and Mister Hurdstrom. Rio had gotten up most of the blood; he didn't think the stain was overly noticeable. "Dang mystery, though, I'll tell you."

"At the hotel, they said your fellow deputy—the young man—was accused of shooting someone in a fit of jealous rage! When I met him, he seemed so nice."

Earlier, Rio had introduced her to Joe Mannion and Stringbean as well as to several of his other pals here and there about Del Norte. A friendly soul who'd lived here several years, Rio was friends with quite a few—everyone from barmen to blacksmiths to muleskinners. He'd enjoyed showing Toni around the town and, even more, showing the lovely lady off to his friends.

"He *is* nice," Rio said of Stringbean. "He's a good kid. I don't believe a word of what that A.J. kid said about him. Somethin' smells darn fishy in Denmark. I'm sure

Joe will get to the bottom of it. He rode out to bring Stringbean and the girl back to town. I'm sure Stringbean has a much more believable story than the one that kid, McClarksville, and Hurdstrom told." He scraped at his stubbly chin with a fingernail. "Just can't figure why'd he'd ride out like that...lookin' so dang guilty."

Rio had been suspicious about A.J.'s accounting, which he'd heard when he'd returned to the jailhouse after hearing about the shooting at the Spider Web. All three—Hurdstrom, McClarksville, and A.J. Lamb--had been here alone together, and before Rio had gone into the office, he'd heard them talking in low, conspiratorial tones.

They'd concocted that story, all right, or Rio was a monkey's uncle.

Joe would get to the bottom of it.

"I'm sure he has a good explanation," Toni said. "I hardly know him but, still, I can't imagine that fine, polite young man doing anything half as nasty as what those men are accusing him of."

"I know him well, and I can't imagine, it either."

"Tell you what, Rio? I think you could use some time away from the office. One of these fine days, why don't we take a buggy ride together in the country and have a picnic along a lovely creek?" Toni smiled up at him, her brown eyes glinting beautifully in the lantern light.

Rio was a little shocked by the suggestion. He felt his cheeks warm, suddenly self-conscious. He glanced down to make sure his shirt was properly tucked into his pants, wincing again at his bulging belly that had his belt buckle staring damn near straight down at the ground. He ran a hand through his thinning hair then regarded the hat on the desk. The Stetson had seen far better days. But then, he'd been wearing it for the past fifteen years.

Why in hell hadn't he thought long ago of getting himself a new one?

He chuckled again to himself as he returned his attention to Toni gazing up him, the skin above the bridge of her nose wrinkled curiously.

The reason he hadn't purchased a new hat was because he was tighter than the bark on a tree and he hadn't expected to find the former Antonia Greer rolling into his fair city!

"What are you chuckling about?" Toni asked.

Rio's felt his cheeks warm. "Oh, I was just givin' myself a little lecture."

"A lecture about what?" She canted her head to one side.

"Ah, well, just how you must see me, Toni. Me with my ragged hat an' ragged clothes and this blame big belly of mine!"

"Aw, Rio, there's nothing wrong with a big belly on a man. Just means you appreciate good cooking, that's all. As for your hat and clothes—what do you say we go shopping for a new wardrobe today?"

He looked at her in surprise. "Well, I, uh...well, I, uh..."

"It's a date, then!" she said, beaming. She rose up on her toes and planted a kiss on his lips.

His lips.

Not his cheek.

His lips.

Still beaming, she wheeled, and flounced jauntily out the door and down the porch steps. She strolled off down the street, humming.

Rio just stood there, feeling the tenderness of her lips on his.

———

MANNION STEPPED DOWN FROM RED'S BACK AND looked down at the man lying belly down before him. He kicked the man over onto his back. The man's slack face owning several day's of gray-brown beard stubble was as familiar as those of the other two dead men.

"Herman Kibble," he and Stringbean said at the same time.

Kibble occasionally worked as a market hunter or at one of the smaller ranching outfits. He'd also been accused of rustling, which Mannion wouldn't put past the man at all. Kibble had grown up in the Sawatch with a widower father and three brothers—all four of whom had been hanged by one of the larger ranchers in the region when they'd been caught with running irons. Likely only by sheer luck had Herman avoided the same fate as his kin.

"What the blazes was he doin' out here, gunnin' for us, Marshal?" Stringbean asked, thoroughly befuddled.

"I'd like to know the same damn—"

Behind him, Molly's voice cut him off.

"Henry...?" she said.

Mannion and Stringbean turned to her. She was standing in the half open doorway, leaning against the doorframe. Her eyes appeared pain-racked, and her knees were quivering. "I'm scared, Henry," she said in a thin, quavering voice. Tears dribbled down her cheeks. "Really, really scared!"

"Oh, honey—it's all right. Come on—let's get you back inside. I'll get you another cup of coffee. It'll all come back to you in a minute, I'm sure."

"What'll come back to her?" Mannion asked.

Stringbean only cast a dire look over his shoulder at the lawman as he ushered the girl into the cabin.

Brows furled with deep curiosity, Mannion followed them inside.

Stringbean had righted the table, and now he sat Molly down at it. She looked deeply scared, which would make sense after all the bullets that had caromed around inside the cabin. But...

"What'll come back to her?" Mannion asked again as Stringbean poured the girl a cup of coffee from the pot on the table, the lid and handle of which had taken deep dents from one of the drygulchers' bullets.

Molly looked up at Mannion. Tears shone in her eyes as she said, "I don't have any idea what I'm doing here, Marshal!"

"What?" Mannion said.

"Lost her memory," Stringbean said. He rubbed the girl's back. "I threw her to the floor too hard. She hit her head. Now she has no memory of the last couple of days." Still rubbing her back, Stringbean said, "I'm so sorry, honey."

Molly looked up at him and asked in a puzzled, little-girl's voice, "Why did you throw me to the floor, Henry?"

"He saved your life, Molly," Mannion said, stepping up to the table and tucking his thumbs back behind his cartridge belt. "You don't remember the attack?"

"What attack?"

Mannion and Stringbean shared a dark look.

"I have no idea how I got here," Molly cried with beseeching up at Stringbean standing over her.

"What's the last thing you do remember?" Mannion asked her.

She frowned, swabbed tears from her cheeks with the backs of her hands. She hiked a shoulder and said,

"Riding to town in the surrey to get material for a new dress with Mother. After that..." She frowned, shook her head. "Everything is fuzzy...or just not there altogether."

"You don't remember Adam?" Mannion asked. "Or the trouble in the jailhouse?"

"Adam? *McClarskville?*" Lori said, indignant. "What about him? I haven't seen him in over a year and I never hope to again!"

Again, Mannion and Stringbean shared a dark look.

Mannion said to Stringbean, "Stay with her. I'll saddle your horse. We'd better get back to town."

———

THEY RODE INTO TOWN AN HOUR AND A HALF LATER.

As usual, the town was bustling in the late morning.

All heads swiveled toward the threesome riding down the middle of the street—Mannion and Stringbean side by side, the forlorn looking Molly riding double with the young deputy on Stringbean's dun.

A large group of horseback riders was gathered outside the San Juan Hotel & Saloon. They were all looking up at Hurdstrom and McClarksville and A.J. Lamb standing on the San Juan's high front stoop. McClarksville was yelling and gesturing. He wore a gun and cartridge belt around his waist. He held a smart-looking, new-model Winchester in his right hand. He was gesturing with that, too, until his head swung toward Mannion, Stringbean, and Molly.

Then he froze and stopped talking. His mouth opened and his lower jaw sagged.

"You got him!" he barked out suddenly.

Then Hurdstrom and A.J. turned their heads toward the threesome, and Hurdstrom said, "*Thank God!*" and hurried down the porch steps, making his way through the horseback riders clumped before him.

"Stringbean!" came a boy's voice from the boardwalk to Mannion's right.

Little, tow-headed Harmon Hauffenthistle came running down off the boardwalk fronting a grocery store, the mail satchel hanging off his shoulder.

"Did you do it, Stringbean?" the boy called, blue eyes wide and bright with exasperation. "Did you kill the Eastern fancy-Dan? Didja?"

He stopped beside the dun and gazed up at Stringbean.

Stringbean stared down at him. He glanced over his shoulder at the puzzled-looking Molly and then at Mannion, who beetled his brows severely at him.

Stringbean looked down at Harmon again, drew a deep breath, and said, "Yes. Yes, I did, Harmon. Sorry to say...I killed the fancy-Dan...in a fit of jealous rage!"

Voices rose along both sides of the street and in the street itself in astonishment.

Hurdstrom, who'd come running, stopped dead in his tracks and stared at Stringbean, as surprised as everyone else around him.

He glanced over his shoulder at McClarksville, who was still standing on the San Juan's veranda.

McClarksville and A.J. shared a glance. Then McClarksville turned back to Hurdstrom and hooked a cunning smile.

CHAPTER 20

"WHAT THE HELL ARE YOU DOIN', YOU CORK-HEADED young scudder?" Rio Waite berated Stringbean through the bars of the cell Mannion had had to lock the young deputy in. "You know you didn't kill that Eastern fancy-Dan. You couldn't kill a man in cold blood if you lived a hundred years. And now you might very well be tried for murder and hang by the neck until you are dead, dead, *dead* in only a few weeks!"

Stringbean was sitting on the cot of his cell in Hotel de Mannion's basement cellblock. Buster sat on Stringbean's lap. Stringbean was petting the loudly purring mouser, who was seemingly oblivious of the tension in the echoing cellblock but concentrating only on the strokes he was getting and on a young spring rabbit flitting through the brush outside of a near barred, ground-level window over which fine, steel mesh had been stretched to keep anyone from tossing a pistol or a nail file into the cellblock to an eagerly waiting prisoner below.

Rio had his fleshy face pressed up between two bars of Stringbean's cell door, his fleshy hands wrapped around a bar to each side of his face so tightly that his knuckles had turned white.

Mannion stood beside Rio, also studying the lad on the cot through the bars.

"Rio has a point, kid. Are you sure this is worth it? I mean, it's a brave thing to do for your girl. Right chivalrous. But you do know, don't you, that if she were tried for that fancy-Dan's murder, she'd likely only get a slap on the wrist and sent home? She was only trying to save your life, after all. If you're found guilty, you, as Rio so aptly put it, will hang until you are dead."

Stringbean looked up grimly at the two men as he continued to run his big, long-fingered hand down Buster's back. "What the heck am I supposed to do, fellas? Let Molly suffer for savin' my bacon? She don't even remember what she did. I can't let her try for murder. Sure, sure, she might only get a slap on the wrist from the judge, since she was savin' me, worthless as I am, but still, her parents would send her away to that reform school again and with that scandal houndin' her for the rest of her days, her life would be ruined."

"What about *your* life?" Mannion asked him.

"Mine don't count for near as much as Molly's," Stringbean said.

Rio clucked and looked up at Mannion in deep frustration.

Joe shook his head. He was as frustrated as Rio. What's more, it galled him to think that Hurdstrom and McClarksville and that lying little sissy A. J. Lamb might just get away with murder.

The murder of Stringbean McCallister.

What burned Mannion even more than that was believing that Hurdstrom and McClarksville had sent those three no-accounts after him, Stringbean, and the girl last night to trim their wicks, apparently not minding if the girl's wick got snuffed, as well. Probably be better to be out one troublesome daughter, Hurdstrom likely figured, than to have to endure a scandal that might keep him and McClarksville from political office...not to mention the wealth that such a position would likely earn them.

Why, in a few years, they might be the richest, most powerful men in the territory.

What was the loss of one troublesome daughter?

Hell, the voters would likely sympathize with him no end and throw every vote his way on account of his being a bereaved father of a daughter murdered by a crazy-jealous deputy town marshal!

Mannion had always sensed Hurdstrom had a black heart. Now he knew it to be true.

"Son," Mannion said to Stringbean now, "is there no way we can talk you out of this?"

Still stroking Buster, Stringbean looked up at him through the cell door bars. "Nah, I don't think so, Marshal. That Eastern fancy-Dan is dead, and someone needs to account for it. I'd rather it be me than Molly. She was just tryin' to save my hide."

Mannion and Rio shared another fateful look. Mannion sighed.

It was one hell of a pickle. Mannion understood the young man's feelings, but it was hard to watch him sacrifice himself. He hoped Stringbean would come around and make the right decision. If not, Mannion would have to. He wouldn't watch Stringbean hang for a crime he had not committed.

Even if it meant putting the girl on trial for the murder she *did* commit?

Yes.

A judge would understand, given the circumstances.

The only problem, however, with the girl's memory gone, it would be Stringbean's word against the Eastern fancy-Dan's Eastern fancy-Dan friend, A.J. Lamb, who had about as much spine as an angleworm.

"Marshal Mannion, is Molly back home with her parents?" Stringbean asked.

"Yes."

Stringbean drew his mouth corners down with worry.

Mannion drew another deep breath, released it slowly, then turned to Rio. "I'm gonna head over to the San Juan for a cup of coffee, maybe a plate of eggs...if I can hold 'em down," he added with another dark glance at his younger deputy. "Hold down the fort till I get back then I'll spell you."

"You got it, Joe."

Mannion headed down the cellblock hall to the stairs, climbed them heavily. A few minutes later he knocked on Jane's door in the Rio Grande and had to wait a minute before she answered. It was around ten o'clock in the morning but when she had a late night, which she often did, she slept in.

Finally, the latching bolt clicked.

The door opened a foot, and Jane frowned through the opening. She wore a soft, light lemon robe with matching slippers, and her face was lined from sleep. She blinked groggily.

"Joe...what are you doing here?" she said, gravelly voiced.

Her tone bit him. He was often here at all hours. Even when she'd been asleep, he'd never received such a cold greeting from her before.

"I have trouble, Jane." No, "honey" this time. He could tell she would have rebuffed the endearment. Her feelings about him had changed, but he had other things to worry about just now. He needed her advice.

"When do you don't have trouble?"

"Never mind, Jane." Mannion turned and started to head back down the hall toward the stairs.

"Joe, wait."

He stopped, turned back around.

"Meet me for coffee downstairs. I'll be there in five minutes."

As he descended the stairs, Mannion heard the thunder of laughter and a man's voice that was all too familiar. He turned to see Longshot Hunter Drago standing with five other men—prominent Del Norte businessmen—at the bar with morning beers on the mahogany before them.

They were talking and laughing and having a good ol' friendly time. A beer breakfast between friends. Prominent friends, each one dressed to the nines in a business suit. Drago wore his long, black, leather duster. His high-crowned black Stetson was on the bar before him.

Drago's eyes drifted to Mannion in the back bar mirror, standing halfway down the stairs, glaring at him. The killer, whose face bore the discoloration and swelling of Mannion's attack, raised a dimpled beer schooner high and smiled his one-eyed smile, and roared, "No hard feelings—eh, Joe? Just a little disagreement between friends!"

The others including Mayor Charlie McQueen turned toward Mannion, casting the town lawman disapproving gazes.

Mannion continued down the stairs.

"Come on, Joe," McQueen said, raising his own beer high. "What do you say? No hard feelings?"

"Go to hell--all of you," Mannion growled, and kicked out a chair at a table. He looked at the red-vested barman standing behind the bar with pomade in his hair and who was just then cracking an egg into a beer schooner and sliding it in front of Drago. The apron, too, looked at Mannion reprovingly, mouth corners drawn down.

"Two cups of coffee, Les," Mannion called to him.

Les didn't respond but merely took Drago's money and dropped it into a money box under the bar. He turned and disappeared through the swing door into the kitchen then returned a minute later with a silver tray on which two cups of coffee and a silver server steamed.

Jane was coming down the stairs just as Les brought the coffee to Mannion's table. Jane greeted the apron and the men at the bar with her customary cheer, already dressed fetchingly in one of her trademark low-cut gowns and a pleated skirt with a knit cream shawl wrapped about her shoulders. She'd pinned her red locks into a prettily messy bun atop her head, sausage curls hanging down to jounce against her cheeks. Pearls set in gold dangled from her ears.

She no longer wore the bandage around her head but a much smaller one over the healing wound. It did little to detract from her attractiveness.

Drago glanced at Mannion in the back bar mirror then turned to Jane and pinched his hat brim to her. "Miss Jane, you look every bit as wonderous in the morning as you do in the evening. I don't know how you do it, but we all thank you for it."

"Here, here!" said one of the other men at the bar.

"Oh, thank you, Hunter, you charmer!" Jane returned throatily, genuinely blushing.

Mannion couldn't believe it. He ground his jaws at Drago, who'd already turned his back to him.

The old killer certainly was making friends around

town. Mannion would give him that. But then, a rogue wolf will often make fast work of a flock.

Jane avoided Mannion's gaze as he rose and pulled out a chair for her. She didn't thank him but just sat in the chair and poured them each a cup of coffee from the steaming server.

"He comes in here a lot, does he?" Mannion couldn't help asking her, casting another steely-eyed glare toward Drago and the other jovially conversing men at the bar.

"Never mind, Joe. Let's get down to brass tacks, shall we?" Jane blew on her coffee and sipped. "What happened with Stringbean?"

Mannion doffed his hat and set it on the table. "You're not gonna believe it."

She gave an impatient sigh and raised her steaming cup to her lips.

Mannion grimaced inwardly at her coldness then told her what had happened last night, including the bushwhack and Molly Hurdstrom's loss of memory.

"So Stringbean's in *jail*?" Jane said, incredulous.

"He took the blame."

"But you're sure he didn't do it."

"Despite his temper tantrum in the San Juan earlier that night, yes. The girl wasn't lying."

Jane stared at Mannion, blinked once. "In that case, Joe, you can't let him take the blame."

"I know."

"What're you going to do?"

"I'm a simple man. I was hoping you'd have the answer. Remember, it'll be Stringbean's word against the word of that Eastern fancy-Dan who is taking a break from *Yale*. The son of a prominent Easter businessman— one who could very well be the next territorial governor— is dead."

"You're in an awful position, Joe. You're only choice is to either watch Stringbean hang or blame the killing on Hurdstrom's daughter, who has no memory of last night at all."

"Her family likely has her believing she actually accepted the hand of the dead fella. She's probably so confused, she doesn't know which end is up. And then if I go over and arrest her for murder..."

"Oh, God," Jane said, slowly shaking her head.

Mannion sighed and sipped his coffee.

"Who do you suppose sent the bushwhackers?"

"Who do you think?"

"*Hurdstrom?* Even though his own *daughter* was in the *cabin*?"

"Who else? It would be too much of a coincidence for it to be someone out for only my head alone."

"My God." Jane shook her head again, slowly. "The evil here in Del Norte..."

"Well, it's growing," Mannion said. "That's what happens. Evil grows right along with it."

Jane wrinkled the skin above the bridge of her nose. A thought had suddenly dawned on her. She turned to Mannion.

"What is it, Jane?"

"I just remembered something. You know, Joe, Hurdstrom and Keel Brandywine have been meeting here a lot. At least two times a week. They always sit by themselves at a private table."

She glanced toward a line of booths blocked off by room dividers with colored glass in their upper panels at the rear of the room, under an enormous painting of a buffalo herd being chased by feathered, buckskin-clad Indians wielding spears and bows and arrows.

"Brandywine—the lumberman?" Mannion said.

Jane nodded. "The other day, when I walked over to the Wooden Nickel to invite Ernie Drake to a card game I was arranging between the town's various saloon owners, I saw Brandywine sitting at a table having what appeared a very private conversation with three well-armed no accounts. Men I'd never seen in Brandywine's company before. The contrast between him and them was stark. That's why I noticed it."

"One of those no-accounts wasn't Herman Kibble, was it?"

"Why, yes, Joe," Jane said. "Yes, it was."

"Hmmm." Mannion nodded slowly. "Brandywine, eh?"

"Didn't you throw a punch at him not long ago?"

"Yes," Mannion said, giving a wolfish grin. "Yes, I did. Maybe I'm gonna get the chance to do it again."

Jane set her right hand on Mannion's left one. "Joe, please *try* to keep your wolf on its leash?"

Mannion looked down at her hand on his.

Flushing self-consciously, she slid her hand away.

"Breakfast?" Mannion said.

Jane shook her head. "Not hungry."

Mannion placed his hand on hers. "Jane..."

She pulled her hand out from beneath his. She finished her coffee and rose. "I have to get the girls up. We'll have the lunch crowd soon."

She swung around and headed for the stairs.

Mannion sat staring down at his coffee, feeling empty inside. When he looked up, he saw Hunter Drago staring at him in the back bar mirror.

Drago grinned.

CHAPTER 21

STRINGBEAN SAT BACK ON HIS BUNK, STARING UP AT THE window high in the outside wall of the cell.

A bird—some sort of sparrow—sat in a sage shrub growing up just outside the window. The bird poked its beak through the wire mesh, peering in at the prisoner below and peeping as though jeeringly, mocking the prisoner's lack of freedom when the bird had all the freedom in the world.

Leastways, that's how Stringbean saw what the bird was doing. He might have been wrong. He'd been in the jail of his own accord for only two days, and already the walls were closing in on him.

He didn't know how he was going to make it all the way to trial, which would be held whenever the notoriously unpredictable circuit court judge got here. There was no courthouse here in Del Norte, so the trial would likely be held in one of the saloons. That's where they were usually held.

Stringbean had sat in on a lot of them.

But never as the defendant.

His chest felt tight. His palms were sweaty.

He didn't mind admitting to himself that he was scared. He didn't want to hang, but he didn't see any other way. He truly loved Molly Hurdstrom. Till now, he hadn't realized how much. But he realized it now and that was the one thing about this whole thing that made him feel good.

He purely loved the girl.

And she loved him.

That made the whole nasty affair worth getting his neck stretched.

Didn't it?

Sure, it did.

Deep down in his bones he shook.

He shook again, this time with a start, when he heard the key in the lock of the cell block door at the top of the stairs. There was the grinding sound of the locking bolt being drawn back and then squawk of the heavy door's iron hinges.

"String...er, I mean, Henry?" Marshal Mannion called from the top of the stairs.

Stringbean dropped his feet to the floor and sat up. "Yes, Marshal?"

"You have a visitor."

"I do?"

Stringbean frowned curiously toward the stairs running up the wall at the front of the cellblock, which was empty save Stringbean. There'd been four prisoners in here last night for drunk and disorderly, one for stealing a wagon wheel, but they'd all been released this morning, including the fellow who'd stolen the wagon wheel, since he'd claimed he'd stolen it for a joke—off a traveling preacher's wagon—and had vowed to give it back. The punishment might have been more severe if Mannion hadn't had a notorious disdain for sky pilots.

The marshal put them in the same category as tarot card readers and snake oil salesman.

"You do," Mannion said.

He muttered something too quietly for Stringbean to hear. Then there was the light tapping of footsteps on the stairs. They were not followed by the closing of the cellblock door. The marshal must have left it open. He, Rio, and Stringbean only kept it closed and locked out of habit, but since only Stringbean was down here, and Stringbean wasn't going anywhere, he kept it open.

As for the door of Stringbean's cell, Mannion had closed and locked it, he said, not because he was afraid Stringbean might try to escape but to give him the full experience of being incarcerated. In time, that hemmed in, locked up feeling, might get him to change his mind.

It wouldn't, to Stringbean's way of thinking, but Stringbean knew that the marshal and Rio were hoping it would.

The tapping continued until Molly appeared at the bottom of the stairs, her hair shining in the light of a lamp hanging from the ceiling. She wore a pretty, cream day dress with a brown shawl, and a matching, little felt hat pinned atop her head. A brown reticule hung from her right wrist.

Stringbean's heart nearly broke at the sight of the girl.

"Molly," he said, rising from the cot and moving to the door.

"Oh, Henry."

She strode down the cellblock's central aisle, hands clasped down low in front of her, the reticule sliding back and forth as she walked. Concern shown in the pretty brunette's gray eyes.

As she approached, Stringbean said, "You shouldn't be here Molly. I know your parents wouldn't like it."

"No, they wouldn't, but I had to see you." She frowned as she studied him closely. "Henry, you didn't kill Adam McClarksville. In a jealous rage! That's not you. That's not who you are."

Stringbean hesitated, averted his gaze. It was hard to lie to the girl he loved. Hard for him to cause her to see him in the light she must see him in in order for her to believe his story.

"I'm sorry, Molly. I had a bad night, and...I don't know what came over me."

"What really happened that night, Henry? Please, tell me."

"That's what happened, Molly. I'm sorry."

"I don't believe you anymore than I believe my parents when they tell me I accepted Adam's hand in marriage. I wouldn't have done that. I don't like the man. *Didn't like him*, I should say. He was mean. He was a thug. When he was here last time, calling on me with his father, we went walking by the creek near my family's house and two boys were fishing.

"Adam thought one was watching me too closely, and he went over and punched him. The boy was maybe fourteen or fifteen. He was just fishing. Adam was twice his size. It was right then and there I decided I'd never, ever marry that man. I told my parents what had happened, and they said he was just protecting me."

Molly pursed her lips and slowly shook her head.

"I'm sorry, Molly," Stringbean said. "It has to be this way."

"Why does it have to be this way? *Tell me!*" She bent her knees and straightened them quickly, venting her bitter frustration. Tears rolled down her cheeks. She closed her hands and pressed the ends of her fists to her temples. "Oh, why can't I remember? The last several days—I have no memory of them! They're all blank, sometimes a blur, but mostly blank! But I know you're lying to me! You're all lying—even you, Henry! *Why?*"

"All I can tell you, Molly," Stringbean said softly, sadly, "is that it has to be this way."

"All right, then," Molly said, sniffing, lifting her chin resolutely, and taking one step back away from the cell door. "Have it your way, Henry. You're lying to me, and that saddens me, but it also makes me angry. You stay here, then, and you get tried for a murder I know you didn't commit. Because you couldn't have shot anyone in cold blood even on the worst night of your life.

"But you go ahead and stick with your story and pay the consequences for your lies. But if at any time you decide to tell me the truth—between now and the day they hang you—send Harmon or some other boy for me, and I will come back to you—to hear the truth. Till then, I will not see you again. Either at your trial or your *hanging!*" she added with a shrill sob and a face twisted in agony.

She slapped a hand across her mouth as she wheeled and strode off down the cellblock toward the stairs.

Watching her, Stringbean drew a deep breath, let it out slowly.

He backed toward the cot, sat down on it, and stared at the floor between his scuffed boots, his heart swollen with grief.

———

MANNION STOOD IN THE JAILHOUSE OFFICE'S OPEN doorway, smoking a cigarette and sipping a cup of coffee. He stared out into the dusty street where a ranch wagon was clattering by, two bearded, middle-

aged drovers in big felt sombreros, billowy necker-
chiefs, and tooled leather chaps sitting on the wagon
seat, faces stoic, eyes narrowed against the roiling dust
of Main Street now at high noon. A rangy German
shepherd followed close behind the wagon, tongue
drooping.

The squeal of mental agony echoed up from the cellblock, jolting Mannion out of his reverie.

The squeal was followed by the clattering of soft-
soled shoes on the cellblock's stone floor. Mannion
turned toward the cellblock's open door through which
the sounds emanated. Feet marched angrily up the
wooden steps until Molly Hurdstrom stepped through
the door and into the office, her pretty face crumpled in
grief.

Tears rolled down her cheeks.

"Say, now," Mannion said. "What's all this about?"

"As if you don't know, Marshal Mannion!" the girl
hissed at him, eyes narrowed in scorn.

He stepped quickly to one side as she marched past
him and out onto the stoop and then down the steps
before swinging south and marching away. Walking
straight backed and stiff-armed, she was the picture of
bitter sadness.

For a few seconds, Mannion felt the urge to call her
back to tell her the real story.

But he couldn't do it.

What would hurt her more? Not knowing or
knowing?

"Joe? Say, Joe!"

Mannion swung his head to the left and blinked his
eyes as if to clear them. He was hallucinating. Must be
from lack of sleep, tossing and turning all night, his mind
spinning away on his myriad of current problems.

He closed his eyes once more, dragged fingers over the lids, and opened them again.

Nope. Sure enough.

The dandy in the new, store-bought three-piece brown suit walking toward Mannion, with a fawn vest and a crisp bowler hat was, indeed, Rio Waite. Why, even a gold-washed chain dangled from a pocket of the middle-aged deputy's stylish waistcoat.

Rio's age-tarnished badge glinted on the coat's left lapel, and his old, brown cartridge belt was buckled around his stout waist, the square, gold buckle facing the ground. Rio's old Remington in an equally old, gray-brown holster rode low on his right hip, the wooden grips splintered and cracked from having been used to hammer coffee beans around cook fires over decades.

Rio strode up to the bottom of the porch steps, stopped, spread his coat open and looked up at Mannion, grinning. "How do I look?"

"Good Christ, man!" Joe said, having taken a sip of coffee during his appraisal of the man walking toward him and half-strangling on it. "You look like too much German worst stuffed into too little sausage casing, and you're bleedin' out both ends!"

Rio looked down at the bulging vest and chuckled. "Ain't exactly me, is it? But Toni likes it, so I reckon I'll wear it and endure the abuse of my peers."

"No, no," Mannion said. "You really don't look too bad. It's just that...well, it's gonna take some getting used to. Like looking at a pair of new boots while still remembering the old ones worn over twenty-five years to the worn softness of Injun moccasins."

"Pshaw!"

"This is Miss Price's idea, eh?" Mannion mused. "Sure, sure. It'd have to be." He frowned suddenly. "Say, you two have gotten right close, haven't you? Obviously," he added with a laugh.

Rio seemed as surprised as Mannion. "Well," he said, turning to gaze out into the street and scratching the back of his head. "I ain't sure, but I'll be hanged"—he turned back to Mannion again, his freshly shaven cheeks coloring with a blush—"if it don't seem like it."

Mannion smiled.

"You know what, Joe?" the deputy said. "It feels good. You know—to have a woman to take places, to have meals with...to watch sing an' dance. I haven't had that for years an' years."

"It don't hurt that she's easy on the eyes."

"No, no," Rio said, chuckling. "That don't hurt, either."

"You know what's even better?" Mannion asked.

"What could be better than that?"

"She's headed this way now."

Rio swung around to face the street again to see the former Miss Antonia Greer angling toward the jailhouse in a fine, leather carriage, a high-stepping white horse in the traces. She pulled the horse and the carriage up in front of Rio, smiled up at Mannion and said, "Good afternoon, Marshal!"

"Good afternoon, Miss Price!" Mannion said, doffing his hat and giving a lavish bow.

"How do you like Rio's new wardrobe?"

"Well, I don't normally say clothes make the man, but I might have to rethink that."

Toni laughed and looked at Rio. "Ready, you handsome devil?"

"Me?" Rio said, climbing up into the carriage, making it sag precariously to the near side on its springs. "Heck, this handsome devil was born ready!"

"Where you two kids off to?" Mannion asked.

"Picnic in the country!" Toni yelled above the din of the street including a pair of braying mules just passing in a particularly thick cloud of dust as they pulled a dray heaped with freshly cut pine logs past the jailhouse. "Good day to you, Marshal!"

She waved. Rio smiled.

Mannion saw a picnic basket on the carriage's rear seat, covered with a red-and-white checked oilcloth. He'd already eaten lunch, but he could smell the fried chicken from here. His mouth watered.

He watched the pair roll off down the street, happy for Rio but bitten by a sharp tooth of sadness, as well. He remembered such afternoons, picnics by the creek with Jane—happiness unsurpassed now lost in the swirl of time.

CHAPTER 22

RIO SAT BACK IN THE CARRIAGE'S QUILTED LEATHER seat and smiled as he regarded the lovely woman sitting on the seat to his left, handling the white horse's reins as adeptly as any veteran jehu.

Toni smiled as she drove, brown eyes sparkling in the midday sunshine. She was achingly beautiful in the frilly white picnic dress she wore—sleeveless and with a low-cut bodice, a thin silk wrap covering her shoulders against the slight spring chill, two corners tied loosely together at her neck. On her head was a large, floppy-brimmed, woven white hat that matched the frock.

Her skin was olive against the whiteness of the dress, her eyes a rich, light brown that seemed to glitter as though with a light from within.

God, it was good to be back in her graces.

To be with her again. He'd forgotten how much he'd enjoyed her company twenty years ago. How much he'd loved her.

There you had it. He'd loved this woman.

He had to be careful not to do that again. His heart had ached for years after she'd pulled out on him with

Brent Price. In fact, he believed Toni was the reason he'd never had another woman in his life. At least, not a regular one. Over the years, when he'd needed his wheels greased or his ashes hauled, as the sayings went, he'd visited hurdy-gurdy houses.

So less complicated. So less dangerous. No chance you could fall in love though there'd been a couple of pretty whores he could have tumbled for if he'd been stupid enough to allow himself the indiscretion.

He turned his head forward, resting his left arm on the back of the seat, letting the sun and leaf shadows wash across his fleshy, craggy face on which he could still feel the cool slickness and smell the mint of the barber's balm.

He had to be careful, he warned himself again. The admonition tempered his happiness, bringing himself back to reality, as it did. But a man had to be careful. He was too old to go getting his heart get broken again.

"Tell me what you're thinking about," Toni said, turning her toothy smile on him.

He glanced at her with a wry smile of his own then turned his head back forward. "A fella's got his secrets."

"He does, does he?"

"He sure as hell does," Rio said, chuckling, watching the dark blue of the stream flash in the aspens fifty yards ahead.

The trail forked, one tine curving off to the left. The other tine jogged straight on through the aspens and crossed the creek at a wooden bridge before continuing on to Burial Rock and the first front of the Sawatch Mountains beyond. This was a pretty, rugged country of shelving dikes, small mesas, and haystack buttes peppered with pines and cedars under a big, cobalt arch of the clearest sky imaginable.

"That's Burial Creek," Rio said.

"I know," Toni said. "Not the most romantic name for a creek but I've heard it's a pretty place to picnic."

"It is pretty," Rio said. "Named after Burial Rock—that big stone pillar jutting up ahead, above those rocky knobs. The Utes used to bury their dead up there, keep 'em away from the predators 'ceptin' birds, of course. They believed the sky and the wind took them first."

"How poetic."

"How did you know about this place? You ever been out here before?"

Toni glanced at him as the carriage clattered along the tine that led to the creek. They were in the open now and the sunshine was almost hot. "A lady has her secrets." She smiled.

Rio laughed.

"I asked Jane Ford back at the San Juan for a romantic place to picnic. She told me about Burial Creek."

"Ah," Rio said. "I'm sure she and the marshal have been out this way more than a few times."

"Likely no more in the future, though," Toni said, frowning as shadows swept over the white gelding and then over the carriage as they entered the pines and aspens sheathing the creek. "She told me she'd broken it off with the good marshal."

Rio clucked his regret. "Had a feelin' that was comin', after the business with Hunter Drago."

"I heard about that."

"Poor Joe." Rio wagged his head. "He can be his own worst enemy sometimes. Well...make that most of the time." Again, he wagged his head.

"Lest you should think me a shameless gossip," Toni

said, "I saw Miss Ford having coffee with Mister Drago earlier. Breakfast, in fact."

"Oh, you did, did you?" Rio winced. "Just hope Joe doesn't catch wind of that. Gravels him, Drago does."

"He doesn't think folks can change, eh?"

"Leastways, not Drago."

"Mister Drago seems nice enough to me. He sent flowers to my dressing room after the show the other night. Included a note assuring me he meant nothing too familiar but was just so affected by more performance he felt the need to send a note of appreciation and to wish me the very best in the future."

"Dang," Rio said. "Now I feel like throwin' a punch at that old regulator myself! Silver tongued *and* silver-penned! Who'd of thought?"

Toni laughed as she turned the wagon off the trail to the right and headed downstream, the creek murmuring over rocks to the left of the faint, two-track trail they were on. "Don't worry," she said. "I'm a one-man kind of gal."

She winked.

Rio felt his cheeks burn. He glanced away.

Damn.

"I heard there was a nice swimming hole ahead," Toni said as they bounced along the trail, the wheels occasionally barking off rocks.

"Holy moly—you intend to go swimmin' out here, Toni?"

"Yes, and you are, too. It's far too nice a day to spend trussed up in these stuffy clothes!"

Rio chuckled again, disbelievingly, and shook his head.

She hadn't changed one damn bit in twenty years...

Ah, what might have been.

"Here we are," Toni said, and pulled the white horse off into a grassy clearing with aspens, pines, and spruces arcing around its right side, the deep dark-blue pool of the creek on the other side, at the base of a large, intricately woven beaver dam that had created a pretty, splashing falls.

Rio had been out here before but only when fishing. Not on a romantic jaunt into the country. He'd caught some big, red-throated trout in the pool. He hadn't considered swimming in it, however. Heck, he hadn't even dipped a toe. Now, however, he was feeling so happy again not to mention adventurous and just downright filled with vim and vinegar that he might just dip a toe.

But that's all he'd dip.

If he tried swimming, he'd likely sink like a rock and they'd have to drag him up, dead as a boot, from the bottom.

He clambered down from the carriage and, as Toni set the brake and wrapped the reins around the handle, he walked around to help her down.

"Why, thank you, kind sir," she said, planting another kiss on his cheek. "What a gentleman you are." She stepped back, considering him closely while nibbling a thumbnail. "And, hmmm...a natty dresser, to boot."

Rio laughed. "I gotta admit—I had a little help with that."

"Oh, you did, did you?"

They both chuckled and then Tony asked him to grab the picnic basket and the large, red velvet blanket it was sitting on. Soon, Rio had spread the blanket in the shade of a sprawling spruce and Toni had emptied the basket, which, she said, had been filled by Jane Ford herself in the kitchen of the San Juan. There was fried chicken, baking powder biscuits, potato salad, dill pickles, pickled beets, sausage, a wheel of cheese, and a loaf of crusty brown bread that had been baked in the San Juan kitchen early that very morning.

There was even a bottle of French wine hand-picked by Jane herself.

Rio had four pieces of the cold chicken—two thighs and two legs—and a good-sized helping of the potato salad and everything else. He washed it all down with a glass of wine and when he was through and feeling as swollen as a tick, Jane poured them each a second glass of wine.

Feeling dreamy and drowsy from the heavy meal and the sunshine and the somnolent sound of the running water beneath the piping of birds and the occasional chitters of an angry squirrel, he sat back against the broad bole of a spruce and sighed with contentment.

Toni sank back against the same tree.

"That was heavenly," Rio said. He patted Toni's hand. "I do thank you, Miss Toni. You're as thoughtful as you are purty."

"Miss Jane provided the meal. Sweet lady."

"It was your idea. As was this suit." Rio had removed the suitcoat and vest and had rolled the sleeves of his white cotton dress shirt up his forearms. He'd loosened the tie, as well. He chuckled as he looked down at his new attire.

"Do you really like it, Rio? I'm not trying to change you. I just thought you might think better of yourself if you dressed a little...well...better."

"And you were right. I believe I been holding my head a little higher ever since I walked out of Kaufman's." Kaufman's was the men's clothing and accessory shop in which he'd laid down a half a month's wages for the new attire. Toni had almost talked him into a silver-capped walking stick.

Almost.

He'd received enough jeering whistles and good-natured catcalls from his friends and sudden admirers just walking down the street to Hotel de Mannion. If he'd been wielding the walking stick, he likely would have been tarred and feathered and dumped in a stock trough.

He chuckled at that.

"What?" Toni said, elbowing him.

He chuckled again and glanced at her. "I told you—a man has his secrets."

"The walking stick?"

Rio snorted.

"All right, that might have been one step too far," Toni allowed.

They laughed.

They sat back against the tree, sipping the wine.

"I haven't had such a wonderful afternoon in a long, long time," Toni said with a contented sigh, letting her head loll against Rio's shoulder.

"I second that," Rio said.

"Let's cap it off right. Let's make it really memorable." Toni finished her wine and pushed to her feet.

"What?" Rio said. "How?"

Toni leaned toward him and brushed the tips of her fingers over his eyelids. "Close your eyes."

"Huh?"

"You heard me."

Rio closed his eyes. "What're you gonna do?"

"Just keep your eyes closed." Rio could hear the blanket-covered grass crinkling and her dress rustling as she rose and moved around.

"Oh-oh," Rio said when he heard her remove her shoes and drop them to the ground.

"You just keep those eyes closed, Mister. I have a pistol in the buggy!"

"You do?" Rio laughed.

"A girl can't be too careful."

Rio laughed again and tried like hell not to peek as he heard her stumbling around on the blanket before him. He heard the tell-tale rustling and snapping and unlacing of a lady disrobing.

Of course, he hadn't heard such a sweet song in a long time outside of the hurdy-gurdy houses—and doxies didn't have all that much to remove--but out here, accompanied with the warm sunshine and bird song and the sonorous muttering of the creek, it was a bewitching...downright alluring...song, indeed.

Splash!

Rio opened his eyes.

Toni's head just then broke the surface of the water, rising from below. She blew water from her lips, swabbed it from her cheeks and turned to Rio still sitting back against the tree.

"Get in here, Mister!"

She leaned back in the water and kicked toward the far side of the creek. As she did, Rio caught a tantalizing view of her bosoms cutting through the creek just below the surface.

Rio chuckled and heaved himself to his feet. He walked to the edge of the stream and said, "If I jump in there, I'll drown. I can't swim a lick."

"You don't need to swim a lick," Toni said, reaching the creek's far side and stretching her arms out on a giant root to each side of her, gently kicking her feet, the first planes of her breasts visible above the water, making

Rio's blood run warm. "It's shallow enough you can stand."

She slid forward and swam back out to the middle of the creek, stopped, and raised. her hands above the water. "I'm standing."

Rio winced. "You are, are you?"

"Get in here but be careful taking those duds off. Fold them up nicely and stack them in a nice pile."

"You're bossy!"

She lowered her chin alluringly, sucked in a little water, and blew it out. "It's a prerequisite for being a woman."

Rio looked at her, his apprehension cutting deep rungs across his forehead, powder white where his hat covered it. "All right. But you gotta turn around. If you so much as take one peak at this fat body, the deal is over."

He didn't like seeing himself naked, much less a woman. He even had the doxies turn the lamps way down or out altogether.

"All right, all right." Toni turned around, giving her back to him. The water came up to just below her shoulders.

Rio stumbled around, grunting and cursing as he skinned out of the new duds. Hearing him, Toni laughed.

"You better not get grass stains on that suit!"

Rio continued to stumble around, cursing, grunting, sighing, occasionally chuckling with deprecation, until he had his hat, boots, tie, shirt, pants, socks, and summerweight longhandles off and piled neatly atop his coat and vest.

"Keep those eyes closed, woman. I'm comin' in!"

Rio got down on all fours, wincing at the creaking in his tired, old bones, and slipped slowly off the bank and into the water. "*Ohh!*" he cried when his feet were firmly ensconced on the muddy bottom. "You didn't tell me it was cold!"

"It's a mountain creek in May, Rio." Toni turned around, smiled, and swam toward him.

She took long, fluid strokes, keeping her beguiling, brown eyes on his, her wet hair pasted against her head, sleek as an otter's hide. The long ends floated behind her in the water. Rio watched her with hushed, growing interest. The closer she came, the harder his heart thudded in his ears.

He kept expecting her to stop.

She didn't.

She swam right up to him, wrapped her arms around his neck, and closed her mouth over his, kissing him with deep, hungry affection.

Oh, Lordy, Rio said to himself, wondering if he was asleep and dreaming.

But no. Her body, cool and smooth and naked in his arms, was very real, indeed.

CHAPTER 23

"STRINGBEAN, YOU WANT A CUP OF COFFEE?" MANNION called down the stairs to the cellblock filled with weak yellow light and shadows. "Just made a fresh pot!"

"No thanks, Marshal," Stringbean replied, his tone concerningly forlorn. "I think I'm gonna try to sleep a little."

"All right," Mannion said. "Let me know. Sleep well."

"Thanks, Marshal."

Mannion glowered down the stairs. Having been locked up for four days now had been taking a lot out of the lad. The circuit judge was still likely a week away. Via telegraph, Mannion had heard he still had two murders to try up around Silverton and four stagecoach robbers, former miners having tired of picks and shovels, apparently, to lay the gavel to in Gunnison. Mannion wasn't sure if he should hope the kid held up during the wait or if he broke. If he broke, he might see the error of his ways and change his mind about taking the blame for Adam McClarksville's death.

On the other hand, if he didn't take the blame, Molly Hurdstrom would have to.

Mannion couldn't see Stringbean letting her take the blame. The young man just wasn't cut that way.

A soft thud sounded on the porch fronting the jailhouse.

Mannion turned his head toward the office's front wall. In the curtained window above his desk, a shadow moved.

Mannion frowned. There was another soft thud. Someone was skulking around out there.

Sliding his right-side Russian from its holster, Mannion moved to the door. He stood to the right of it for a moment, hand on the knob, waiting for a possible bullet. When one didn't come, he opened the door quickly, stepped out through the opening, and side-stepped to the right again, putting his back to the jail-house's front wall.

He looked around. The street before him was dark save for orange glows around burning oil pots and board-walks illuminated by lamplit saloon windows. From somewhere to Mannion's right along the street came the hum of voices from one such saloon. Beneath the hum was the patter of an off-key piano and the singing of a girl trying her best to be heard above the din.

More voices off to the left and on the other side of the street, fronting Hunter Drago's Three-Legged Dog. A few men were standing out front of the place, talking jovially with a girl, likely one of Drago's three whores. The girl was talking and laughing with the men until she cursed suddenly and said sharply, "Ronnie, you can't put your hand there unless you pay first! Those are the rules, you idiot," she admonished with a laugh.

Ronnie chuckled and said something too quietly for Mannion to hear.

Mannion glanced toward the window on his right, in

206 / PETER BRANDVOLD

which he'd seen the shadow move. Another shadow moved now quickly, an object darting toward him from the windowsill in a blur of fast motion. Mannion's heart thudded as he raised the Russian but held fire when the object thumped onto the floor at his feet with a shrill MEOW!

"Damn, Buster!" the lawman said, lowering the Russian and easing the tension in his trigger finger. "You're gonna be the death of me yet!"

The cat purred as he pressed his fat, furry body up against Mannion's left boot.

Mannion chuckled his relief.

He sheathed the Remington and checked his time-piece. Almost midnight. Time for his witching hour rounds, to see if any shops were being broken into or if any bar fights needed breaking up.

He reached into the office and drew the door closed, latching it with a click, then adjusted the set of his high-crowned black Stetson, and walked down the porch steps and into the street. He crossed to the other side at a slant and began tramping along the boardwalks over there, some raised, some not, some roofed, some not. As he did, he glanced cautiously into the dark breaks between build-ings in which a shooter or shooters might lurk.

Just ahead lay the Three-Legged Dog. The three men and the girl Mannion had heard earlier conversing out front, turned to him now, having heard his approach. They glanced at each other edgily and then two of the men and the girl turned and stepped through the saloon's batwings. The third man took a quick sip from the dimpled schooner in his hand, glanced once more, cautiously, at Mannion, and then pushed through the still-swinging doors himself.

Mannion stopped to peer over the batwings.

Inside, the three men and the girl were just then taking seats at a table. Only two other tables were occupied. Only one man stood at the bar, slouched over a shot glass a bottle of whiskey, his battered Stetson on the bar to his left. He was just then yawning widely into the backbar mirror, dragging a hand down over his open mouth.

One of the two occupied tables was occupied by Hunter Drago and Jane Ford.

Mannion stared at the pair, his insides twisting around like venomous snakes.

They were both slumped forward in their chairs, having what appeared an intimate conversation, both smiling understandingly. A labeled bottle stood on the table between them as did two brandy snifters.

Jane and Hunter Drago were having a heart to heart.

Drago suddenly glanced toward the batwings. He glanced away and then, seeing Mannion, returned his gaze to the batwings and held it on Mannion. He moved his lips, saying something to Jane. She turned toward the batwings, as well, her own gaze finding Joe.

Her eyes turned dark. They stayed on Mannion for about five seconds and then she turned her head toward Drago. Her lips moved as she said something, dropping her gaze to the table and wrapping both hands around her snifter as though for comfort.

Drago gave Mannion a two-fingered salute and a crooked smile and returned his attention to Mannion's woman.

Former woman.

Jane had a new man.

Joe continued walking past the Three-Legged Dog, but his mind was on Jane and Drago. A dark rat of dread nibbled away at his guts as though they were chunks of discarded bread in an alley.

What the hell was Drago up to?

Or was he up to anything?

Was Mannion really out of his mind like most of the town thought, and the old killer really was here, coincidentally in Mannion's town, to run a saloon and start a new life?

Maybe so. Maybe he was.

Maybe Mannion had gotten it all wrong.

Maybe Joe really was the suspicious, contrary old devil everyone, including his own daughter, thought he was.

He walked on, feeling a little shaky with self-doubt. It wasn't a pleasant sensation. He'd rarely doubted himself.

Boots thudded behind him suddenly. "Marshal Man--! Yikes—*hold on, hold on!*" yelped the town's tall, blond, sharp-nosed, mustached undertaker, Marvin Bellringer. He held up a beer mug in one hand while holding up his other hand, palm out, in supplication.

He squeezed his eyes closed as he turned his head to one side, urging, "Don't shoot, for Godsakes!"

Mannion had wheeled suddenly, raising both Russians, cocking and aiming them straight out from his shoulders.

"Sorry, Marvin." Mannion depressed the hammers and lowered both hoglegs.

The undertaker lowered his beer and his hand slowly, giving a relieved sigh. "I was just havin' a beer in the Sundowner when I seen you walk by. Remembered somethin' I forgot to tell you days back. Between you an' Hunter Drago, I've had so much business that--"

"Just get to the point, if you please, Bellringer."

"Oh, sure, sure." The undertaker took a sip of his

beer then scrubbed his hand across his mouth. "Remember them three fellas who tried to snuff your wick at Miss Ida's café a few weeks back?"

"How could I forget? One of their bullets found Jane."

"Well, I had 'em out in the street in front of my place, like you wanted. Left 'em out there a little too long, an' they started to smell. A muleskinner drove by one day, smelled 'em and gave 'em a gander. After he got done givin' me hell about keepin' 'em out in the street so long, he said he recognized all three."

"He did?"

"He did."

"Well?"

"They were regulators who usually worked for the rich mine operators around Leadville. All three had plenty of notches on their pistol grips. He didn't know their names, but he, having staked small claims around Leadville himself, sure 'nough knew them by sight. They were right good at either killin' fellas who got crossways with the bigger outfits or scarin' ya so bad you tucked tail and ran. The muleskinner tucked tail an' ran...all the way to Del Norte. That's why he's drivin' ore drays now for the Cloud Tickler Mine up around Uncompahgre Peak."

"I see," Mannion said, tapping his thumb and index finger pensively against the grips of his right-side .44. "I see..." There were plenty of businessmen around Del Norte who had interests up at Leadville and who might very well have known the three hardtails who'd tried to trim Mannion's wick.

Known and employed them.

Mannion's trouble might very well be local. He'd had that suspicion since the black-vested rider with the high, cream Stetson and black horse had tried to perforate his hide when he'd been riding out to inquire with Garth Helton. There were enough men right in town here who'd love nothing more than to see Bloody Joe dead. Some businessmen—especially the newer ones—saw his somewhat archaic ways of enforcing the law as bad for modern business.

After how efficiently and thoroughly he'd tamed Del Norte when he and Vangie had moved here from Kansas, damn their ungrateful hides to hell!

"Thanks, Marvin." Mannion fished a nickel out of his pants pocket, flipped it to the undertaker. "Not that you haven't made enough money of late, but here—have a beer on me."

Bellringer caught the coin against his chest and smiled.

He turned around and strode back toward the Sundowner, casting one cautious gaze back over his shoulder at the notoriously unpredictable Mannion.

Joe continued walking along the street to the south, peering in breaks between buildings and twisting doorknobs, making sure the shops were locked. He peered into the break between a harness shop and a feed store and froze. A shadow moved back toward the break's far end.

At least, he thought so. Like the shadow in the jailhouse window.

But that had only been Buster.

Right?

Mannion stared into the break, murky with dense shadows relieved only by light from an oil pot burning on the opposite side of the street, behind Mannion, and the stars, it being a starry, moonless night.

"Anyone there?" Mannion called, his voice pitched with suspicion.

No response. But then, he hadn't expected one.

Except maybe one voiced in lead.

Mannion unsnapped the keeper thong from over the big Russian holstered for the cross-draw on his left hip and continued forward, pricking his ears extra intensely for any sound of movement around him. He'd had a weird feeling ever since he'd seen that shadow in the jailhouse window. Even after Buster had leaped out of the same window, making him wonder if the shadow he'd spied hadn't only been the cat.

But maybe Buster had only been trying to warn him of trouble.

Buster was a good cat that way. He'd lived around three lawmen long enough to have honed his own keen sense of danger.

Mannion reached the south end of town, all the way to where the original cabins and stock pens and barns hunched darkly in the sagebrush and willows. Only the rare light in the rare window out here. Most of the old-timers, Del Norte's original settlers, who lived out this way had long since gone to bed.

Mannion walked back into the business district, again rattling doorknobs and peering through dark windows, looking for suspicious movement inside.

He paused out front of the San Juan. He stared up the veranda's broad front steps.

The big, curtained windows of the saloon were still lit but Mannion saw no shadows moving behind them. Probably only a few itinerant horse or cattlemen still drinking inside after making business deals, preparing to hop the morning stage to head back to wherever they'd come from. Mannion had found that most such businessmen were from Denver, but they were coming from as far away as Kansas City and Chicago to seal deals these days, too.

Del Norte and the area around it were growing.

Joe stared up at the windows of his and Vangie's suite, which they'd occupied since their house had been burned by Whip Helton and the toughnuts he'd ridden with—all dead now. The windows were dark. Vangie was asleep.

Mannion grew dark himself, pondering his daughter. She'd been especially cool to him ever since he'd braced Hunter Drago. Not as cool as Jane, but cool. Vangie usually left the suite early to work with the wild stallion, returning to have supper with her father and to retire early, for Vangie was early to bed and early to rise. She spent most of her time with her beloved horses. She and Mannion used to spend an hour or two reading together and talking after supper, but these days Vangie usually repaired to her room to read by herself and to go to sleep.

Self-doubt made Mannion feel shaky again.

Had he been wrong about Drago?

Was he as crazy as everyone thought he was?

He continued forward, rattling doorknobs, pausing to peer over batwings, looking for trouble, finding none. It was a quiet night.

He paused to peer over the batwings of the Wooden Nickel Saloon. Finding the place nearly deserted, he turned away and started forward again but stopped and turned back to peer over the doors once more.

Four heads turned toward him. The heads of the only four people in the place aside from the husky barman who appeared to be asleep standing up behind the bar, arms crossed on his lumpy chest.

Those three heads belonged to Mayor Charlie McQueen, Ralph Hurdstrom, Malcolm McCarksville, and the lumberman, Keel Brandywine. All four sets of eyes widened in surprise as they studied Mannion. Charlie McQueen's lower jaw dropped a little, and his cheeks above his immaculately trimmed beard colored.

All four men sat staring, speechless, at Mannion.

Sitting at a table in the middle of the otherwise empty room, they were nervous.

In fact, as Mannion regarded them, a sweat bead popped out on Hurdstrom's forehead. It glistened in the light of a near hurricane lamp and dribbled down into his right eye, which he blinked against the salty sting.

Mannion stepped through the batwings, stopped just inside.

"Gentlemen," he said, spreading his feet a little more than shoulder width apart and planting his fists on his hips. "Burnin' the midnight oil?"

McQueen's right eye twitched. All eyes remained on Mannion.

"Is that a crime, Mannion?" Brandywine asked, cheekily.

"Not at all. Just making conversation," Mannion said.

He gave a smile that he knew did not make it to his eyes.

All four men, he silently pondered as he stared back at them, had reason to see him dead. McQueen had helped Joe out in the old trouble of last year, taking down Helton's men on Main Street. But Brandywine was one of those newcomers who likely wanted Mannion out—even *before* Mannion had tattooed his cheek days back, after he and Jane had been ambushed in Miss Ida's café.

Had Brandywine convinced McQueen to join in his efforts?

It wouldn't have been too hard. McQueen was a weak-minded popinjay.

Hurdstrom had likely been in cahoots with Brandy-wine and McQueen even before the mud storm had erupted involving his daughter and the deceased Adam McClarksville. He was one of those rich, wealthy newcomers. He had business interests in Leadville and Joe had heard that McClarksville, who had big political ambitions, did, too. Their killing Mannion would have the additional benefit of making sure the charges against his deputy stuck.

They were all in *something* together. That was for sure. Mannion could see it in their eyes.

What were they doing up so late?

Maybe they thought that tonight, with almost the entire town against Mannion because of Hunter Drago, was a most opportune time to finally kick the lawman out with a cold shovel. Maybe they were staying up late to finally see it through.

Mannion smiled again suddenly, pinched his hat brim to the four nervous popinjays. "Goodnight, gentlemen. Best go home soon. God knows you need your beauty sleep!"

He winked, turned around, and pushed back out through the batwings.

He resumed his trek, looking for trouble, finding none...until he stopped at the bottom of the jailhouse steps.

The window left of the door was dark.

Mannion had left a lamp burning.

He reached down and unsnapped the keeper thong from over the hammer of his cross-draw Russian.

CHAPTER 24

Mannion ratcheted back the Russian's hammer.

He walked up the porch steps, not trying to be quiet. He took one step onto the porch then lurched to his left and slammed his back against the office's front wall, left of the door. He'd no sooner made the move than a deafening blast issued from inside the office. A pumpkin-sized hole appeared in the door, wood from the vertical panels flying out across the porch and down the steps where Mannion had been standing a second before.

Joe turned to face the door. He thrust the Russian through the hole and fired round after round into the office, hearing screams and loud grunts of agonized surprise followed by the thudding of feet and the heavier thuds of bodies striking to the floor. He'd just gotten off his sixth shot when a bullet from behind him punched into the doorframe to his right.

A gun blasted on the other side of the street.

He saw the flash in the corner of his right eye.

He pulled the empty Russian out of the door and twisted around to his left, dropping to his butt on the porch floor and slamming his back against the office's front wall. He drew the right-side Russian from its holster, aimed straight out away from him as another bullet slammed into the office wall just above his left shoulder.

He triggered the Russian at the flash—once, twice, three, four times.

The man-shaped silhouette jerked backward. He fell on the boardwalk fronting the barbershop. Mannion fired again but his slug plowed harmlessly into the building behind the man as he gave an enraged bellow, heaved himself to his feet, and ran into the break to the left of the barber shop.

"Yellow dog!"

Mannion quickly reloaded the smoking Russian in his hand then leaped off the porch and ran across the street. He stopped at the mouth of the break near where a high-crowned cream Stetson lay on the boardwalk, crown up. Mannion crouched, raised the Russian, and fired three quick shots into the darkness before him. A man yelped. There was a crunching, rustling thud as the man fell somewhere deep inside the break.

Mannion strode into the darkness before him, inadvertently kicking old newspapers and discarded bottles and airtight tins, sage shrubs and grass crunching beneath his boots. Ahead, a shadow moved on the ground. The man lay writhing and cursing.

As Mannion approached, the man, who wore a black vest, rolled onto his back and glared up at his assailant. He had a broad face with a thick handlebar mustache to which sand and bits of weed seeds clung. "How many damn lives, you got anyway, Mannion, you bloody bastard?"

"One more than you!" Mannion holstered the Russian and kicked the man in the side. "Get up!"

"I'm all shot up!"

"Then I'll help you up."

The man screamed as Mannion crouched, grabbed the front of the man's vest, and pulled him to his feet.

"*Ohhh!*" the man cried.

Mannion could feel the greasy blood through his gloves.

Mannion grabbed the man by the back of his shirt collar and half-dragged him back through the break and into the street, the man groaning and grunting and cursing as he shambled along, half-falling, sometimes falling to his knees before Mannion jerked him back to his feet and they resumed their trek south along Main.

"Who are you?" Mannion asked as they approached the Wooden Nickel out front of which four men stood in silhouette against the lamplight issuing from the saloon behind them.

"Go to hell!"

Mannion stopped, let the man drop to his knees in the street. Joe kicked him in the belly, hard.

The man screamed and said in a quavering, guttural voice: "Jeremiah Craig!"

Mannion laughed. He knew the name. Regulator from Wyoming. Worked for top dollar which had likely come from the four men just then scurrying back through the Wooden Nickel's doors likes rats to their holes.

"Up you go!"

Mannion grabbed the back of the man's collar and jerked him back to his feet.

Again, the man cursed as he was half-dragged onto the boardwalk fronting the Wooden Nickel and then through the swinging doors and inside. McQueen, Hurdstrom, McClarksville, and Brandywine were sitting where they'd been sitting before. Even as Mannion noisily dragged the drygulching killer into the saloon, violently kicking chairs and tables out of his way, they did not look at him but kept their sheepish gazes on one another, each with one hand on his shot glass, hilariously trying to look casual.

As Mannion drew to within two feet of the four men, he gave one more, hard thrust, twisting around at the waist, and thrust Craig onto the table where the killer lay belly up, dark eyes glassy with pain. The bottle and shot glasses flew in all directions. The four dandies scrambled to their feet, knocking over chairs, and scurried back away from the table.

"What is the meaning of this?" yowled Charlie McQueen. "Joe, my God!"

Mannion unsheathed his cross-draw Russian, clicked the hammer back, leaned over the table, and thrust the barrel into Craig's mustached mouth. "Who sent you?"

Craig choked on the barrel, bulging eyes turning even more horrified, body spasming violently, flopping his arms and legs.

Joe removed the barrel from the man's mouth. "Who sent you?"

The man made strangling sounds as he blinked in horror up at Mannion, spittle foaming on his lips.

Again, Mannion thrust the Russian's barrel into the man's mouth. "Who sent you?"

He withdrew the barrel from the man's mouth. "If I don't get an answer," he said, "I'm gonna blow a through the back of your throat!"

The man looked around wildly at the four men staring down, aghast, at him. He raised one arm feebly, pointing desperately with one black-gloved hand, "*They did!*"

Mannion smiled. "That's what I thought."

"Holster it, Mannion. You're done!"

Joe turned to see Keel Brandywine holding a cocked Lady Derringer on him to Joe's right, three feet away.

Mannion laughed and smashed the Russian down hard against the Derringer, which cracked and sent a slug into the floor between Joe's boots. Brandywine yowled as he dropped the Derringer and grabbed the hand with which he'd been holding the feminine little popper with his other one. He crouched over the injured appendage. As he did, Joe smashed his right knee into the man's face, feeling the wetness of the man's blood through his denims as the man's nose exploded like a ripe tomato.

Brandywine staggered backward, straightening, blood oozing from his smashed nose, eyes rolling back in his head. Joe holstered the Russian and used the fist that had been holding it to deliver a savage roundhouse to Brandywine's left cheek.

Brandywine yelped and flew back and sideways before landing on a table.

Joe crouched over him, lifted him up by his shirt collar and delivered one savage blow after another to the man's face. When the man's face was ground burger, eyes already swelling, there was a girlish shriek behind Joe and suddenly Charlie McQueen leaped onto Joe's back, entangling his arms around Joe's neck, squeezing.

"You're a bloody savage, Joe! A bloody damn savage! You *must* be stopped!"

"Oh, Mr. Mayor," Joe raked out, twisting around so suddenly that McQueen was forced to release his womanish hold on his neck. He flew backward, staggering on his brogan-clad feet, thrusting his arms out to his sides to help him regain his balance. "You got no idea!"

Joe punched the man in his impeccably bearded face,

causing the man's glasses to fly off, bounce off the floor, and clatter away. He rammed his fist into the man's belly and then into his face once more before another man came bulling into Joe's side, mewling hoarsely, thrusting Joe onto a table to his right.

The man—Hurdstrom, face swollen and red with foppish fury—tried to punch Joe in the face, but Joe easily deflected the blows with his arms and landed two solid jabs to the man's mouth, tearing his lips. Hurdstrom had no sooner sagged to the floor than McClarksville was on top of Joe. He was bigger than Hurdstrom and had probably taken a few boxing lessons in whatever college he'd gone to back East—probably Yale, since that's where Joe understood his son Adam and A.J. Lamb were going.

Had been going, in the case of Adam..

Nothing taught the art of fisticuffs better than the Wild Western Frontier, however.

Joe easily absorbed the blows, feeling only a slight crack on the corner of his lower lip before he head-butted the man off him. McClarksville groaned and went staggering backward. Mannion pushed himself up off the table with his elbows and followed the man's backward retreat, hammering McClarksville's face and then his belly and then his face again and then his belly again before the man rammed up against the bar and, out like a blown lamp, eyes rolling back in his head, he sagged straight down to the floor with a resolute thud.

McClarksville's descent to the floor gave Mannion a good view of the barman, Romer Diggs, who was no longer sleeping on his feet. The only change in his former position, however, was that he'd merely opened his eyes. His thick arms were still crossed on his lumpy chest.

"Thanks a lot, Joe. They're regulars."

"Ah, hell." Mannion chuckled as he strode over to the

table on which his hat lay. The other three dandies groaned on the floor and spat blood from their lips. "They'll be back."

He wasn't going to haul them over to Hotel de Mannion. He'd already given them the best punishment possible. Besides, he didn't want them cluttering up his cellblock while they waited for the judge. They'd learned their lesson. When they met Joe in the street from now on, they'd hold their hats in their hands and likely offer to shine his boots.

Mannion chuckled as he reshaped his hat and set it on his head. He looked at the four dandies lying in heaps around where Josiah Crag lay belly up on the table, apparently dead from his own many injuries. Mannion said to McQueen, "If you send any more men after me, Mister Mayor, I'm gonna kick the stuffing out of both your soft ends and hang you from the nearest tree—*slow*. That goes for the rest of you fellas!"

He turned his head forward as he continued to the batwings.

He stopped suddenly.

Jane stood between the open swing doors, staring at him, holding a spruce green shawl about her slender shoulders.

Her eyes shone with no little disgust and reproach. Her upper lip twitched then curled.

Mannion continued toward her. He didn't say anything. She didn't, either.

She just stepped back and to one side and looked up at him warily as he pushed through the batwings and turned right, heading back to the jailhouse to clear out the fresh beef he'd left inside.

He supposed Stringbean might be wondering what all the fuss had been about, too.

Despite himself, he smiled.

Helluva night, Blood Joe. Even for you...

———

JANE FORD WOKE THE NEXT MORNING AT SEVEN o'clock, early for her, feeling refreshed despite how late she'd gone to bed. But then, she'd always been a night owl. She'd enjoyed the drinks and stories she'd shared with Hunter. She'd slept relatively well despite an hour or so of tossing and turning, as she usually did lately, over the matter of Joe.

The truth was she still loved the man. You couldn't change such feelings on a dime.

But what she'd seen—the *unseemly scene* she'd witness in the Wooden Nickel last night—had further enhanced her resolve that Mannion was not the man for her. Of course, she didn't know what had led to the dustup—if you could call it that—in the Wooden Nickel, but surely another man of more controlled passions might have handled it better. Especially a man who'd been given the privilege of wearing a town marshal's badge as well as that of a deputy sheriff though Joe rarely wore the second badge but kept it in a drawer until trouble called him outside Del Norte's town limits and he needed broader jurisdictional authority.

The county sheriff had come calling for that badge the previous fall, during Joe's row with Garth Helton, and Joe had sent the sheriff packing without it.

So like Joe.

That remembrance gave Jane the urge to quirk a mouth corner in a devilish grin but she managed to contain herself and to retain the seriousness of perspective warranted by the throwback character of Bloody Joe

Mannion. He was a brigand. A thug. He'd beaten up three of Del Norte's most prominent businessmen last night. And the man he'd treated so harshly last week had not deserved the thrashing Joe had given him right out on Main Street for all to see.

In fact, the Hunter Drago whom Jane had come to know was quite the civilized, even sensitive and philosophical man. Twelve years of prison had, indeed, changed him for the better. Made him soulful, kind. He'd even kindled a relationship with his Maker, and he could quote long passages from the Good Book itself.

So unlike Joe.

Yes, Jane reflected as she dressed in her best riding gear—slacks, cream silk blouse, vest, and soft doeskin jacket with bone buttons and whang strings hanging from the sleeves—she'd become quite attracted to the man.

She quickly brushed her hair and gathered it into a mare's tail secured with a round, silver clip. She pulled on her riding boots, stuffed the cuffs of her soft cotton slacks into them, then knotted a green bandanna around her neck. The green of the bandanna matched the green of her felt riding hat.

She gave herself quick appraisal in the standing mirror and smiled. Jane liked what she saw, sure enough.

More importantly, she hoped that Hunter Drago would like what he saw, too.

Jane left her suite, locked the door behind her, and descended the stairs. A good dozen or so men were breakfasting in the big main drinking hall. As Jane dropped down the stairs, feeling a little breathless and flushed, all heads turned to her and then the men— mostly men but a few of Jane's working girls, as well— rose from their chairs and gave her a warm round of applause.

A couple of them whistled.

Jane stopped, frowning curiously.

Then she shuttled her gaze out the window left of the door. Hunter Drago was sitting his handsome cream horse out there, holding the reins of Jane's saddled chestnut mare.

She smiled as she returned her gaze to her fawning admirers.

They were all giving her their tacit approval of Jane's apparent switch in affections from the uncouth rebel, Bloody Joe Mannion, to Del Norte's newest, respected businessman...

Hunter Drago.

Unsuccessfully fighting off a blush, Jane continued down the stairs, strode across the room while the applause continued, and then pushed out through the batwings.

Hunter smiled from beneath the brim of his black, bullet-crowned hat. He raised the mare's reins in his left hand.

"As promise, here I am." Hunter's smile broadened. "Now, shall we see some of this beautiful country, Miss Jane?"

"We shall," Jane said, smiling delightedly as she strode down the porch steps and accepted the reins.

Hunter winked and pinched his hat brim to her.

CHAPTER 25

Riding stirrup to stirrup, Jane and Hunter Drago galloped out of town to the north.

They rode hard for several miles then slowed their mounts as they began climbing the forested first front of the Sawatch Range. Towering stone monoliths began rising around them.

They climbed up and over two watersheds and, now at ten thousand feet above sea level, the air thin and cool, they rode through the bustling little mining town of St. Elmo, nodding at the bearded prospectors standing knee deep in Chalk Creek, panning for gold. Here, dirty snowdrifts remained between the small, tin- or brush-roofed cabins issuing blue smoke from their brick or tin chimney pipes. Jane and her riding companion left town but not before buying a picnic lunch of roast beef sandwiches and hard-boiled eggs from the La Plata Saloon then continued northwest in the forested mountain bastion, toward Mirror Lake and another burgeoning mining camp on the other side of yet another high pass, called Tin Cup.

They were following a trail between a steep mountain

shoulder and a deep canyon threaded by yet another creek when clouds rolled in, and a cool wind picked up. Distantly, thunder rumbled.

"Oh, my," Jane said, hipping around to watch the swollen, purple clouds tumbling toward her from the southeast. "We're going to get a storm. Best head for lower ground!"

"Now, now, Miss Jane," Hunter said, narrowing that beguiling lone eye of his and spreading his mouth with a wolfish smile. The tails of his black duster were blowing up in front of him. "You don't seem to me like the sort of woman who'd balk at a little afternoon storm."

Jane grimaced. "I don't?" The problem was few storms this high up in the mountains were "little."

"No. And neither does that mare of yours."

Jane looked down at the four-year-old chestnut she'd named Pandora. When Jane had time to read, which was rare, she preferred Greek Mythology. The mare appeared calm despite her tail blowing up between her legs and the continuing rumble of distant thunder. Pandora merely lifted her long, fine snout to sniff the breeze as though savoring the smell of distant rain, pine resin, brimstone, and sage.

"Well, I don't need to be shown up by my horse," Jane said with a laugh. She winced when more thunder rumbled, growing louder as the storm approached. "Besides," she said, "we're only about a mile from the next pass. We'll have more cover down the other side. We might see some bighorn sheep over there!"

"I would indeed love to see a bighorn sheep. Never have before."

"They're a real treat," Jane said, touching boot heels to Pandora's flanks and continuing forward.

They'd ridden only a hundred more yards when it started to rain.

The sky just spit at first but, as though someone were pushing the rain throttle steadily forward, it came down harder and harder very quickly. Thunder rumbled louder and then, just as Jane and Pandora were within sight of the rocky crest of the pass, riding ahead of Hunter on the narrow horse trail, a witch's finger of pale blue lightning flashed out of nowhere and a Ponderosa pine standing along the trail maybe fifty feet ahead and left suddenly exploded as though it had been filled with dynamite.

Thunder followed like the hammering of a giant, empty tin pot, making the world shudder.

The crown dropped down over where the lightning had split the tree nearly in two, burning. Bark and wood chunks flew in all directions.

Pandora gave a high, shrill whinny and reared sharply, clawing her hooves at the purple sky. "*Ohh!*" Jane said, reaching for the horn with both gloved hands but missing it as gravity shoved her back over the mare's arched tail. She turned a backward somersault in midair then watched the gravelly ground come up fast to smack her hard.

She'd no sooner struck than she began to slide down the steep slope toward the canyon.

"No!" she cried, digging her gloved fingers desperately into the gravely ground, unable to find purchase.

"Jane!" Hunter yelled.

"Help!" Jane cried as she felt her feet and then her legs drop down over the lip of the canyon.

Then the rest of her dropped over the edge and the ridge wall was a red-tan blur in front of her as she dropped straight down, facing it, until she landed so hard on something protruding from the ridge wall that the air in her lungs was slammed out of her in a loud, raking WHUSH!!

The sudden landing dazed her, scrambling her brains, blurring her vision, and causing bells to clang in her ears.

She groaned and lifted her face from the ground and looked around to see that she'd landed—at least the upper half of her body had landed—on a three- or four-feet knob of sloping ground, slick from the pounding rain and protruding from the ridge wall. A stout but stunted cedar grew out of the base of the knob, between the knob and the ridge, and it was this that she had automatically wrapped her arms around.

That's why she hadn't slid down off the knob and into the canyon yawning wide two hundred feet below.

She glanced into that chasm. She swooned, her stomach rising into her throat.

The stream wended through the canyon below the veil of slanting rain, the water stitched with white rapids.

Somewhere, a hawk screeched beneath the storm's roar, as though mocking the poor woman's dire predicament.

"Oh," Jane heard herself say, her legs dangling over that deep, yawning crevasse threatening to suck the rest of her into infinity if only her desperately clasped hands should unclasp, tearing her arms free of the anchoring cedar and hurling her into oblivion. "*Oh, God!*"

"Hold on, Jane."

She was able to lift her head just enough to see Hunter standing atop the ridge, peering expressionlessly down at her, arms hanging straight down at his sides. Rain hammered his stoic, black-clad figure.

"I'll be right with you."

He turned and disappeared.

"Oh, God," Jane said, resting her chin on the wet, sloping knob.

Fear engulfed her. Every muscle and sinew in her body was trembling.

That terror grew even more expansive when she heard the crackling of the cedar in front of her. The tree bowed forward. Bark dribbled down its trunk, which was about as large around as one of Joe's corded forearms. The cedar was stout but brittle; it was not going to take the pressure Jane was putting on it much longer. If it didn't break, she was going to tear it out by its roots!

Neither were her hands going to take the pressure she was putting on them. They were slick from the rain, and they ached miserably through the knuckles, which bulged from the strain of keeping her fingers so fiercely entangled.

Again, the tree crackled and lurched forward a little more.

"Oh, God!" Jane gasped, her body jerking back toward the chasm trying so desperately to suck her into it.

Again, the hawk gave its mocking cry beneath the storm's roar.

"Oh, shut. up, for Godsakes!" she shrilled.

"I didn't say anything."

Again, Jane gasped with a start.

The voice had come from just above her. She looked up to see Hunter Dago walking down the face of the ridge, a stout rope wrapped around his waist and slip-knotted before him. He glanced down at Jane.

"How are you doing, Miss Jane? Holding up well?"

"Reasonably well for someone who is about to die, I should think," Jane said, tears rolling down her cheeks, mixing with the rain.

Hunter glanced up the ridge and yelled, "Back a little more, Herod!"

More rope paid down from the lip of the ridge, and Hunter took three more steps down the ridge until he was directly to Jane's left.

"Oh, God!" Jane said, when the cedar gave another sudden jerk.

Jane jerked as well. She looked at her fingers. They were white. They were sliding apart.

"I don't want to die!" Jane wailed as her slick, wet fingers continued to slide apart.

"Don't blame you a bit," Drago said.

Again, the cedar jerked forward.

"Oh, no!" Jane screamed as her hands came apart and she lurched down toward the chasm opening its mouth to receive her.

Her head had just dropped down over the lip of the knob and she was beginning that long, inelegant fall into the jaws of death when she felt a strong arm wrap itself around her, stopping her fall and drawing her toward Hunter. He used both arms to pull her over onto his lap.

"There, there, Miss Jane," he said. "Now, see—it wasn't your time, was it?" He gave an amused chuckle. "No, not yet." He looked up toward the lip of the ridge and whistled. "Ahead, Herod—*easy does it*!"

As the rope tightened and Hunter began walking his polished, squared-toed, black boots up the face of the ridge, Jane clinging to him for dear life, her arms around his neck, he said, "Won't be long now."

Jane shuddered as she stared horrifically into the weather-fogged chasm that had nearly taken her before shuttling her gaze up toward the crest of the ridge where the taut rope was sliding up over the lip, causing sand and gravel to dribble down the ridge's face, some of it peppering her sodden face and hair.

Jane was speechless with fear. The fear seemed to intensify as she and Drago neared the ridge's lip. Would they actually make it up and over to safety?

And then the dogged Herod pulled them up and over it. Heart in her throat, Jane watched the hindquarters and tail of the cream horse walking forward toward the forested slope beyond, her feet and Hunter's feet following the rest of them up out of the chasm.

"Stop, Herod," Hunter calmly called to the mount, who stopped immediately.

Jane stopped sliding painfully along the ground. Her heart slowed. She looked up to see Hunter on top of her, straddling her. He smiled down at her, flicked a gloved thumb across her lower lip. "'Riches do not profit in the day of wrath,'" he quoted, "'But righteousness delivers from death.' Proverbs, chapter eleven, verse four."

He winked. The rain sluiced off the slight funnel in his Stetson's brim.

"Well said," Jane said, still trembling. "Better yet—well delivered."

Hunter twisted around, loosened the rope's slip knot, then lifted the loop up and over them both, tossed it aside.

Jane was soaked to the skin, and cold. So cold. She didn't mind. Not one bit.

She'd fully expected to be dead by now.

"In other words," Jane said above the roar of the storm. "Thank you."

"Oh, don't thank me, Miss Jane." Hunter rose, straightening his long, lean legs then crouched to wrap one arm around Jane's shoulders and took her right arm in his right hand, gently lifting her to her feet. "I almost got you killed for my mulishness. Let's see how fit you--"

"Ow," Jane said. As she placed weight on her left ankle the appendage gave a fierce bark of agony.

"Ah," Drago said. "The ankle."

"Yes."

As Jane leaned against him, he gentled her back down to the ground.

In the hammering rain, the water continuing to sluice off his hat brim, Hunter dropped to a knee beside her. "I tell you what, Miss Jane. Why don't we get ourselves out of this weather? I spied a cave back a couple hundred yards. Why don't we take cover in there, and then we'll get warm and check out that ankle of yours?"

Jane nodded. She leaned forward to squeeze the appendage in question. It ached fiercely and she thought she could feel it swelling inside her boot.

Hunter rose then crouched over Jane, drawing her up into his capable arms. He carried her over to Herod and set her up on the horse's back, settling her snug in the wet saddle.

Jane looked around, frowning. "Where's Pandora?"

Hunter climbed up onto Herod's back to settle himself behind Jane. He looked around through the slashing rain as thunder continued to hammer the heavens and lightning flashed, bright as exploding kegs of dynamite. "I don't know," he yelled above the storm's cacophony. "Must've headed for home."

He reined the cream around and clucked to it. "Let's get you thawed out and safe, Miss Jane," he said. "Thawed out an' safe. Yessir."

He winked at her.

CHAPTER 26

JANE FELT SAFE WITH HUNTER BEHIND HER, HIS ARMS wrapped around her as he manipulated Herod's reins.

Herod?

Jane chuckled to herself.

In prison, Drago must have taken his Biblical readings a little too far, to a far too imaginative degree. But who wouldn't, Jane supposed?

The Good Book was probably the only thing he'd had to read, and she was sure the walls—or bars—had closed in on him. If Jane remembered correctly from her own rudimentary Biblical teachings from Sunday School when she'd been growing up in a wealthy, modestly God-fearing family in St. Louis, King Herod was the monster King of Judea who tried to kill baby Jesus and, when he couldn't find him, killed every other infant in Bethlehem.

Jane chuckled. Herod must've been quite the contrarian before Hunter had managed to train him so well, thus the name. Likely an appalling exaggeration of the horse's real character, but Jane knew how frustrating half-broke horses could be. She should probably suggest Hunter change the name now. After all, the horse had saved both their lives, so unlike what the Biblical Herod would have done. But she'd let it go for now.

There might be time later. Yes, there might just be time later, she thought as Hunter put Herod up a well-worn trail climbing the side of the forested slope on their right. Jane leaned back against Hunter as the horse climbed, wending around large rocks, toward the oval, dark mouth of a cave opening beneath a stone overhang about fifty yards up from the main trail below.

At the top of the slope, Hunter checked Herod down, stepped down from the saddle, then reached up and eased Jane into his arms. Shifting her weight, settling her against his chest, he climbed the slight, stony rise that rose to the cave.

"Oh, Hunter, your poor back," Jane said, her arms around his neck.

"Pshaw!" Hunter said. "I carried rocks in prison for twelve years. Yessir, from one pile to another pile to another pile. The guards were notional—don't ya know? Kept changing their minds about where they wanted them piled. Compared to those stones I was forced to move around under threat of a bullwhipping, you're light as a feather, Miss Jane!"

He laughed then crouched to peer cautiously into the cave through the billowing, pale curtain of rain. Jane looked, too, relieved to see no menacing, copper eyes staring out at them, for she knew that wildcats often called these caverns home. The cave was about the size of a small parlor, the ceiling slanting down toward the back until the rear wall, barely visible in the murky shadows, was only about three feet high.

What caught the brunt of Jane's and Hunter's attention, however, was a modest-sized pile of firewood stacked against the right wall, with a fruit crate filled with what appeared tinder of twigs and crushed pinecones. Beside the fruit crate sat three airtight tins—two of beans, one of stewed tomatoes.

In the center of the cave lay a blackened stone fire ring and a small mound of gray ash.

"Not only abandoned but supplied!" Jane cooed in approval.

"Yessir," Hunter allowed. "Many folks must overnight here and keeping fuel for such times as these is the custom of the country."

Drago grunted his satisfaction then crouched to enter and gently sat Jane down against the left wall.

"Oh," Jane said, flexing her ankle inside the boot then crouching forward to squeeze the swelling limb with both hands. "Hurts bad, Hunter. I hope you brought some whiskey."

Hunter laughed and patted Jane's shoulder as though the question were too absurd to warrant a response. "Let me fetch my possible, an' we'll get that ankle tended."

Hunter left the cave, crouching against the storm. Jane sat back against the cave wall, cursing her stupidity. She should not have let him convince her to keep climbing higher on the pass. Not with a storm on the way. She knew better. Hunter did not. He'd spent the last twelve years in federal prison. Still, she'd let him convince her to keep going because he was a man—a big, burly man.

The type of man who'd always caught her eye and had ensnared her heart over the years.

Not unlike Joe himself.

Yes, unlike Joe. Hunter was far different from Joe. Hunter was still a man, but he had a tender heart and a vibrant spirit and it was she who'd let him convince her to keep riding when she'd known better. With him as with every man, she just needed to put her foot down and keep it down. She was no wilting hothouse flower, after all.

But there'd be time for that, she thought, smiling as she watched the tall, lean, rugged man lead the horse into the shelter of some rocks down the slope. Plenty of time.

Had her heart already been ensnared? She hoped not. She needed more time after Joe, to be able to completely let him go. Just as she was no wilting hothouse flower, she was no teenager, either. She should know better.

But was it so wrong to let your heart be ensnared? She had to admit she'd been lonely after Joe, and she wasn't getting any younger. She'd gone long stretches without a man in her life. She was, deep down, independent. But she felt the years catching up to her. And with each day that passed, each night she slept alone grew longer and longer...

"Penny for your thoughts, Miss Jane?"

Jane looked up to see Hunter standing before her, his rain-beaded saddlebags draped over his shoulder. She shook her head as though to clear the reverie, feeling her cheeks warm then warm still further when she imagined the pink flush that must be rising in them.

"Oh, it's nothing," Jane said.

Hunter smiled down at her, knowingly, and Jane averted her gaze, embarrassed.

Hunter removed his hat, swatted water from it against his leg, set it down on a rock then dropped to a knee beside Jane. He unbuckled the flap of one saddlebag pouch, dipped his hand inside, and pulled out a hide wrapped bottle.

"Here," he said, removing the hide from the bottle and held it up, smiling. "That should take the sting out of that ankle."

"Oh," Jane said in surprise. "My favorite brandy!"

Hunter smiled and winked. "Would I bring anything less?"

It was Jane's turn to smile. "I had a bottle of red wine in my saddlebags. But Pandora's probably half-way back to Del Norte by now."

"Then I reckon this will have to do." Hunter pried the cork out of the bottle, handed the bottle to Jane, and placed his hands on her left boot. "This is going to have to come off."

"Good luck," Jane said, taking a liberal pull from the bottle. "It's swelling." She winced. "Believe me—I can feel it."

"Think it's broken?"

"Just a bad sprain," Jane said. "At least, I think so. I've had them before." She gave Hunter an ironic look and hooked a crooked smile at him. "This is not my first rodeo, unfortunately."

"Tough woman," Hunter said. "I like that. Better take another pull, though. This is gonna hurt."

"All right." Jane held up a finger and took a pull. She lowered the bottle and said, "Wait, wait." She took another couple of deep pulls from the bottle, sighed, and ran the back of her hand across her mouth.

Both hands on her foot, preparing to tug, Hunter looked up at her from beneath his brows, mouth corners quirked in an ironic grin.

"All right," Jane said.

"Here we go!"

He'd no sooner started to pull than several bayonets of raw, burning pain shot upward from her ankle to impale her heart. The world spun, grew dim, then as dark as the bottom of a very deep well.

Warm sunlight soothed her. She dreamed she must be

lying in a sunny glade in the deep of summer. But then she opened her eyes and saw the crackling fire in the stone ring before her. Immediately, she felt the pain in her left ankle and looked down to see the appendage in question wrapped tightly in several lengths of tough cotton cloth. Her toes sticking up out of the wrap were purple. They, too, were swelling. Her right boot stood before the fire, drying.

Jane shuttled her gaze across the warmly leaping flames.

She frowned. Apprehension touched her.

Hunter knelt on one knee back near where the wood had been piled, a steaming tin coffee cup in his hand. He was clad in only his white cotton longhandles. His outer clothes including his duster and his hat were spread out on the ground near the fire. He'd pulled the top of his longhandles down to expose his pale chest and belly, his chorded belly button. He didn't have any fat on him. It was all tight muscle and sinew, giving his bony, tight-muscled chest a concave appearance.

He gazed through the flames at Jane with the oddest expression. His lone eye was darkly pensive, and his face resembled a death's head mask of deep, bitter reverie.

He seemed to stare right through Jane to the depths of her soul, and as though he didn't like what he saw.

"Hunter?" she said.

He continued to stare at her as though he'd gone into some dark trance.

"Hunter?" Jane said again, hearing a thin tremor in her voice.

Maintaining that same expression, he said tonelessly, "I was just wondering if you had any idea how long twelve years is."

Jane stared at him. She hoped that she was still asleep and dreaming, but she didn't think she was.

Despite the heat from the flames, she felt the cool touch of the outside air—it had stopped raining but was still gray and cloudy—against her chest. She glanced down in horror to see that the top six buttons of her blouse had been undone, and the blouse had been partly peeled down her shoulders. She could see her white chemise that was still wet from the rain. Enough of it was exposed to expose her cleavage. The garment was still so wet that she could see right through it, like a second skin.

She gasped and flicked her shocked gaze across the fire again.

Drago's broad, chiseled features crumpled in a bizarre mental agony. "Twelve years!" he bellowed, his voice painfully assaulting Jane's ears in the tight confines.

"Oh, God," Jane heard herself mutter.

"I waited twelve years for this!"

"Oh, God," Jane heard herself mutter yet again. Her heart beat like that of a frightened baby swallow.

"Gettin' your eye dug out by savages," Hunter said. "You know what it's like with only one eye in prison, Jane? Never able to see who's comin' up on your blind side until you feel the blade slide into your ribs?"

The uncorked brandy bottle stood near his left knee.

He lifted it, dumped some brandy into his coffee, and swirled the solution as he stared with that haunting expression across the fire at her. "Spendin' all day...*every day*...using picks, chisels, and shovels...boring train tunnels. Then, just for the guards' kicks an' giggles at night...spending extra time turning big rocks into smaller rocks. If you so much as hesitate, they take the bullwhip to you."

Jane had seen the snake-like pink scares atop his

shoulders. But now he turned slowly, giving her his back. She grimaced and slapped a hand to her mouth. His back was a grisly network of long, curving, overlaid scars. It was covered with them so thoroughly that she didn't see so much as a postage stamp-size of unmarred flesh. The scars appeared to continue down into his pants.

Slowly, that dark, death's head stare still in place, he turned back to her.

"Twelve years," he said with quiet menace. "Night after night, imagining the man who put you there enjoying his freedom. A hot steak, a swallow of whiskey, a warm bed...a soft woman."

He took another sip of his coffee and brandy and nodded slowly as he returned his gaze to Jane. "Twelve years... I figured Joe could wait a few weeks, wondering why I was in Del Norte." He smiled with cold lunacy. "*Knowing* something was going to happen but not what. Wondering what it was. Just what form my eruption would take."

The cold, crazy smile broadened. "He'll know soon, though, won't he Jane?"

"Hunter..."

"I'm going to kill you, Jane. I'm going to kill you in front of him. And then I'm going to kill him, too—*slow!*"

That last word roared out of him even louder than the claps of deafening thunder from earlier.

He set his cup down and then he rose and strode quickly over to Jane, dropping down before her and taking her arms in his hands, squeezing them painfully and thrusting her back against the cave wall.

"But first I'm gonna have what I haven't had in twelve long years. I'm gonna take that from him, too!"

CHAPTER 27

MOLLY HURDSTROM WOKE FROM A NAP WITH A GASP.

She sat up on her bed, the coverlet sliding down her chest. She stared across her bedroom lit in the afternoon by two large windows but saw little but the fog inside her own head. No, not inside her own head. The fog of partially remembered images inside the jailhouse the night that Adam McClarksville had been killed.

She remembered holding something heavy in her hands and the smell of rotten eggs in the air around her. The sensations were frustratingly fleeting; she couldn't get enough of a hold on them to gain clarity.

She couldn't have been holding a gun. She'd never held one before, much less fired one.

Her heart pounded in terror, as though even awake now from a half-remembered dream, she was still reliving that night.

Terrified of *what*?

For the life of her, she couldn't remember.

She looked at her small, pale hands in her lap. They held nothing. Neither now nor, suddenly, in her memory.

All she could remember from that night was raised voices, her own included. What those voices were saying, she did not know. It was as though she were hearing a heated argument between herself and two or three men from the far end of the house. Those voices seemed to be growing more and more distant until they faded altogether, the fog consuming them.

Molly clearly remembered one thing, though. The feeling of fear.

Not fear for herself but for Henry.

Why?

What danger was he in?

He and Adam must have fought because Henry's face had been badly bruised.

Had Henry shot Adam after they'd fought?

That must have been the case. She couldn't fathom it, though. But maybe that was because she didn't want to fathom that Henry, the young man she had come to know and love despite their hailing from two far different worlds, was capable of jealous rages and murder.

But maybe she didn't know Henry half as well as she thought she did.

Her heart continued to hammer against her breastbone.

She tossed aside the afghan she used on her made bed when she lay down for afternoon naps and dropped her silk-stockinged feet to the floor. Her lungs felt tight. She couldn't seem to breathe. Her shoes...

She found them, walked over to them, stepped into them, and buckled the gold buckles. She grabbed her leather jacket off the wall by the door, drew it on, automatically ran her hands through her hair, checking to see if she looked respectable. She felt the ribbon she'd tied in it that morning. Her hair was good enough, a minor consideration. She had to get out of the house.

She opened her bedroom door, looked both ways down the dimly lit hall, and called, "Mother?"

No response.

"Mrs. Broadmoore?" Clara Broadmoore was the Hurdstroms' part-time housekeeper. She usually only came in the morning and was gone by one, as she apparently was now. Molly suspected her parents had instructed the woman to keep an eye on Molly while she was here. They didn't want her leaving the house without them knowing where she was going and when she would be back.

Well, Mrs. Broadmoore was gone now and so was Mother. Mother was likely at the office helping with the month-end accounts. Molly absently remembered the commotion that had filled the house one recent early morning when Father had returned home with his face badly discolored and swollen. Mother had summoned the doctor to stitch father's lower lip.

Father had yelled and cursed for the next hour.

Molly did not know what kind of trouble Father had gotten into—and didn't care—but she assumed he must have been confronted by a disgruntled former employee or employees in the Wooden Nickel, her father's favorite watering hole in Del Norte, where he enjoyed fleecing men of the lower classes at poker. He'd been confronted there before.

Every man had his bad habits, or his "sport," as Mother called them. Fleecing the lower classes was her father's, her mother had explained when Molly had caught word of her father's regular visits to the humble dive.

Molly wasn't worried about Father. She had no love

for him anymore. He was cold, stern, an arbitrary disciplinarian. He still treated Molly, at seventeen, like a child. Or like a piece of property whose future he would dictate and whose future husband would be up to him and her mother to decide. Molly had been made to understand a couple of years ago that whom she would marry would be a business decision.

Thus, it had been decided that Molly would give her hand to Adam McClarksville when he'd graduated Yale and that was all there was to it. They'd allowed her the dalliance with the young deputy to keep her occupied and amused, unable to believe she would actually tumble for someone so backwards—at least, in their eyes.

What Molly could not believe, however, was that she had finally agreed to the proposition. She had promised herself that, despite what her parents and the McClarksvilles wanted, she would not marry Adam. She would marry the man she loved even if it cost her being "cast out on her own in the cold, cruel world she knew little of, so spoiled she'd been," as was her father's way of putting it.

Yes, she was a headstrong young woman. It had cost her time in a terrible place, but so be it. She knew enough from what she'd read and from her own instincts that life was short and precious, that love was everything, and that what her parents expected of her was not only unreasonable but unconscionable.

She went downstairs, relieved to confirm that she was, indeed, alone. The cabinet clock ticked in the living room, accentuating the house's quiet abandonment.

Molly strode through the quiet, neat, recently cleaned and tidied kitchen to the back door, and stepped out onto the back porch. Her heart was still beating fast, and her lungs felt tight. What she needed was a walk.

She stepped off the porch and strode down the stone-paved path past the springhouse, the privy, and the woodshed, around her mother's vegetable garden, which she'd been ordered to weed this afternoon—anything to keep her busy and out of trouble, which seemed all the more important after the other night when Adam was killed—and into the woods beyond in which the creek murmured in its verdant sheath of wild berry bushes.

She'd just crossed the creek at a shallow ford, climbed the opposite bank and was walking into the pines and sage beyond when a man's sing-song voice rose behind her, "Oh, Miss Mol-lee!"

Molly swung around with a frightened gasp and stared back beyond the creek and through the pines. "Who's there?"

"Ohhh...Miss...Mol-leee!" came the sing-song voice again, a little louder this time.

The mocking yell was followed by the slow thuds of a horse's hooves.

Molly gazed back through the pines. Her heart had just started to settle down once she'd crossed the creek as though by leaving her yard she'd crossed into safe territory, but now it was starting to hammer again. It hammered harder when a horse and rider appeared, back about fifty or sixty yards through the trees, moving slowly along through the pines.

"Who is it?" Molly said, raising her hand to shade her eyes from the sun glare. "Who's there?"

She hadn't managed to raise her voice loudly enough to be heard.

"Mol-leee?" came the rider's voice. She couldn't make him out. He was too far away, and he was silhouetted against the sun. "That you up there, Miss Molly?"

Molly recognized the voice if not the rest of him.

A.J. Lamb--Adam's friend from Yale.

"G-go away," Molly said, managing to get some volume behind it. "I don't want any company, Mister Lamb. Besides, it's not proper. I'm alone. My parents are not home."

She turned and continued walking through the trees, quickening her pace, her heart continuing to drum and bang against her breastbone. She was following an old walking path. She didn't know who had made the path; it had been here for as long as she could remember. Someone had once told her the Indians had made it when this area had belonged to them. She had also heard that much farther along the trail sat an old, abandoned mountain man's cabin. Molly didn't know for sure. She'd never walked more than a half a mile or so along the trail, to the place where the trail crossed yet another creek.

"That's all right," A.J. Lamb called behind her. "I won't tell if you won't!"

He laughed. There was the sound of splashing water. Molly looked back to see Lamb and the horse crossing the creek, the water splashing up white and making several small rainbows in the sunlight. Lamb whistled sharply. The horse lunged up the near bank and then Lamb booted it into a trot, whipping his reins against its left hip until it was loping.

Molly stepped to one side of the trail and stopped, anger mixing with her fear now. She hadn't seen Lamb only briefly two nights ago, when he and Mister McClarksville had come over to the Hurdstrom house. She and Lamb had exchanged the briefest of glances, his a strangely meaningful one, before all three—her father, McClarksville, and Lamb--had disappeared into Father's study. Molly had met Lamb only once before, two years ago, when she and her parents had taken the train to

Denver and they'd met the McClarksvilles—Malcolm and Adam—with A.J. Lamb there, as well.

She didn't know for sure, of course, but she assumed that Adam and Lamb were very close friends, and that apparently close college friends went everywhere and did everything together. She hadn't liked the quick, furtive smirks they'd shot at each other that night in the Larimer Hotel's natty dining room. She hadn't known what the smirks had been about, of course; she had just assumed that smirking and kicking each other under the table a lot was how young men their ages behaved regularly, which is to say childishly.

Now she watched angrily as he rode up to her, smiling beneath the narrow brim of his black bowler. He was not an unattractive young man, but she did not like how he always seemed to be smiling as though he knew a secret about you, and wouldn't you just like to know what it was? He'd been like that during their brief meeting two years ago, and he was like that now.

He was also overly stylishly dressed in a black, three-piece suit with a white silk shirt, paper collar, and burgundy necktie. Molly had never known any young man other than Adam McClarksville and A.J. Lamb to dress this way, daily. She thought it silly and rather showy not to mention phony. But then, she supposed, even at their young ages, two years older than Molly, they were being groomed to fill their fathers' shoes and they might as well learn early how to dress the part.

"I told you," Molly said, "I'm all alone"—she threw her arm out to indicate that no one else was around —"and you're being here is most improper, Mr. Lamb."

"Ah, heck," Lamb said, dropping athletically down from his saddle. "Who cares what's right and proper, anymore? Besides, I've been going stir-crazy over at that stuffy hotel while Mister McClarksville spends all his time with Mister Hurdstrom. I don't know what they're cooking up. Or rather what they *were* cooking up...until McClarksville came back to the hotel one morning with his face all swollen up like he'd been bit by one of those western rattlesnakes I was warned so much about back East before I headed out here with Adam."

Lamb walked up to Molly, holding his horse's reins lightly, smiling, showing a full set of very white, well-tended teeth.

Lamb shrugged. "I don't know...I just figured maybe I'd ride over and see what you were up to, Miss Molly. No one answered my knock on the front door, so I walked around back and saw you walking into the woods." He shrugged again. "Figured I'd trail along, is all. Maybe have a conversation."

"About what?"

"About *what*?" Lamb seemed surprised. He gave a tight, little chuckle. Then he frowned curiously and canted his head to one side. "You really don't know—do you? I mean, this act of yours—it's really not an act, is it?"

"If you mean about my not remembering what happened the night Adam died—I don't." Molly hesitated, not sure she wanted to ask what she found herself about to ask. Did she really want to know? Suddenly, she wondered. "You know, don't you?"

Lamb smiled his knowing, oily smile. He let his male eyes roam over her body clad in a plain gingham dress, a simple frock for an afternoon close to home. He tied his horse to a tree then stepped up closer to Molly and held out his hand to her. "Come on, Miss Molly. Let's us take a walk together. You know what? I have a feeling you and I could be friends. Who knows? Maybe you'd like me more than you liked Adam. Truth be told, he and I were good friends, but he had more than a few shortcomings."

He snickered and kicked a rock then opened and closed his waiting hand. "Come on, now. You don't have to be afraid of me. I'm harmless enough. Let's walk, Miss Molly."

CHAPTER 28

MOLLY SCOWLED UP AT A.J. LAMB, HER FACE WARMING
with anger. "I'm not going to hold your hand, Mr. Lamb!"

Lamb beetled his chestnut brows with indignation.
"No needing to get your bloomers in a twist, Miss Molly.
I was just trying to be friendly. After all, I know something about you that you likely don't want anyone else to
know."

"What do you know about me?" she said, gazing up at
him, her heart fluttering.

Now he gave that arrogant, knowing smile again.
"Why, it was you who killed Adam. Not the deputy. No,
sir—it was you. *Pow! Pow!*" he bellowed loudly, his voice
echoing around the woods. He thumped himself twice in
the chest, hard. "Twice through the heart, *dead*!" he yelled
again.

Molly stared up at him, aghast. She stumbled heavily
backward with the force of what she'd just learned. As
she did, it all came to back to her. Deep down, she'd
known, hadn't she? Yes, deep down she had known.

Suddenly, she saw it all before her as though it were
playing out again right now.

The gun in her hands aimed at where Adam and A.J. Lamb were mercilessly beating Henry.

"*Adam, stop it!*"

The man hammering Henry stopped suddenly and whipped around.

"*Molly—put that gun down, you whore!*"

Molly screamed and squeezed her eyes shut as the gun she was holding in outstretched hands flashed and roared.

Adam flew back against the wall, groaning. He looked down, and his eyes widened at the blood oozing from the dead-center of his chest.

"*Ohh!*" *he cried, casting his frantic, exasperated gaze at Molly.* "*You...you killed me, you* whore!"

She screamed again as she ratcheted the hammer back and fired again, the gun report sounding like a cannon blast in the tight confines.

Adam grunted and looked down in horror at the second hole in his chest. He stood against the wall for a time, back arched, grinding his heels into the floor. Then, as though he were a marionette whose strings were suddenly cut, he dropped to the floor in a quivering heap.

Molly slapped a hand to her mouth in horror.

The rotten egg odor she'd smelled earlier had been the smell of gun smoke. Smoke from the gun that had been in her own hands.

Grinning like the cat that ate the canary, A.J. Lamb walked up to Molly. "Don't worry, honey. I'll never tell...as long as you do something special for me."

"*What?*"

"Oh, come on—don't play innocent with me." Lamb smiled insinuatingly. "I've heard the stories...about why you were sent away to that school for wayward girls."

Molly felt her lower jaw drop. She stared up at Lamb, who was a whole head taller than she was, in mute shock.

"Come on, pretty girl," Lamb said, shoving Molly up against a tree. He learned toward her, trying to kiss her.

She wriggled away from him, screaming, "No!" And slapped him across the face.

It was his turn to stare in shock. Quickly, that look became one of exasperated anger. In a blur of quick motion, he drew his right hand back behind his left shoulder then sent it flying forward until the back of it smashed against Molly's mouth. She screamed as she twisted around and fell.

She lay belly down on the ground, dazed, the coppery taste of blood on her lips. Before she knew it, Lamb was on top of her, thrusting her onto her back and laughing as he nuzzled her neck and pawed her breasts through her dress.

"No!" She thrust her left knee up into his groin.

He grunted in agony and for a moment seemed paralyzed, lying stiffly on top of her, mouth drawn wide, face red, a forked, blue vein throbbing just above his nose. Molly screamed again, pushed him off her then scrambled to her feet and ran as fast as she could straight into the forest.

"Whore!" Lamb bellowed behind her. "You'll pay for that, you whore!"

Molly screamed hoarsely, venting her own rage. She ran as fast as she could, but cold fingers of dread walked up and down her spine as she heard his heavy, thudding, crunching footsteps growing quickly, loudly behind her. She could hear him raking air in and out of his lungs fiercely as he closed the gap between them.

Those sounds, too, grew louder until his shadow slid quickly up on her right and then his hands were in her hair. He pulled her head back savagely, cursing, then gave her a hard shove. She flew forward and hit the ground hard and rolled. She'd no sooner come to a stop, lying belly up, than Lamb threw himself on top of her. He straddled her, grabbed the front of her dress with both hands and, his face a red mask of savage fury, ripped it down the middle with a single, powerful thrust, revealing her chamise and heaving breasts pushing the fabric out from behind.

He grabbed the top of the chemise and, with an enraged, hoarse grunt, spittle flying from his lips, ripped it down the middle, as well, laying her pale breasts bare.

"You bastard!" Molly screamed, vaguely surprised that she'd found the word in her vocabulary.

She tried to kick at the assailant on top of her, but he was too high up on her body. She tried to punch him but received only another savage backhand across her cheek for her efforts.

That dazed her, caused her vision to dim, the world to tilt around her.

He grinned down at her goatishly as he lowered one hand to the fly of his twill trousers, began undoing the buttons. "You know what, Miss Molly—you murderin' whore? I think you're gonna like it. Why don't you just like back an' stop fussin', an'..."

He stopped, frowned suddenly, looked around.

Molly had heard it, too, the loudening thuds of a horse approaching fast.

Molly looked up in time to see a galloping horse and rider appear out of nowhere, approaching in a blur through the pines, long brown hair bouncing on the rider's slender shoulders. Closer and closer horse and rider came until, screaming angrily, the rider flung herself from the saddle and into A.J. Lamb with a fierce, enraged cry, knocking Lamb off Molly.

The rider rolled off Lamb and was just gaining her

knees, turning to face him, when Lamb said, "What in holy hell...?"

His own renewed rage overtaking his momentary confusion, he threw himself onto the girl clad in a checked wool shirt and blue denims. She'd been wearing a tan felt hat, but it had flown off her head when she'd unseated herself from the calico mare she'd been riding.

Lamb shoved the girl onto the ground, yelling, "You want some, too, little girl?" He laughed and whooped. "The more the merrier!"

The girl—whom the awestruck Molly recognized as Marshal Mannion's daughter, Evangeline—looked up over Lamb's shoulder at Molly and yelled, "*Rock!*"

Lamb shoved her down and slapped her. She fought him fiercely, matching blow for blow, her body quivering defensively beneath his thick, lumpy body.

A rock was in Molly's hand before she'd even thought about looking for one. She held it taut in her right hand, digging her fingers into it, tightening her jaws.

She gave a deep-throated, enraged scream as she threw herself atop Lamb and smashed the rock against the back of his head with a resolute *thud*!

"Oh!" Lamb cried, his body suddenly falling still atop of Miss Mannion.

Slowly, he turned his head to one side. His face was red and swollen, his eyes suddenly bright with pain. He gritted his teeth and was about to say something to Molly still holding the rock, when Vangie looked up from behind him again and screamed, "*Again!* You have to kill them! It's the only way to stop them!"

Molly gave another enraged scream and slammed the rock down on Lamb's head again, this time across his right temple.

He turned his head away with a grunt and started to

turn toward Molly again, the gash on his temple oozing dark-red blood, when Molly gave another scream and smashed the rock down against his head again, in the same place as before.

Lamb flinched, yelled, started to raise his head again. He also raised his right arm to shield himself from another blow...to no avail.

Smack!

Again, the rock in Molly's hand slammed against his head.

"Oh!" he said again, more softly this time, his eyelids appearing to grow heavy. He started to roll off Vangie and then Vangie kicked him all the way off and grabbed a rock of her own.

Screaming bitterly with otherworldy anger, the girls knelt over Lamb, taking turns smashing his head with their rocks.

Again and again, the stones came down with solid thuds...until Lamb's head looked like nothing more than a smashed, red pumpkin. His body lay on its side, limp against the ground, knees bent as though he were only napping.

But already flies were starting to buzz around the man's ruined skull.

The girls stopped their assault.

Breathless, they stared down at the dead man before them.

They stared down in silence for a long time, raking air in and out of their lungs, holding their bloody rocks.

Finally, they turned to each other.

Molly frowned, curious. Though they were the same age, she'd never exchanged more than two words with Vangie Mannion in her life.

"I heard what happened," Vangie said. "Decided to

ride over, see how you were doing." She glanced down at the dead man before her. "Glad I did. I heard your screams..."

Dully, Molly nodded.

She looked off, thoughtful, then returned her gaze to Vangie. "I have to see Henry."

Vangie nodded, swallowed, licked her lips. "Well, we both know where he is."

————

AT HOTEL DE MANNION, JOE PULLED THE STEAMING coffee pot down off the stove's warming rack and filled two stone mugs, one with a jagged crack running down its face. The crack had been in the mug for as long as Mannion could remember. He didn't worry about it. It was still a stout mug.

He set the pot back onto the warming rack, picked up the mugs, and stepped out onto the stoop. He handed one of the mugs, the one without the crack—he seemed to favor the one with the crack, for some unconscious reason—to Rio, who sat kicked back in his usual chair near the door. Rio wore the new, three-piece suit that made him look like an overstuffed sausage or a slightly more successful than usual whiskey drummer.

Mannion wasn't sure which.

"Here you go," Mannion said. "Fresh pot. Put hair on your chest."

"Gracias, amigo," Rio said, accepting the cup while lowering his boots from the edge of the porch rail on which, as usual for this time of the day, they'd been resting, crossed at the ankles. "Speaking of which"—he poked a finger into his shirt and gave his chest a scratch, stretching his lips back from his teeth—"this shirt sure does make my chest itch."

Mannion sagged down into his chair to Rio's right. "Tell the Chinaman not to put any starch in it."

"Oh, I haven't had it laundered yet."

"Oh." Mannion blew on his coffee. "Well, maybe that's the problem."

"Nah," Rio said, blowing on his own black brew. "My chest is more used to the old one."

"Just take some time, then," Mannion said, sipping his coffee.

"Yeah."

Mannion glanced at him. "Unless you want to just go ahead and switch back. Truth be told, every time I look at you in that funeral garb, my whole body itches."

Rio sipped his own coffee, smiled. "Yeah, well..."

"What we don't do for women," Mannion said with a dry chuckle. Switching subjects, he said, "How the kid holding up?"

"Stringbean?" Rio said. "Well, he's got a complete count of all the stones in the back wall of his cell and in the cells around him. I think he said somewhere around five hundred and thirty-six though there was a crack in one that might officially make it two rocks instead of one. He even wanted my opinion on the matter. Seemed to nag him."

"Well, at least he hasn't hanged himself by his belt."

"Not yet." Rio took another sip of his mud. "Sure wish the judge would—" He stopped when something on the street caught his eye. He turned to Mannion. "Hey, Joe."

Mannion followed Rio's gaze to where Vangie was riding toward the jailhouse on her calico mare from along the street on his left. Vangie wasn't the only one on the horse. Mannion canted his head for a better look, scrutinizing the second rider.

The girl riding behind Vangie, wrapped in a blanket, was Molly Hurdstrom.

Both girls wore sullen, ashen expressions. Their faces appeared splattered with what could only have been blood.

Mannion's interest was piqued when he saw blood on Vangie's right hand. He rose quickly, concern building in him. Rio lowered his boots from the rail to make way for Joe, who stepped past him to stand at the top of the porch steps, gazing incredulously, worriedly toward the two girls.

Vangie reined up before him, stared down at him with that ashen look.

Molly stared down at the lawman with the same expression. Both girls were badly disheveled. Dirt and sand clung to Vangie's denims, even to her hair hanging down from beneath her cream hat. Her bottom lip was cracked and swollen, and her right eye was discolored.

Molly looked even worse. They both looked like they'd been in one hell of a fight.

"Good God," Joe said.

Molly swiped her own bloody right hand across her mouth, streaking her lips with red. Her voice and eyes eerily distant, she said, "Marshal Mannion--can I please see Henry?"

CHAPTER 29

HUNTER DRAGO CLOSED HIS MOUTH OVER JANE'S, chomping down hard on her lower lip.

A bright red veil of pain closed over her eyes.

She reached down with her right hand, closed it around the grips of the big .45 holstered for the cross-draw on Drago's left hip. While the man continued to mash his mouth down on hers, chewing her lips and grunting like an animal, Jane unsnapped the keeper thong from over the .45's hammer. She slid the gun from its sheath, flipped it in her hand so that she held it by the barrel then, using her free arm, thrust him slightly back away from her.

When she had enough room to maneuver, she cursed loudly and slammed the butt of the gun against the killer's right temple.

Drago cried out and rolled off her, closing one hand over his forehead, which immediately oozed blood from the deep gash, while reaching out weakly but angrily with his other hand for one of Jane's legs. She scuttled back away from the man, kicking at him, groaning against the pain in her broken ankle. She heaved herself to her feet, trying to keep weight off the bad ankle. She turned the .45 in her hand and, steadying herself with one hand on the cave wall, clicked back the hammer and aimed the big popper down at Drago's head.

He glanced up at her, his jade eye widening when he saw the gun yawning down at him. Placing his hands flat against the cave floor, he gave a bellowing wail and scissored his left leg wildly, kicking Jane's right leg out from under her. She screamed and triggered the .45 into the cave ceiling just before she struck the floor on her head and shoulders.

The Colt went flying out of her hand.

She hit the ground hard, braining her, knocking the wind out of her, paralyzing her. When she managed to suck some air back into her lungs, she looked over to see that Drago was in as bad a shape as she or worse. He sat back against the cave wall, clamping both hands to his bloody temple and yowling like a gut-shot coyote.

Jane gave a satisfied curl to her upper lip. She'd put everything she had into that smack...

She rolled onto her belly, looking for Drago's .45. She didn't see it. She must have tossed it down the soggy slope fronting the cave. Damn. If she could get her hands on the revolver, she'd finish the bastard right here and now.

Drago had the same idea in reverse.

"I'm gonna kill you, woman," he raged, his voice pinched with pain. "I'm gonna kill you *slow* an' *hard*!"

Jane heaved herself to her feet and turned to run, her terror causing her to forget about the broken ankle. Agony bit her hard and she fell instantly, groaning, pain shooting up from her foot. She glanced back at Drago. Holding one hand to his bloody temple, he slid a big bowie knife from the sheath on his left side and dipped his chin to cast Jane a glare a spine-freezing malevolence.

Jane groaned, heaved herself to her feet, settled the bulk of her weight on her good ankle and hobbled out of the cave. She moved down the slope fronting the cavern too quickly, fell, and rolled, sobbing.

The bad ankle was on fire.

Still, her determination to get away from the lunatic killer was stronger than any pain she might endure. She pushed to her feet again. She found a deadfall branch she could use as a crutch and, leaning into the branch, continued hobbling down the slope.

"*Kill you, woman! Damn near blinded my other eye!*" Drago bellowed behind her, his inhuman voice echoing around the cavern behind Jane.

She hobbled down the slope, faster. She was coated in mud from her tumble down the stone declivity fronting the cave. She slipped and slid in the slick sand and gravel now and in the spongy forest duff. Seeing the trail again through the trees below, she moved too quickly again, inadvertently put weight on the broken ankle, and fell with a horrified, indignant wail of her own.

———

"GIMME ANOTHER HIT O' THAT, WILL YA, WILL-JOHN?" asked Max McCorkle as he sat in the driver's boot of the big Pittsburgh freight wagon, the ribbons of the four mules in the traces held deftly in his gloved, bear-sized paws.

"You had enough," Will-John LaSalle said, holding the unlabeled bottle of who-hit-John tightly between his legs. "We still got us a good two hours to Del Norte and the trail is wet. Eyes on the trail, my friend. Eyes on the trail!"

"Oh, go to hell! I'm still cold an' wet from the rain and I need the 'John to thaw my bones!" McCorkle took the reins in his left hand and extended his right to the burly LaSalle.

"Oh, hell, ya big crybaby," LaSalle said, thrusting the bottle into his friend and colleague's hand. "Go ahead an' drain it. Drive us into a canyon. See if I care. I got five mouths to feed an' and a howlin' woman to give me the what-for if I'm late again, so, hell, yeah—drive us into the nearest canyon, Will-John!"

LaSalle howled crazily, drunkenly, stomped his knee-high, cork-soled, lace-up boots on the splintery wooden floor of the driver's box, and tugged on the tangled, gray, tobacco-stained beard that hung nearly to his bulging paunch.

McCorkle pulled the bottle down after two or three good tugs and thrust the bottle back at his partner. "I told you not to marry that woman. She's half-Comanch, an' the Comanch is more notional them rock-worshippin' heathens. The Comanch women have the final say. They're the law o' the land. Now, me, I once had me a Navajo girl. Oh, damn, she was sweet. Plump an' sweet an' *fine!*"

The driver grinned lustily, narrow-eyed, at his partner, and leaned over to say, "An' she knew how to please me right fine in bed, Rainbow did..."

"Oh, really, Max?" LaSalle said. "That why she ran off with that saloon owner from Tucson?"

"Dammit!" McCorkle complained. "Now, why'd you have to go remind me o' that, an' spoil the memory?"

"Just keep drivin', Max. I might got me five ungrateful mouths to feed back in Del Norte, but I got a bottle o' the good stuff in the wood pile, so--" He stopped suddenly, turned to frown curiously at the driver. "Did you hear that?"

"Hear what?"

"Sounded like a scream."

"Ah, hell," McCorkle said. "You're just imaginin' your woman's already givin' you the what-for once you--" He stopped suddenly and cast his squinting gaze off the right side of the trail ahead. "I heard that!"

A woman's scream. A garbled, pleading cry for help.

LaSalle lurched to his feet, pointing. "There!"

McCorkle followed his partner's pointing figure toward where someone was crawling through the trees on the trail's right side. A woman, all right. A fella could tell that even for all the mud and pine needles she appeared to have bathed in. A redhead. She was just now coming down out of the trees, pushing up on her arms and thrusting herself forward then collapsing, then steeling herself again, lifting her head high until the chords stood out in her neck, groaning loudly, and pushed forward once more.

"Stop the wagon, Max! Stop the wagon!"

"All right, all right," McCorkle said, drawing back on the ribbons.

LaSalle corked the bottle, shoved it under the seat, and then clambered down from the driver's boot and onto the muddy trail. He thrust his arms out to both sides for balance. He'd had a pull or two too many of the tangleleg he'd bought in the mountain mining camp of Tincup after the weather had started to sour, he realized.

The woman shoved up on her hands again, pushed herself forward, kicking with one leg but sort of dragging the other leg behind her. She turned toward LaSalle and her eyes widened hopefully. "Help me!" she cried. "P-please help. He's going to kill me!"

LaSalle approached cautiously, peering up the forested slope behind the woman, apprehension touching him. "Who...who's gonna kill ya, ma'am?"

She'd collapsed face down and said something into the ground. LaSalle couldn't make it out.

He dropped to a knee beside the woman. He placed a hand on her back and frowned down at her. "Who...who...?"

The woman lifted her mud-streaked face and turned to him, her brown eyes cast with terror. "Hunter Drago!"

"Miss *Jane?*" LaSalle exclaimed in shock, jerking his head back suddenly.

He turned to where Max McCorkle was just then shambling bandy-legged around the snorting, braying team, heading toward where LaSalle was hunkered in the brush beside the woman. "Max, it's Jane Ford!"

"*Jane Ford?*" McCorkle said, half to himself, bushy brows beetling beneath the brim of his battered sombrero. "You mean, from the *San Juan* in *Del Norte?*"

"Sure enough, it is!" LaSalle turned back to the woman. "What're you doin' way out here, Miss Jane?"

"Will-John," the woman said, reaching up to place a hand on LaSalle's knee. "Do you men have a gun?"

"Sure, sure—we got a gun," McCorkle answered for LaSalle, hitching up his patched canvas trousers at the thighs and squatting before the woman. "We got us a double-barrel shotgun under the seat yonder." He hooked a thumb over his shoulder to indicate the wagon sitting on the two-track trail behind him. The mules eyed him, his partner, and the woman skeptically.

"Good!" Jane said. "There is a very bad man behind

me. He's trying to kill me. I have a broken ankle. Can you gentlemen help me into your wagon?"

"Sure, sure, Miss Jane," both men said in tandem, casting their wary gazes up the forested slope behind the woman. "Who's, um...who's this bad fella you're talkin' about...?"

"Hunter Drago," Jane said.

"Mr. Drago?" McCorkle said, scowling incredulously. "He's up there? What in blue blazes is *he* doin' out here?"

"I told you," the woman said, impatiently. "He's trying to kill me. Now, gentlemen, please..."

McCorkle and LaSalle shared a skeptical look.

LaSalle turned back to the woman and said, "Mr. Drago...he ain't so bad. Always been friendly enough to us. Are you sure it's *him* back there?"

"Look, gentlemen, *please*," the woman said, growing even more impatient as she set a hand on one of McCorkle's upthrust knees. "We must not tarry."

"Tarry?" LaSalle said.

"Get me into your wagon and let's get the hell out of here before he comes to finish the job he started!" the woman intoned, desperately, throatily.

Again, the men shared a look.

Had Miss Jane gone off her nut? Some women did way out here in the mountains. Happened all the time. Usually in the winter when the snow was titty-deep, but a few even...

"Gentlemen!" the woman intoned, casting a dire look back over her shoulder again. *"Please!"*

"All right, all right!" McCorkle said, glancing at LaSalle then taking one of Jane's arms in both hands and glancing at his partner. He winked as though to say it was best to humor the gal until they could get her back to town. The sawbones might need to look at more than her ankle, however. "Come on, Will-John. Let's get Miss Jane into the wagon."

"All right, all right," La Salle said, returning his partner's knowing look and taking Jane's other arm.

Gently, they helped her to her feet. She leaned against LaSalle, putting very little weight on her bandaged foot and ankle. Glancing behind her, giving a frightened shudder, she turned to McCorkle. "Max, fetch your shotgun."

"What?"

She swallowed, drew a calming breath though it didn't appear to calm her much. "Please...fetch your shotgun and keep an eye out for Drago. He'll be coming up behind me soon, I have no doubt. At least, we have to assume he will."

McCorkle shared another skeptical look with his partner then turned and ambled back to the wagon. "Sure, sure—whatever you want, Miss Jane."

While McCorkle continued to the wagon, the mules watching the humans as dubiously as the two freighters had been regarding the muddy, injured woman, LaSalle started helping her toward the wagon, as well. It was a slow, difficult task, because she could put almost no weight at all on the injured ankle, which LaSalle could see was badly swollen behind the muddy bandage.

The woman heaved a sigh of relief when McCorkle reached under the wagon seat and pulled out a long-barreled, double-bore shotgun. She glanced behind her once more then turned to McCorkle and said, a little breathlessly, "Good...good."

"Don't you worry, ma'am." McCorkle broke open the double-bore to check the loads then snapped it closed and held it up high across his chest. "Any bad fellas try to hurt you again, I'll blow a hole in 'em large enough to drive a freight train through!"

"Good, good," the woman said again, breathless with relief, as LaSalle helped her up to the big Pittsburg's right front wheel, which rose as high as LaSalle himself, who stood well over six feet tall. "Very, good, gentlemen. Thank you."

"We'll get you up onto the seat, Miss Jane," La Salle said.

"Yes, thank you," she said, casting yet another fearful glance back in the direction from which she'd come.

McCorkle climbed up in the driver's box and then pulled Jane up while LaSalle pushed from behind. She groaned when she had to put some weight on her injured foot as she climbed the steel rungs just behind the wheel, but she seemed no more worse for the wear than she already was when they finally had her in the box. She sat down and then LaSalle climbed up to sit beside her, McCorkle to her left.

McCorkle handed the double-bore over the woman to LaSalle, saying, "You ride shotgun, Will-John. Careful now you don't blow your foot off." He leaned toward the woman and said with amused insinuation, "He ain't near as good with that barn blaster as I am."

"Please, Max," the woman said, tensely. "I don't mean to sound ungrateful, but I really wish you would get a move on. You gentlemen really don't seem to understand the direness of the situation."

"All right, all right—we'll get movin', Miss Jane," McCorkle said, untying the reins from around the brake handle then shoving the handle forward, releasing the brake shoes from the wheels.

LaSalle frowned down at the woman, saying, "Miss Jane, are you sure you didn't just take a tumble from your horse." He twirled a finger in the air beside his ear.

"Maybe got addled a bit an' just *imagined* Mr. Drago was out to kill ya?"

She gave a weary sigh. "Yes, yes—I'm sure that's all it was. I'm just addled. Nevertheless..."

"Here we go," McCorkle said, removing the black-snake from the steel whip socket by the brake handle. He loudly cracked the popper over the mules' backs. "All right, now—step it up, ya mangy varmints. We got us a lady here, so show her how well you mind me!"

He guffawed and cracked the popper over the team a few more times, and when they were rolling along, he returned the whip to its socket and leaned forward, elbows on his knees, holding the ribbons lightly in his gloved hands, humming, "Sweet Betsy from Pike."

———

JANE HEAVED A RELIEVED SIGH WHEN MCCORKLE finally got the wagon rolling.

Several times, she looked back toward where the secondary trail climbed the ridge through the trees toward the cave but saw nothing—no movement whatever. No sign of the lunatic killer, Hunter Drago.

Jane wondered if she'd hit him hard enough to kill him.

Possibly, he'd bled to death. She knew from her own experience that head wounds could bleed profusely. She likely would have bled out herself after her run-in with the men out to kill Joe at Ida Becker's Good Food if Joe hadn't gotten her straight to the doctor.

Joe...

For the first time since her near-deadly encounter with Drago did she reflect on Joe's intransigence regarding Drago.

He'd been right. She'd been wrong.

So wrong...

Would he ever forgive her?

Again, she glanced behind. She could no longer see the trail that led up the ridge to the cave. More relief washed over her.

She turned her head forward. Ahead lay a rise, a low saddle.

With each turn of the wagon's iron-shod wheels, Jane felt safer until she felt her lips quirk a relieved smile. More and more distance was being stretched between her and her would-be killer.

Once the wagon reached the top of the rise and started down the other side, she could let her guard down. Drago was either dead or passed out. At least, injured too badly to come after her.

She looked at the big, double-bore shotgun resting across the canvas-clad thighs of Will-John LaSalle.

Again, she smiled.

Soon, she would be back in Del Norte. She'd have to eat crow, of course, but she'd do so gladly, just knowing she was safe.

Joe would gloat. Let him.

The wagon lurched and jostled up the rise.

When the team reached the crest, it started down the opposite side almost immediately. The wagon reached the top of the saddle and started down, as well, the next valley opening before Jane—the rocky, two-track trail threading the narrow gap between the evergreen forest on the left and a steep, rocky ridge on the right.

Jane's spine stiffened. She saw him only now as the team and the front of the wagon dropped down to open the view before her...

The lone, black-clad rider sitting the fine, cream stallion between the forest and the rocky ridge, at the very base of the rise seventy yards away.

"Whoa! Whoa! Whoa!" yelled McCorkle, drawing back on the team's reins.

Sharing wary looks with LaSalle, he got the team stopped, and set the brake.

Before Jane could suck a terrified breath down her throat, Drago lifted the Henry repeater in his hands and shot both men out of the driver's box to either side of her.

One second, the pair had been sitting beside her.

The next second, they were gone without either making a sound.

Drago wasn't called "Long Shot" for nothing.

Jane closed her eyes. She wished he'd go ahead and kill her now, but she knew he wouldn't.

No. She'd die long and hard, indeed.

Oh, well. It was better than she deserved.

She opened her eyes to see Drago riding toward her casually, grinning.

CHAPTER 30

MANNION STUCK THE KEY IN THE LOCK AND turned it.

"You have a visitor, kid," he told Stringbean through the bars of the young deputy's cell.

Stringbean sat up on his cot and dropped his feet to the floor, frowning. "I do?"

"Yep." Mannion turned and strode back along the cellblock toward the stairs. "Come on up."

"Who is it?" Stringbean called behind him, rising from the cot and moving through the open cell door.

"You'll see."

Mannion climbed the stairs and stepped through the open cellblock door into his office. Molly Hurdstrom stood looking at him, dourly. Her face was splashed with blood. Her right hand was covered with it. Mannion had checked her and Vangie both over, and for the life of him he hadn't been able to find a single injury.

Which meant the blood on them was not theirs.

Neither of them had looked much in the mood for talking so he didn't press them. He'd just gone down to fetch his prisoner who, as Mannion stepped past the silent girl toward the office's front door, stepped into the office behind him.

"Molly?" Stringbean said in surprise just before Mannion opened the office door and stepped out onto the porch.

Vangie stood before him, looking much as Molly did. Face splattered with blood. Her right hand was covered with the stuff.

"What happened?" Joe asked.

"You'll find a young man dead near the Hurdstrom house. Maybe a hundred yards behind it. In the woods."

"A young man..."

"Molly said his name was A.J. A.J. Lamb." Vangie's upper lip fluttered with emotion as her eyes turned hard and angry. "He attacked her. I heard her screaming and rode over to help."

Mannion drew a deep breath as he studied his daughter's hard, stricken eyes. Eyes that still bore the pain and fury of what she had gone through last fall then only a few days earlier when she was riding alone in the mountains...and what, it seems, Molly Hurdstrom had gone through just a short time earlier.

"Is she...all right?" Mannion asked his daughter.

"I got there in time," Vangie said tightly.

Mannion nodded. "Did he tell her what happened here, in the jailhouse, or did she suddenly remember on her own?"

"I don't know." Vangie shrugged. "She said she just want to see Stringbean, so I grabbed a blanket from her house—her clothes were almost ripped off of her," she added with another bitter curl of her upper lip, "and rode her over here."

"I see."

Vangie shuddered but her eyes were gimlet hard as

she said, "I'm going to go over to the hotel and have a bath."

"Good idea." Mannion placed a hand on his daughter's shoulder. "You all right, honey?"

Vangie looked up at him, her gaze resolute. She gave a faint, hard smile. "I couldn't be better, Pa. Mister Lamb has seen far better days, however."

Mannion drew another sharp breath, taken aback but also pleased by his daughter's stalwart savagery. Sometimes that's what it took.

It was a savage world, after all.

He watched in silence as Vangie moved off down the porch steps, mounted the calico, and booted it off down the street in the direction of the San Juan.

She just disappeared around a string of mining supply drays likely heading for the Lucky Seven or the Lonely Loretta mines that lay south of Del Norte, when hoof thuds rose behind Joe and a man called, "Marshal Mannion?"

Joe swung around to see the proprietor of Warren H.G. Griggs Livery & Feed Barn riding a stout brindle mule toward the jailhouse, a look of deep concern on the man's eyes beneath the floppy brim of his battered, low-crowned felt hat. Griggs was stout with a big, square head and shaggy silver-and-brown muttonchops framing his broad face. He wore a grisly horse-shoe-shaped scar on his right cheek. It was not uncommon for liverymen—especially ones who also worked as farriers—to wear similar scars, a trademark of sorts of their hazardous trade.

Griggs reined in the mule before Mannion and said, "Thought you should know Miss Jane's chestnut showed up at the barn a few minutes ago...without Miss Jane herself. The mare looks a little wild-eyed and her saddle was hanging down her side. She was a little damp and the saddle's wet...like maybe Miss Jane and Mister Drago mighta got caught in a storm up in the mountains."

Griggs hooked a thumb over his beefy left shoulder to indicate the large, gray hump of the Sawatch Range rising out of the plains to the north.

"Jane and Mister Drago?" Mannion said, scowling, jealousy mixing with the old anger inside him.

Griggs flinched as though he'd been slapped. "Yeah... well, uh...they rode out together early this morning. Drago came for both their horses. He said Miss Jane was gonna show him around the Sawatch."

Again, knowing the nature of Mannion's and Jane's relationship—or their former relationship, at least—the liveryman flinched.

Mannion turned away, drawing his index finger and thumb down his jaws to his chin. "Yeah, well, they can both go to hell," he growled.

"All right, then, Marshal," Griggs said, reining the beefy mule around. "Just thought you should know."

"Yeah, yeah," Mannion muttered and slowly, pensively climbed the porch steps, continuing to massage his chin with his thumb and index finger.

Anger burned in him. But concern did, too. It built quickly to worry.

Jane's mare had returned to town without Jane.

What did that mean?

Had Jane fallen prey to the storm Mannion had seen shrouding the Sawatch earlier in the afternoon...or to Hunter Drago?

"Ah, shit," Joe said, wheeling and turning to where Griggs was riding off to the south, about to turn down the next side street to the west. "Griggs!"

The man reined in the mule and looked back over his shoulder.

"Saddle Red for me. I'll be over for him in a few minutes!"

Griggs threw up an acknowledging hand then booted the mule on around the corner and out of sight.

Mannion continued across the porch. He tripped the latch, opened the door, and stepped into the office. Stringbean and the girl stood in the middle of the room. Stringbean had his arms around her and was rocking her gently from side to side as she sobbed into his shoulder.

Mannion walked over to where his saddlebags hung from a chairback by the open cellblock door.

"Marshal...what's gonna happen to...?" Stringbean let his voice trail off as he glanced down at the girl in his arms.

Molly turned to face the lawman then as well, eyes shiny with tears but wide with expectance, as well.

"Go home, young lady," Mannion said, dropping a couple of boxes of .44 shells into an open saddlebag pouch then buckling the flap. Slinging the saddlebags over his shoulder, he turned to the pair. "I'll talk to the county prosecutor. No charges will be filed. If your father tries to ship you off to reform school again, he'll be the one behind bars." He gave the girl a pointed look. "Tell him that."

Joe would file charges, all right—for conspiracy to commit murder.

Under the circumstances, Mannion doubted he'd get any kickback from Hurdstrom. From now on, he'd have Hurdstrom, McQueen, and Keel Brandywine fighting each other to dust his suit. As for McClarksville—he was about to get kicked back to where he came from, the body of his son's perverted friend in tow. If McClarksville squawked, he'd get those same charges filed and he'd be going away to the territorial pen with the others for a long time.

Mannion almost hoped they squawked.

Stringbean and the girl staring at him in shocked silence, Mannion picked up his Yellowboy and headed for the door. "Take over, kid. I'm off to find Jane."

As he stepped through the door, Stringbean called behind him, "Miss Jane...?"

"Long story."

Mannion tramped across the porch, down the steps, and headed off in the direction of Grigg's Livery. Fifteen minutes later, he was mounted up and galloping north toward where the Sawatch humped, dark, banner-like clouds of the previous rainstorm that had assaulted that stony bastion remaining around it, scarf-like.

Mannion knew Jane's usual route, which she took once or twice a week to free herself body and soul of the stress of running a business the size of the San Juan, so he knew where she and Drago had likely headed. Her destination was usually Mirror Lake, where she'd have a picnic lunch—usually all by herself but apparently this afternoon with the cunning killer, Drago—and then continue to Tincup and then start the return trip, heading down into the Arkansas Valley and following the river back to the south toward Del Norte.

Beautiful country.

Damned foolish of her, however, to ride off alone with Drago. Joe had tried to tell her, but she hadn't listened. No one had listened. Anger nettled him but he was not surprised to find that worry was what he felt most. Almost to the point of desperation. No, he wasn't surprised. He still loved the woman.

What buoyed him on his hard ride with the ridges

rising around him casting long afternoon shadows across the rugged terrain he and Red traversed, was knowing that Drago hadn't likely killed her.

Not yet, at least.

No, Drago would want to save that for when he had an audience of one:

Mannion.

Fortunately or unfortunately, Joe knew how sadistic killers like Hunter Drago thought.

As he and Red climbed into the first front of the Sawatch, it began spitting rain again. Whatever trail Drago and Jane had left had been wiped out by the previous storm. While Joe figured he knew where Jane had been headed, he stopped in St. Elmo and inquired at the La Plata Saloon--a long, low, mud adobe building on the main drag's north side, across from Chalk Creek in which a few bearded prospectors were still panning though the light was fading quickly. A small collection of children, mostly boys, were collected along the shore of the creek, taking turns skipping stones while a little brown dog sniffed along the shoreline.

As Joe had suspected, Jane and Drago had stopped at the La Plata for a picnic lunch, as Jane often did when riding alone up here, then continued northwest toward Tincup and Mirror Lake. Mannion stepped back into the saddle and continued in the same direction.

"Hyahh, boy...*byahhh*!"

Red thew his ears back and lunged into a lope, the little dog running along behind, barking and nipping at the horse's scissoring hooves before stopping abruptly and returning to the children, little tail wagging.

A half hour later, following a wagon trail along the shoulder of a steep mountain, Mannion checked Red down quickly and cast his questioning scowl ahead along the trail and up a hill sixty yards away. A Pittsburg freight wagon with a tarp-covered box stood near the crest of the ridge, on the near side, four mules in the traces. The mules stared dully at Mannion, a couple switching their tails and curiously flicking their ears.

Joe clucked Red ahead along the trail and up the hill. He swung Red off the trail's left side and stopped the horse to stare down at the bearded man lying belly down in the sage. He was a big man in canvas trousers and ragged buckskin coat. A battered hat lay in the sage beside him.

Mannion swung down and kicked the man onto his back.

Two brown eyes stared up at him, unblinking. Blood bibbed the man's hickory shirt between suspenders.

"Will-John LaSalle," Mannion muttered.

LaSalle always rode with Max McCorkle.

Mannion walked around to the other side of the wagon and found McCorkle in much the same condition in which he'd found LaSalle:

Dead with a single bullet through the dead center of his chest.

Mannion looked around until he found fresh horse prints scoring the wet sand and gravel leading up the trail behind the wagon.

Joe swung up onto Red's back, the nettling worry nettling him even more severely—he was sure the two dead freighters had been killed by Drago though he had no idea why he would have killed them—and continued up and over the hill and down the other side. He stopped when he spotted the relatively fresh tracks of a horse and rider angling off the trail to the left and climbing a steep, forested ridge toward where the dark, oval-shaped mouth of a cave shone at the base of a stone wall under a large, craggy overhang.

Sliding his Yellowboy from its boot and cocking the rifle one-handed, Mannion continued up the ridge. He looked around carefully, expecting a bushwhack. He reined up in front of the cave. It was getting dark, so he had trouble seeing inside.

He dismounted, climbed the stone shelf rising to the cave mouth, then fired a lucifer match on his thumbnail. He used the weak, umber light to peruse the cave's interior. He frowned when he saw scratch marks in the cave's floor, near a flame-scorched fire ring in which a pile of gray ashes smoldered.

Mannion stepped into the cave. He fired another match and held it over the scratch marks in the cave floor. His heart kicked when he saw that the scratch marks formed large, capital letters forming the words: REVENGE AT BURIAL ROCK.

Mannion dropped the match and ran out of the cave.

CHAPTER 31

An hour later, Mannion rode up to the lip of a deep badlands area stippled with mounds and pinnacles of rock and scored by the twisting, turning line of an ancient riverbed. The riverbed was a dark line at the heart of the badlands beneath Joe, the chasm dappled by the pearl light of a full moon flickering behind the last of the scudding, tattered storm clouds.

The badlands were all shadows and light, the light ever so slowly sliding the shadows across the foreboding, rocky formations.

Mannion sat astride Red, close beside an ancient, dead aspen whose roots spidered out of the side of the canyon beneath Joe, hanging down over the chasm. The tree's broad shadow should absorb and conceal horse and rider from anyone watching. And Joe knew they...or *he*, rather...was watching. A slight, chill wind blew, nudging the branches of the dead tree. The soft moaning and ratcheting sounds made Red tense his muscles beneath the saddle.

"Easy, boy," Mannion said, reaching forward to run a

calming hand down the horse's long neck. "All's well, all's well..."

Who was he kidding?

Of course, it wasn't.

The cold-blooded killer had Jane.

Revenge at Burial Rock...

Mannion cast his gaze toward the giant anvil of granite rising on the far side of the canyon, straight out away from the lawman and Red, three or four hundred yards away.

Burial Rock.

The escarpment stood a good two hundred feet above the canyon floor, forming a high back wall. At the very crest of that craggy bastion, the orange flames of a fire flickered and glowed against the starry sky above and beyond it. The firelight flickered across the poles of a Ute burial scaffold flanking the fire.

Mannion reached back and pulled his field glasses out of a saddlebag pouch. He raised the glasses and adjusted the focus until the two spheres of magnified vision became one. He adjusted the wheel a little more and then he saw the two human-shaped shadows in front of the fire—one shadow larger than the other one. Drago and Jane. They were sitting or kneeling. Drago appeared to have his hands raised. Orange light flickered across the lenses of the glasses he held in his hands, surveying the canyon below.

Jane sat beside him. She appeared to be resting her head on her upraised knees Probably feeling stupid and afraid not only for herself but for the trap she'd allowed Drago to set for Joe.

Despite his fury at her for not listening to him, for so easily falling for Drago's ploy, Mannion could understand how she'd done it.

Drago was cold and cunning. And Jane wasn't as harsh a judge of character as Mannion was. She wanted to believe the best about people.

No sin in that.

Mannion lowered the glasses, returned them to the saddlebag pouch.

He clucked Red straight back away from the chasm and into the trees behind them.

When he was sure that the shadows of the forest concealed them, Mannion turned Red to the left and booted the horse into a walk, angling down the slope toward where Joe, having hunted outlaws in this area before, knew a game trail dropped down the side of the ridge.

The steep trail was sheathed in large boulders that blocked the moonlight, so Joe was relatively certain that when he and Red bottomed out on the canyon floor twenty minutes later, he hadn't been seen from the top of Burial Rock, which now loomed nearly straight up above him from roughly a hundred yards ahead.

Steering by moonlight, Mannion and Red followed the twisting course of the ancient riverbed for a good twenty minutes between conical bluffs and jutting pinnacles of rock before the bed swung sharply right to follow the base of Burial Rock off to the south. Mannion put Red up out of the bed to the left, following a notch in the rocks and boulders sheathing the watercourse, and around to the northwest side of the formation.

As he rode, he looked for a way up the steep face.

He followed the rock around to its backside and found it far less steep than the front. He'd never been on this side of the rock before. He decided that Drago had to have been. The old killer had likely scouted it thoroughly before he'd come to Del Norte. He'd wanted to find the best spot for affecting his long-harbored desire for revenge.

Drago was cold and cunning as well as imaginative.

Damned imaginative.

He must have secretly scouted Del Norte and had discovered the saloon for sale. He'd likely purchased the place through attorneys and through the mail or via wired bank draft, swearing to secrecy all involved in the transaction. That's why Mannion hadn't learned ahead of time who the new owner of the Three-Legged Dog was until Drago had ridden into town that day with the three dead men draped belly down across their saddles.

Mannion put Red up the slope, heading for the crest of Burial Rock. Horse and rider wended their way around rocks and cedars. Joe was glad for the concealment of the darkness on this side of the rock, for the moon was still quartering up the opposite side.

When Joe figured they were roughly halfway to the top, a horse's shrilly whinny rose from just ahead, from the concealment of heavy shadows on this side of a low escarpment. Mannion ground his molars, pulled Red into another such pocket of shadows, and jerked Red to a stop. He stepped down from the saddle, dropped the reins, placed a hand on the bay's left wither and said, "Stay, boy."

He heard the tremble of anxiety in his voice.

Drago had strategically positioned his horse so that it would signal him when Mannion came. Well, now the killer knew Mannion had come.

Joe edged a look around the left side of his covering rocks. He could see the moonlight-limned top of Burial Rock from here, including a couple of ancient burial scaffolds, rawhide torn from the scaffoldings' frames blowing in the night breeze, glinting in the moon- and firelight.

Holding the Yellowboy low, his right hand around the brass breech, Mannion hurried out from behind his cover and toward where a large cedar and a cracked boulder lay to his left and up the rise another ten yards. He was halfway there when a bullet spanged loudly off a rock just behind him and was followed a wink later by the hiccupping report of the rifle that had fired it.

Mannion stepped behind the cedar and the cracked boulder, placing his back to them, bringing the Yellowboy up and squeezing it anxiously in his gloved hands.

"Hello, Joe!" came Drago's bellowing voice echoing around the boulders. "Welcome! Welcome! We've been waiting for you, your woman and me!"

Mannion said nothing. He ground his molars and squeezed the Yellowboy in silent rage.

Drago yelled, "Say hello to your man, Jane! He came all this way to save your hide, after all! The least you can do is greet him, thank him for coming!" He raised his voice louder, adding, "For coming all this way to watch you *die*!"

Jane sobbed. A small, faraway voice.

Then she yelled, her voice trembling, "I'm sorry, Joe! I wish you'd go, but I know you won't because it's not the kind of man you are! I wish you would, though." Her voice hardened. "This is my own damn fault. You tried to tell me and I wouldn't listen!"

Mannion edged a look around the boulder and the cedar toward the top of the rock. Drago and Jane were out of sight, likely just back from the lip of the ridge where Mannion couldn't take a shot at the killer. Joe could make out the glow of the fire well back from the edge of the ridge.

He moved to the left side of the boulder and the cedar and ran, crouching, toward a low hump of rocky ground a good distance across the shoulder of the slope. As he ran, two more bullets kicked up sand and gravel behind him. He dove forward, struck the ground, and rolled behind the rocky hummock as another bullet nipped his right boot heel.

Mannion rolled onto his back, half sat up against the low rise.

"Goddamn son of a bitch of a devil!" he breathed.

"Come on, Joe!" Drago said. "The more the merrier!"

Drago wouldn't kill him. He'd try to wound him. But he wouldn't kill him. He'd save that for later. Drago wanted Mannion alive to watch the killer kill Jane.

Joe had to kill Drago before he could do that.

The question was—how?

Mannion turned to face the hummock, doffing his hat. He edged a look up over it toward the top of Burial Rock. No sign of Drago. He was staying low and out of sight.

Mannion cursed.

He had to get closer.

The only problem was, the closer he got to Drago and Jane, the closer Jane would get to death. Mannion was the audience Drago wanted.

Joe was between a rock and a hard place.

He'd been there before.

———

TORN RAWHIDE FROM THE BURIAL SCAFFOLDS BUFFETED in the wind around Jane as she sat back against a rock, staring toward where Hunter Drago knelt behind a rock at the lip of the ridge. He was aiming his Henry repeater down the backside of the ridge toward where Joe was working his way up.

Jane sobbed, hating herself for her stupidity.

She would die and Joe would die, and it would be her fault.

She wished Joe would leave here, wait to kill Drago another time...at a better time for him. She knew he wouldn't do that.

She jerked with a violent start when Drago's rifle lapped flames, the thunder of the loud report knocking her back against the rock.

Drago smiled. "You're doing well, Joe," the killer yelled. "Pretty damn fast for an older fella!" He chuckled as he ejected the spent, smoking cartridge from the Henry's breech and levered another one to replace it. "Come on up! Join the party!"

Jane winced as she pulled at the ropes firmly tying her hands behind her back. She winced again when she looked down at her ankle. It was badly swollen. In the light from the fire dancing behind her, she could see that the toes were purple and swollen.

Even if she could loosen the ropes binding her wrists, which she'd been working on for the past hour, the hemp cutting into her skin for her efforts, she wouldn't be able to maneuver on that broken ankle. After Drago had half-dragged her up the slope from where he'd left his horse in the rocks, the pain was worse now than ever.

Still, she worked at the ropes. She had to do *something* to help Joe.

Again, Drago's rifle lapped flames, and roared.

He chuckled as he levered out the spent cartridge and seated a fresh one in the breech.

"Come on up, Joe," the killer shouted. "The only way to save her is to show yourself!"

Don't do it, Joe, Jane thought. *I'm not worth it...*

Again, the rifle blasted.

Jane ground her teeth as she continued working on the ropes, trying to pull her hands through the loops, feeling the blood ooze from the cuts and scrapes of the hemp carving into her skin.

The wind moaned through the poles of the burial scaffolds around her.

It fluttered the torn pieces of buckskin on which the ancient bones had once lain before the buckskin had given way and the bleached bones now littered the ground beneath the scaffolds, showing bone-white in the intensifying moonlight.

Again, Jane winced, grinding her teeth against the burn of the chafing ropes. She hadn't worked her hands through the loops but she'd inadvertently stretched the hemp between her tied wrists. That gave her more room to maneuver.

Again, the Henry roared, flames streaking from the barrel down the slope to the right in the murky darkness on that sight of the ridge.

Jane gasped, put her head down, and continued to try to free her hands of the tight loops.

"All right, Joe!" Drago bellowed. "You're close enough!"

Drago turned to glare back at Jane, his eyes reflecting the dancing flames of the fire behind her.

Jane froze, bowed her head as though in prayer.

"She's going to die now, Joe!"

Drago heaved himself to his feet and walked stiffly back to Jane.

"*Ow!*" Jane cried as he pulled her to her feet by her left arm.

He jerked her forward. Her broken ankle barked,

shooting bayonets of pain all through her, as he half-dragged, half-carried her forward to where he'd been kneeling behind the rocks.

"Show yourself, Joe!" Drago yelled, setting his rifle down atop the rocks he'd been kneeling behind and unsheathing his big, silver-plated Colt .45. He ratcheted back the hammer and pressed the barrel against Jane's head.

The iron maw was cold and hard. Jane closed her eyes and turned her head away, so that the iron maw pressed against the side of her head over her left ear.

"Show yourself now, Joe, or she dies right here and now!" Drago yelled, his words echoing around the dark canyon below the slope.

"You'll kill her, anyway!" came Joe's reply.

From the almost intimate sound of his voice, he was close. Very close.

Too close.

"I'll kill her right now, Joe!" Drago returned.

"All right."

Jane blinked, frowned.

Joe stood before her, maybe fifteen feet down the slope below her and Drago. He'd just stepped out from behind a boulder, holding his Yellowboy rifle out to one side, his free hand out to the other side in supplication. His craggy, mustached face was drawn with worry. He slid his worried eyes to Jane and then back to the killer.

"Let her go," he urged. "Please, Drago...the war is between you and me."

Jane glanced up at Drago. He grinned in delight. "Drop the rifle."

Joe opened his right, gloved hand. The Yellowboy dropped to the ground with a thudding clatter and slid on the loose gravel.

"Anything to see her breathe for just one more second, eh, Joe?" Drago laughed. "Your lone weakness, Joe. You love the lady."

Joe looked at Jane. She gazed back at him, tears dribbling down her cheeks.

"Twelve years, Joe, I've waited for this."

"I know," Joe said. "I know." He lifted his gaze to Drago. "Kill me, Hunter. She did nothing."

"No, but you love her." Drago ground his teeth until Jane could see his jaws dimpling in the moonlight. "I loved my freedom, Joe. I loved my eye, Joe. Those savages took it from me...because you locked me away in there."

"You're crazy, Hunter," Joe said. "You're not thinking right."

"After twelve years in a place like that, Joe," Drago said, "who does?"

He glared down at Jane. "You're gonna watch her die now, Joe."

"No!"

Drago turned his head to face Jane. He smiled once more.

Jane saw the man's right index finger tighten against the trigger. She gritted her teeth and swung her hands around from behind her back, having just pulled her right hand free of the blood-stained loop and having lost a good bit of skin with the effort. She grabbed the frayed end of the rope dangling from her left wrist with her right hand and shoved the big Colt down just enough that when it roared, the slug tore into the ground between her knees, throwing sand and gravel up into her face.

Jane screamed as she summoned every bit of strength left in her being and ignored the tearing pain in her broken ankle. She sprang up off her feet and, looping the end of the rope twice around her right fist, thrust her arms around Drago's neck from behind him. She drew the foot-long length of hemp coated with her own blood back against the killer's throat and drew him back toward her until they fell back to the ground together...Drago atop Jane, Jane grinding her teeth as she drew the bloody rope back taut against the killer's throat.

Drago dropped the Colt and thrashed wildly, panicked, strangling.

Jane drew the rope even tighter against the killer's throat, pinching off his wind. He fought wildly, kicking his legs madly, spurs ringing raucously, to free to free the taut rope from his neck.

Though he thrashed and fought violently, Jane shut out the pain in her ankle, shut out the crushing weight of the man on top of her, and drew the rope even tighter against the man's spasming throat, seeing from the side his lone eye bulging from its socket and glistening in the moonlight, reflecting the torn hides ripped from the burial scaffolds buffeting in the night wind behind him.

Drago fought the rope. He was strong. But at this moment in time, her and Joe's lives on the line, Jane was stronger.

More determined.

Angrier.

Meaner...

Joe stepped forward into Jane's field of vision, his face beneath the broad brim of his high-crowned Stetson cast in shock in the moonlight. He aimed one of his big Russians down at Drago thrashing wildly atop Jane.

"Kill him," Jane spat out as she pulled the bloody hemp back against Drago's throat. "Kill him, Joe!"

Joe shuttled his gaze to her, shook his head.

"My bullet might go through him, honey." The corners of his mouth quirked in a wry smile. "Besides, you're doing just fine!"

CHAPTER 32

THREE DAYS LATER, MANNION TRIPPED THE LATCH OF the door of Hotel de Mannion, pushed the door wide, and stopped in his tracks, "Hold on, Rio! Don't do it! She's not worth it!"

Except maybe Jane, he vaguely thought now that Jane was well on the way to recovery from her broken ankle over at the San Juan, and that he'd forgiven her for not believing him about the now-dead killer, Hunter Drago.

Before him, his back facing Joe, Rio Waite was shoving the barrel of his old revolver up against his back and grunting with the effort...

With the effort of what, Mannion wasn't sure.

Had the dance hall girl finally driven him to suicide?

Shooting yourself through the back was a damn strange way to go, but there was no telling what a woman might drive a man to do.

Rio glanced over his shoulder at Mannion. "Ah, hell, Joe, I ain't tryin' to shoot myself through the back. I got a scratch right in the spot on my back I can't reach!"

"That new shirt again?"

"Uh-huh. Ah, *God*!" Rio complained, turning his head forward and raking the gun barrel against his back.

"You need to boil that shirt in lye. Boil it a good, long time!"

"It's the only one I got. It takes the Chinaman a good two days to wash clothes and get 'em back to me. What am I gonna wear in place of it? My old shirt wouldn't look good at all with these pants...that vest..."

He glanced over at the new vest and frock coat draped over the back of the chair by the door to the basement cellblock.

"If you insist on wearing that monkey suit," Mannion said, "then you need to get yourself a second shirt."

"I can't afford a--"

Rio stopped and turned to the door, frowning.

"What is it?" Mannion asked.

"That laugh." Rio holstered the hogleg and walked past Mannion. He stopped in the open door and stared out into the street. "I'd recognize that laugh anywhere..."

———

"WHAT IS IT?" MANNION ASKED AGAIN, BEHIND RIO, who continued to stare out into the street.

Or *across* the street, rather.

At a well-dressed couple, a man and a woman, walking jauntily along the boardwalk over there, heading to Rio's left, which was south along Del Norte's Main Street.

"Well...I'll be damned," Rio said, raking his thumb across the numb of his chin.

The man he was staring at was a stranger, albeit a very well-dressed stranger. Impeccably dressed, in fact, in a pin-striped suit that put Rio's new, store-bought duds to shame. He was tall and he wore an ostentatious mustache with upswept, waxed ends. He brashly, proudly wielded a carved walking stick with what appeared a silver horse head handle.

No, Rio wouldn't know the dapper-Dan from Adam's off-ox. However, he *did* recognize the well-dressed, strawberry blonde the man was strolling with, talking with, laughing with as he strolled.

As Rio studied her now, Toni Greer...er, *Price*...half-turned her head toward the man she was walking with, and threw it back, showing nearly all of her white teeth in a throaty laugh before turning her head back forward as she and her male companion strolled off down the street to the south, thoroughly enjoying each other's company. Toni gave the pink parasol she was holding, and which matched the picture hat she wore as well as the lace on her elegant traveling gown, a joyous little spin.

She laughed again, again throatily. As she and the dapper-Dan continued off down the street, the laugh was drowned by the hustle and bustle of the horse and wagon traffic on the busy street.

Rio stared after where the happy couple had disappeared in the crowd on the street's opposite side. Anger burned in him. He felt his upper lip and left nostril curl as he said, "Well...how 'bout that? She did it again!"

"Did what again?" Mannion asked.

Rio glanced over his shoulder at the lawman standing behind him, frowning at him curiously. "Joe, can you hold the store? I got somethin' to tend to."

"Go ahead," Mannion said. "Don't forget about the stage. I just saw it roll into town a few minutes ago."

Rio stepped farther out onto the porch and swung his head to peer down the same side of the street the jail-house was on. Sure enough, the Rio Grande & Company Stage Line's dusty coach sat in front of the company's office two blocks away. Rio would be damned if he didn't just then see the dapper gent in the pin-stiped suit and Toni angling right toward it!

He bunched his cheeks and slammed his right fist into his left palm. "She did it again, sure enough!"

Mannion stepped into the doorway, scowling curiously down at his shorter, older, thicker deputy. "Did what again?"

"That tears it!" Rio said, not hearing his boss's question beneath the roar of rage in his ears and stomped off down the porch steps.

He swung left and tramped furiously off in the direction of the stage office.

He was approaching the white frame clapboard building as Toni and the dapper gent stood side-by-side at the edge of the boardwalk, watching the stage line's half-breed porter pull up behind the parked Concord in the stage line's buckboard wagon, the back of the wagon mounded high with Toni's carpet bags, steamer trunks, and portmanteaus as well as several leather, monogramed bags no doubt belonging to the dapper gent.

Seething, ignoring the dust-caked jehu Lyle Horton's jovial greeting as the driver greased the coach's near front wheel with a long stick, Rio strode forward. Toni and the dapper gent were still talking and laughing as Kenny Two Owls, dressed in his too-tight suit that reminded Rio of his own, were setting their bags on the boardwalk before them. Toni turned her head slightly toward Rio, turned it back forward, then snapped it toward him once more.

Her eyes widened in surprise as they held on the deputy.

"Rio!" she said, slapping a gloved hand to the dangerously lowcut bodice of her traveling frock. "There you are!"

"Yeah," Rio said, stopping before her. "Here, I am." He jerked his chin to indicate the dusty Concord. "Leaving, are ya?"

"Yes," Toni said, haltingly. "My month is up. I tried to find you earlier...to say goodbye, but..."

"I was making my morning rounds...but I was around."

"Oh, sure, sure." Toni glanced nervously at the dapper gent scowling at Rio, the man's otherwise pale cheeks above the upswept ends of his waxed mustache turning crimson.

Toni glanced down, looked at the dapper gent once more then cleared her throat and let her gaze settle again on the stiff-backed Rio. "Uh...Rio...I meant to tell you..."

"You meant to tell me you found another fancy-Dan to run off with? To leave me standing here in my stiff suit with my hat in my hands...er, my thumb up my–"

"Oh, Rio, please—let's be *civilized*! I meant to tell you all about Herman here—we met only a few nights ago, I assure you—but I just wasn't sure how to breech the subject." Toni wrung her hands together and canted her head to one side, manufacturing a pained, sympathetic expression. "I truly do feel awful, Rio...just awful...well... that it happened again, doggoneit," she added with a frustrated stomp of a foot.

She looked up at the dapper gent with a wan half-smile before returning her gaze to Rio. "I'm so sorry, Rio. I hope you didn't take what happened between us too seriously."

"I reckon I did. I reckon I was fool enough to think you did, too."

"Oh, Rio--I was afraid that might happen and yet--"

"Ah, shut up!"

Toni stared at him in shock. "Rio, please! I feel badly enough as it is!"

"No, you don't," Rio said, clenching his right hand into a tight fist and pulling it back toward his shoulder. "But you're about to!"

The right jab connected soundly with Toni's red-painted mouth.

She gave an indignant yelp and flew backward into the arms of the dapper gent, who glared at Rio and said, "What is the meaning of this, you uncivilized brigand?!"

Rio stepped up to where Toni slumped in the dandy's arms, staring up at him in astonishment, holding one gloved hand over her mouth. He hadn't hit her hard enough the crack her lips. Somehow, he'd managed to restrain himself.

He thrust his arm and a castigating finger straight out at her. "Toni, you were right. You are nothing more than a slattern. That's all you are and all you've ever been. I'm just sorry it took me twenty years to realize it."

He cast his glare at the dapper gent, holding the slumped Toni and staring at Rio in wide-eyed exasperation.

Rio pinched his hat brim to the man and said, "Good luck, Dan. You're gonna need it!"

With that, he wheeled and tramped back in the direction from which he'd come.

————

KICKED BACK IN A CHAIR ON THE FRONT PORCH OF Hotel de Mannion, boots crossed on the rail before him, Joe watched his thick-set deputy stride toward him.

Rio's fleshy face was red with anger.

The deputy said nothing as he stomped up the steps,

crossed the porch beside Joe, pushed open the door, and disappeared into the office.

Mannion winced, sighed, shook his head.

A few minutes later, boots thumped around inside the office behind him.

The door opened.

Rio stepped out, setting his old, battered, badly weathered, funnel-brimmed Stetson on his head. He wore his former, age-old garb—faded, red, neck-knotted bandanna, patched canvas breeches, and rumpled hickory shirt that stretched taut over his considerable paunch, offering a peek of his wash worn longhandle top where the shirt gaped open between buttons just above his badly strained cartridge belt.

Rio stood at the top of the porch steps, staring out into the street as he continued to adjust the set of his humble Stetson. The seat of his canvas breeches sagged badly.

He lowered his hands, stepped back, and slacked into the chair beside Joe.

He raised his boots to the porch rail, crossed them, sank back in his chair, crossed his lumpy arms on his lumpy chest, and sighed.

"Feel better?" Mannion asked him.

"Oh, yeah."

CODA

TWO WEEKS LATER, JOE SAID, "YOU SURE ABOUT THIS, honey? You sure he's ready? You haven't been working with him all that long, you know."

Standing inside the breaking corral, tightening the cinch of the saddle she'd just placed on the back of the handsome blue roan she called Cochise, Vangie Mannion glanced over her left shoulder at her father.

She smiled reassuringly, nodded, and returned her attention to the saddling of the stallion, who craned his neck to look back over his left wither at the young lady who'd been working tirelessly, day in and day out, to gentle him while leaving him with what Vangie hoped was a half-wild heart. The roan worked his nose, no doubt detecting the familiar, reassuring scent of his bene-factor then turned his head forward and stomped one rear hoof and gave his tail a single switch.

He had spirit, and he was a little uneasy with the saddle on his back. But he did not try to flee his saddler, Joe noted. Vangie was not holding the reins of the bridle she'd slipped over the stallion's ears. The ribbons drooped straight down to the ground in front of the horse.

Vangie had saddled and bridled the roan several times over the past week, and she'd ridden him around the corral. She had not, yet, however, ridden him outside the corral, which was what she intended to do for the first time this morning.

Mannion stood gazing over the stout rails of the breaking corral that he'd built with the help of Stringbean McCallister for the sole purpose of housing the bronc while Vangie gentled him. Jane Ford stood behind him, leaning on her crutches, her broken right ankle firmly ensconced in a white plaster of Paris cast. The heel of that foot rested forward on the corral's bottom rail. Jane raised her left arm, letting that crutch fall against her, and rubbed Mannion's back with her still-bandaged right hand.

"Worried?"

"Yep," Mannion said with a sigh, lacing his fingers together atop the corral. "He's still wild. She hasn't been working with him that long. It takes a good six months to get a horse like that ready for riding."

"Well, horse and girl have one thing in common." Jane smiled up over Mannion's right shoulder. "They're both wild. Wild at heart." She reached up to flick the brim of Joe's Stetson with her right index finger. "Just like her father."

Mannion snorted a laugh.

Vangie cast another smile over her left shoulder at her father, this time a bemused one. She grabbed the roan's reins, toed a stirrup, and swung up into the leather.

She turned to Joe. "You can open the gate now, Pa."

Mannion winced. "You sure?"

"I'm sure, Pa."

Mannion looked at Jane. She smiled up at him, nodded.

He sighed, walked over to the gate, lifted the wire latch from the gate post, and stepped back, drawing the gate wide as he did. The hinges squawked quietly.

Vangie looked at him. She looked down at the roan, drew a deep breath, and said, "All right, Cochise. What do you say, big fella? Are you ready for a *real* ride?"

Mannion felt the tension in his back; it stiffened the muscles between his shoulders.

The roan stared at the open gate. Mannion could hear the horse breathing, see the glee at the prospect of freedom in his dark eyes. He pawed the ground with his right front hoof, gave his tail another eager switch, twitched his ears.

"All right, then," Vangie said, nudging the bronc gently with her spurred boots.

The horse lurched forward with a slight start.

Mannion sucked a sharp, anxious breath.

He thought the bronc would hump its back suddenly and buck her off.

But he did not.

Eyes on the open gate beckoning him to freedom, the horse walked forward. Vangie rode lightly in the saddle, letting her body move in harmony with the horse, her rump rising gently up and down in the saddle. Her eyes, however, Mannion noted as she and the bronc passed through the gate, were anxious, her cheeks a little pale beneath their suntan.

Horse and rider rode out away from the corral and then Vangie drew back on the reins. The horse stopped.

Cochise turned his head left to stare at the purple humps of the San Juan Mountains rising in the southwest. He lifted his long, fine snout and sniffed the air, gave his tail another eager switch.

He wanted to run for all he was worth back to his home in those mountains, Joe thought. Back to his harem and his colts. To his enemies...

He could if he wanted to. He could buck Vangie off and head that way.

Would he?

Vangie gently neck-reined the horse to the left and nudged him with her spurs, putting him into a fast walk. Horse and rider began riding around the outside of the round corral.

Mannion and Jane watched, both tense, expecting the worst, for the stallion to suddenly pitch, throw Vangie off, and leave her in the dirt while he galloped off to his harem in his beloved mountains, buck-kicking in defiance at the girl's attempts to tame him enough to be ridden.

Cochise did not.

Vangie and the horse circled the corral once and then, as they approached the nervous Mannion leaning against the open corral gate, Vangie nudged the roan into a trot.

They trotted around the corral once.

Then Vangie nudged him into a gallop.

They galloped around the corral twice, the horse snorting, hooves thumping, dust rising.

Horse and rider moved as one.

Mannion and Jane shared a relieved smile.

"All right, then," Vangie said, checking the stallion down in front of her father. She smiled at Mannion, eyes lit with a joy Mannion hadn't seen in a long time. "He's doing fine, Pa."

"He is," Mannion said. "You've done well, honey."

"I reckon it's time to see just how well," Vangie said.

"Do be careful, honey."

"I will, Pa."

Vangie neck-reined the horse to the right. "All right, Cochise," Vangie said, leaning low over the horse's pole. "Let's get us some air, Cochise. What do you say, boy?"

She nudged the horse with her spurs. Cochise lunged forward off his rear hooves and, tail arched, laying his ears back against his sleek head, galloped off to the southwest, toward the purple bumps of the San Juans rising beyond.

The pounding hooves thundered, the sound dwindling as horse and rider grew smaller and smaller in the distance.

Jane hobbled up to stand beside Mannion at the open corral gate.

"They're beautiful, both of them," she said. "And they're doing well together."

"They are," Mannion said, smiling after the girl and the galloping horse. He glanced at Jane. "What about us?"

"What about us?" Jane asked, wrinkling the skin above the bridge of her nose, gazing up at him.

"Will we do well together, you think?" Mannion reached into a pocket of his black denim jacket. He opened his hand. On his gloved palm rested a black leather ring box.

He opened the box to reveal a gold ring with a single, small diamond setting in gold prongs resting on a bed of cream-colored burlap.

"Nothing fancy. It was my mother's. I didn't even know I had it until I was going through an old chest of hers a few weeks back. Right then, it occurred to me..." He frowned down at the ring.

"What did?" Jane asked.

Mannion slid his gaze to her. "You deserve a bigger

304 / PETER BRANDVOLD

diamond, but I'd like you to wear it." He canted his head to one side, giving a foxy half-smile and narrowing one eye. "What do you think, Miss Ford? Are you crazy enough to hitch your wagon to this temperamental fool's broken-down wagon?"

Jane gazed up at him, her eyes pensively probing his. She shook her head. "I'm not worth it, Joe."

Mannion chuckled, slid his thumb across her cheek. "Now, ain't that a coincidence? I'm not, either."

Tears glazed her eyes.

"I'll take that as a yes," Joe said. He leaned down and kissed her.

Jane kissed him back, lifting a hand to the back of his head, tugging on his longish, salt-and-pepper hair.

They both looked up when a loud whinny cut through the quiet, mid-morning air. Jane gave a fearful gasp. She and Mannion both expected to see Vangie on the ground.

The girl was still in the saddle, however, maybe two hundred yards away. Vangie suddenly stopped the stallion and curveted him. The horse rose off its rear hooves, clawed his front feet at the sky, and loosed another loud, wild whinny, shaking his black-faced head, black mane glistening beautifully in the high-country sunlight.

Vangie waved her hat high as she looked back toward her father and Jane. She was too far away for Mannion to see her clearly, but he knew she was smiling—probably as big as she'd ever smiled before.

Mannion smiled, too. He chuckled and returned her wave.

Jane, did, too.

The stallion dropped back down to all fours. Vangie set her hat back on her head, turned the stallion, and galloped off toward the mountains again. She rode maybe another hundred yards then turned back toward

Mannion and Jane, putting the bronc into another ground-churning run.

Mannion gave a relieved sigh.

Jane rested her chin on a slat of the corral gate, gazing southwest as horse and rider grew gradually before her. She and Joe could again hear the thudding of the stallion's hooves. The rataplan grew louder.

As horse and rider came closer, Mannion could see the big smile on his daughter's lovely face as she moved gracefully, rising and falling lightly in the saddle, with the stallion's own natural grace.

"Wild at heart," Jane said. "Horse and girl forever."

"Forever," Mannion agreed.

"Just like her father," Jane said.

"Just like her soon-to-be stepmother," Mannion said, and kissed the scar on Jane's forehead.

Jane looked up at him. "How soon?"

"How soon would you like, Madam Jane?"

"Soon," Jane said, giving a slit-eyed grin. "Before either one of us has time to get cold feet and beat it for those mountains yonder."

Mannion chuckled. "Good idea."

He turned to where Vangie and the wild-eyed bronc approached from fifty yards away, closing fast.

"Vangie," Joe said with a broad wave. "We got news, girl!"

A LOOK AT BOOK THREE: SAINTS AND SINNERS

Town Marshal "Bloody" Joe Mannion is back in this third high-action volume in Peter Brandvold's explosive new western series!

When Jeremiah Claggett, constable of the nearby ghost town of Fury, is murdered by Frank Lord, the kill-crazy leader of a dozen wild outlaws, Bloody Joe has to come to grips with the fact that he's inadvertently to blame. Mannion had turned Frank's brother, Billy, over to Claggett for safekeeping, setting off the chain of events that end his friend's life. Mannion is the kill-crazy one now. Not realizing he's being shadowed by Clagget's beautiful, half-wild granddaughter, Justy, and an inscrutable saddle tramp, Mannion sets out on his vengeance quest.

In typical Bloody Joe style, he storms Lord's gang single-handedly, which nearly proves to be his undoing—until he's set upon by a mystery 'Man of the Lord' and given... *something*. Whether that something is good or bad Mannion has difficulty discerning.

Saints and Sinners is a crazy, dark, storm-ridden ride through the hell of the San Juan Mountains of southwestern Colorado. Whoever manages to ride out alive—saint or sinner, or maybe a combination—will be changed forever, baptized in gun smoke and blood.

AVAILABLE MAY 2022

Peter Brandvold grew up in the great state of North Dakota in the 1960's and '70s, when television westerns were as popular as shows about hoarders and shark tanks are now, and western paperbacks were as popular as *Game of Thrones*.

Brandvold watched every western series on television at the time. He grew up riding horses and herding cows on the farms of his grandfather and many friends who owned livestock.

Brandvold's imagination has always lived and will always live in the West. He is the author of over a hundred lightning-fast action westerns under his own name and his pen name, Frank Leslie.